THE SHATTERED SKULL
The Sugar Skull
Book 3

MANUEL RUIZ

STERLING & STONE

Dedicated to the Round Rock Crew, our friends and family group forged over the last 25+ years. From our many gatherings, events, dinners, and trips together, they keep me grounded and sane when my writing demands a little insanity.

Truth be told, they're a little insane, too. And I wouldn't have it any other way.

Jenny

Lisa

Erica

Vinny & Brenda

Rudy & Angel

Juan & Roberta

And of course, my Daisy

Love you all!

Prologue

In the year 1662 in the colony of Connecticut, two men, one a magistrate and another a member of the prosecutorial tribunal overseeing the accusations and trials of witches, stood over a suspected witch deep in the forest.

An extremely pregnant suspected witch.

Fearing the accused would bear a demonic child, the men stood in wait with a midwife present, each holding a dagger to kill the abomination if necessary.

History would prove that most of the accused women during this time were not actual witches and wrongly accused. But in this case, the tribunal was correct.

The woman screamed as the birth approached and the men readied themselves, each holding the woman's arms with one hand and their daggers with the other.

They told no one what they were doing and knew no one would dare take the woman's word over theirs. They trusted the midwife, as she was married to the magistrate.

But others knew. And they were watching.

Four friends of the woman, also witches, had followed and were lying in wait in the darkness. As the pregnant woman's screams increased, her friends leapt from their hiding places with clubs and sticks.

The men and midwife fell as they were struck. The witches moved quickly. One took over as midwife while the others took out items from the bags they carried.

The three pulled out herbs they burned and poured into liquid concoctions, closing their eyes, chanting and swaying in unison.

The new midwife said, "The child's head is appearing!"

One witch took a mirror and stuck it into the ground, facing the child's protruding crown.

The women chanted faster, pouring their potions into the mouth of the accused. The witch drank between her screams, joining in the chants when she could.

But something else was watching them. Something darker than the forest night answering their chanting call.

As much as the women believed they were true witches and capable of darkness and summoning, this was the first time they had been heard.

The women craved vengeance. They called to the darkness to aid them, and that darkness arrived.

In their haste, they did not realize what they asked. Rarely can darkness be commanded or controlled, and in this case, they knew not what they summoned.

It was evil. The darkness of a demon who had escaped its underworld confinement long before this night but had lost its form and voice as punishment.

Now it was only an essence drifting throughout the world, seeking freedom. And after more than a millennium of being lost, on this day, it heard voices. Voices that beckoned.

The voices led to a visible light emanating from a

human. Within that human's belly, something was about to be birthed. An escape. At long last.

The darkness listened, and the darkness followed the light. The moment it entered the mother's womb, the woman's voice shifted from screams to a deep bellow. The voice the darkness had lost so long ago.

The bellow stirred the magistrate and the tribunal member. The magistrate was on his back, but still unable to move. He glanced at his companion.

"Do you hear? It is true darkness. You must stop it."

The man understood. He got up, crouching, and stepped closer with his dagger in hand, unnoticed by the witches and their ceremony.

The mother's eyes were filled with blackness as the inhuman roar emerged from her mouth.

The man looked at the mirror and saw the reflection of the child's head. It was almost completely out.

The man turned to the magistrate, unsure of what to do, but then the chanting witches turned and saw him.

Startled and panicked, the man whispered, asking for the Lord's guidance, believing his actions were justified. This one time the tribunal so happened to be correct would never absolve all the women he and the magistrate helped wrongly accuse and hang.

Still, he had to act.

Before the women could rise, he ran to the mother, lifted his dagger, and brought it down.

He struck again. Then again, ripping through the woman's outer stomach and penetrating her womb and birth canal.

The other witches grabbed him, but he was a man possessed. He struck over and over, knocking the witches away and stopping only after his exhaustion kept him from lifting his arms once more.

The witches stared for a moment before running away. They knew there was nothing they could do to save their friend.

The woman's insides were split wide, revealing the unborn children within.

Twin boys.

The child's head that was halfway out was now fully ejected on the ground with its dead eyes facing the mirror, while the other still sat in the exposed womb, waiting for his turn to take a breath of life that would never come.

The man fell to his knees, his face spattered with blood.

"What have I done?" he said aloud. "Lord, forgive me!"

His eyes widened as the tiny corpses rose in the air, their birthing cords still attached to their host.

The eyes of the child near the mirror opened, and he continued to stare at his reflection with his black pupils.

The second child held his empty gaze on the man, then opened his mouth, revealing sharp, animal-like teeth. A dark mist surrounded him, and he opened his mouth wider, bellowing loudly enough to frighten any nearby creature.

The twins' skins turned to ash and burst, flaring into the night as their cords fell to the ground.

The mirror cracked. The man saw a face with yellow eyes within each broken glass shard. He screamed and ran. Without checking on the magistrate, he rushed out of the forest. The magistrate's fear took over, giving him the ability to get up and flee.

The darkness remained and escaped from its twin hosts. This rebirth allowed a whisper of the darkness to pass into our world, but something even more unexpected occurred. The twin hosts broke the darkness in two.

The lone wandering darkness was now two separate

entities. Demon brothers bound by their shared origin. One brother dependent on the reflections of the world, with the ability to travel quickly and spread fear, while the other gained strength and control over its darkness.

However, their new existence was limited. They were strong enough to exist, yet not strong enough to escape the confines of the forest.

Over the following centuries, as man conquered and invaded the natural land in the name of progress and expansion, the forest thinned. New inhabitants lived and died within their domain, and the brothers fed off the fear and darkness many of their souls provided.

Then one day, they obtained enough strength to leave their domain.

They yearned for more, spreading throughout the expanded lands of the New World, fulfilling a hunger that could never be satisfied.

But two and a half centuries later, everything changed when they came upon a ghostly child, also living between planes, looking for her cat…

Chapter One

MIA'S MAGIC WAS FLOWING.

She didn't know what it was. The synchronicity. The breathing. The level of concentration that took her somewhere else, even as more than twenty people surrounded her, anticipating her next move. They kept asking her how she did it, but she had no answer. The subjects simply yielded to her will, even as they were on the brink of death. They were without sustenance, yet somehow found a way to live.

The subjects before her might not be human, but they had to be fed by the earth and sunlight or they would die. And they thirsted for water. Always.

The junior year botany class experiment was to take an almost dying plant and test various methods that would help provide some semblance of life. There was no expectation that the leaves would live past the day or even the duration of the class.

Test and observe.

Yet the entire class, leaving their experiments unfinished or unstarted, was quietly vying for a position to witness if Mia might do something none of them could.

Professor Cort stood behind them, no longer wondering if Mia would defy expectations. He knew she would, even without a scientific explanation of how it was possible.

They didn't wait long.

The edges of the wilting plant leaves moved. They waved in a slow motion like they were reacting to a gentle wind. The withered pieces gained color until they matched the darker roots of the leaf nearest the stem. Then the plant, lying flat and bent on the small patch of soil holding the smallest ends of its roots, started to move as a whole.

As the plant gained more of its green shade, Mia felt heat in the pit in her stomach.

Then her temples started to ache. She noticed something approaching from the window side of the room. It wasn't a classmate, though. Maybe someone outside?

Not possible, she thought. We're on the second floor.

Maybe it was just a bird or an owl that had appeared before.

Her eyes shifted in that direction. Nothing on the windowsill, and other than a few smears, nothing on the glass.

The room took in a collective breath without thinking as the leaf slithered upward in a fraction of movements that seemed to strengthen with each effort. Within another two minutes, the leaf was off the soil, and moments later, the plant stood straight, prepared to survive well beyond a day.

The class applauded while Mia and her lab partner, Laura, finally breathed.

Professor Cort smiled. He wanted to tell his fellow Florida State University at Tallahassee colleagues about what he had witnessed over the last semester, but unless he brought them over to see her in person, he knew they'd think he'd lost his mind. There was no way he could explain the plant behavior, but his eyes didn't deceive him. To date, only a handful of other professors had witnessed it.

The professor turned to the door, wondering if anyone else was watching. He noticed several of the student's plants had already withered from being ignored, but the students didn't care. They wanted to see the Mia show.

Mia had been uncomfortable with the audience the first few times, but she was getting used to it. It gave her a small rush of confidence.

The professor tapped a few of the students on the shoulder to return to their work, but many kept staring at Mia's plant.

There were a few whispers of, "How does she do that?" before they dispersed.

Laura smiled. "I'm glad you're my partner. I know I wouldn't get through this without you."

Professor Cort walked to Mia and Laura's table once the students returned to their experiments, trying to keep his composure. It had already taken everything he had to not jump up and down in excitement when the plant reached its pinnacle.

Mia looked up at Professor Cort as he approached her table and smiled nervously. She liked him. She could sense his shock, but he kept his cool and didn't make her feel like everyone was staring, even though she knew they were.

"Mia, just incredible. That's the most fulfillment of color and texture I've ever seen. You brought that back to life."

Mia smiled and thanked him.

"You can walk around the room or take a break if

you'd like," he whispered, so only Mia and Laura could hear. "It'll help get everyone back to their own projects instead of talking about yours."

She nodded and got up. Laura followed. Mia glanced around the room and everyone who had been staring quickly shifted back to their experiments.

She heard a whimper.

She looked ahead of her table and saw Sarah. They attended middle school together, but Sarah had moved to another neighborhood and went to a different high school. They had reconnected in Professor Cort's class and had spoken a few times over the semester.

Mia walked to her table. Sarah's lab partner was out, so she was doing her experiment alone.

"Hey, Sarah."

She looked up at Mia and half smiled. "I wish I was half as good as you. I'm fighting a borderline D right now."

Mia looked back at the professor. He was helping another table.

"What have you done so far?"

"I thought I had done everything right, but my plant looks deader than when I started."

Mia looked at the plant and then back at her. She picked up some of the mix and put a few more pinches in.

As they watched, two of the leaf ends started to turn maroon.

Sarah's mouth was open. "How?"

Mia just shook her head. She really didn't know.

"Thank you," Sarah mouthed to her.

The plant slowly rose. It would never reach the same height as Mia's, but it would be enough to pass.

Mia made sure the attention on her had waned and

moved to the spot on the window where she had felt the pull earlier.

She looked outside.

Mia didn't see anything but a beautiful sky. The sun was out and bright. She saw two squirrels chasing each other up the trees in the quad and some birds flying around, but nothing out of the ordinary.

She figured it was just the anxiety from so many staring at her that made her head hurt earlier. Either that or a brain tumor. She wasn't a hypochondriac, but that seemed like a real possibility versus admitting she was imagining things.

Mia turned back to the class. Sarah was smiling now.

She looked back through the window and then saw a few smudges. One smudged area stood out, spread in several directions.

She remembered her cousins always leaving each other obscene messages on days where the windows would glaze over.

She leaned down and slowly breathed on the mirror.

Something had been drawn on the glass. She breathed on it more. It was bigger than she thought. What looked like it was the size of a quarter now looked like it was as big as her hand. The outline formed and she shook her head. She looked back to see if anyone else could see what she could.

It was a skull.

Not just a smudge that resembled a skull, but with thin detailed lines, like someone had drawn it with some kind of smudge-making pen. It was a decorated sugar skull. had a menacing look to it, and it felt like it was sta right through her.

Mia lifted her fist to rub it out and noticed he shake as heat filled the back of her head.

Someone must have done this in a previous class. It's nothing.

But that didn't explain why she felt like she did. She closed her eyes tight and shook her head.

"Just tired," she whispered to herself and rubbed the skull off vigorously.

She returned to her seat and started thumbing through her textbook.

It was the single oddest day in her favorite class. A class that was filed with more odd days than not lately.

Chapter Two

GABBY AND RICKY WERE EXHAUSTED.

In the five months they'd been traveling together since meeting at Gabby's house in Dallas, their mission to save Gabby's daughter's soul and stop the demons that tried to destroy both of their lives had taken a toll.

During Ricky's time preparing and learning how to hunt and chase his demons, he found an online community of true believers, although true belief didn't always amount to reliable sources. Many claimed to have hunted and killed demons and evil spirits, but he quickly learned most were young wannabes who had never left their hometown or didn't own a weapon more dangerous than a kitchen knife. When he read about the ones that claimed to have wounded a Sasquatch or trapped a chupacabra, he blocked them from his contacts. Ricky figured if you ever did trap something like that, at least one person in your posse would have a phone handy to take a picture.

Even so, Ricky had to prove himself with this community, banking on at least two or three being legitimate. He knew the ones that boasted the loudest were most likely the fakest, but it had taken time.

After almost destroying the city of Stone Creek's downtown as a tool in the demon rampage that took the life of his dear Ellie, Ricky and his family were put in witness protection. But Ricky spent every moment worried that the demons would find him someday, and his sister and mother would pay the price. They were relocated to the West Coast and there had been no signs of any demon activity, but he couldn't shake the feeling they were coming for him. The nightmares didn't help, either. He realized he wouldn't be able to rest until they were destroyed. He felt that tracking down the demons was the only way he could truly protect them all, especially his sister, Myra.

Ricky's path led him to Gabby, and although he had never told the online community who he was, his knowledge had helped the network accept him. Even so, he was still treading carefully.

Gabby had flown back to Texas twice, but after seeing her daughter, Ally, looking weaker and worse, she knew her time was better spent hunting. She still video chatted with her sister and Ally every day, grateful that her sister was caring for her daughter.

The online hunter network had helped them find safe places to sleep when they needed it. Learning which places to avoid was just as important. Ricky was still trying to figure out who he could truly trust beyond finding places to rest, but he had hit a wall.

Although their last two leads in Arizona and Oklahoma were a bust, Ricky wasn't about to quit. He wanted to eliminate the current leads before moving on.

The pair had stopped at a motel on the west border of Alabama. Ricky had a paper map open on the small table in his room. It was marked with the places they'd been and potential next destinations. They had options. There were fat red circles on a couple of places he thought were most likely to yield something.

"Do you really think these could be real?" Gabby asked.

There had been some noise about Huntsville that led them in this direction.

"We got two different groups of kids. First, the three elementary friends, then those middle schoolers reporting being attacked by dark figures."

"What makes you so sure?"

"I'm not sure. Normally I'd think these were BS, but the reports are similar, and the towns are only about 100 miles from each other. I think they're worth checking out. Or maybe I'm just desperate."

They had a few more hours ahead of them. They had hoped to get closer but were exhausted. They needed some solid rest and a good breakfast.

They slept more than six hours, which was rare, then packed up their things and were out by 10 a.m. They stopped at a Waffle House. It was a Tuesday and mid-morning, but the place was still packed.

They hadn't spoken on the way to the waffle house, which was just a ten-minute drive from the hotel. Ricky already knew that Gabby needed coffee before she could have a meaningful conversation, and Gabby knew Ricky needed time to process what he was thinking or he'd break into a jumbled mess of explanation that he'd have to repeat three times before it finally made sense.

They had gotten to know each well after being total strangers just a few months prior. It was easy to gel with someone who shared the same goal.

As Gabby took her fourth sip of coffee, she finally

looked at Ricky, who again had his map spread out on the table. His waffles were getting cold.

"What are you thinking? Continue to Huntsville first?"

He nodded. "Yes, we have to eliminate it."

"It seems like we're lost," Gabby said.

"I know," Ricky said. "It's getting harder to rely on the network, but the new source who gave me this has been doing this for a while. He could be legit."

"After the last few weeks, it's nice to hear you have a little hope."

"Sometimes hope is all that keeps me going."

Chapter Three

MIA'S CLASSES ALTERNATED DAYS, and she returned to her botany class two days after seeing the skull on the window. There was no experiment today. It was primarily a Professor Cort lecture with some questions and answers. Mia enjoyed not feeling the pressure of performing for an audience. The skull on the window had bothered her for about two hours after she saw it, but she had forgotten about it since, convinced it was just something someone had drawn to pass the time.

Mia listened and took notes on plant pathology.

The class time seemed to fly by and before she knew it, it was over. The professor dismissed them fifteen minutes early.

"I'm giving you a gift of an early dismissal and would suggest not asking any more questions and risk the ire of your classmates. Enjoy!"

The class sighed with relief. A few even clapped.

"Don't be too nice to me yet. I know we have a long weekend coming up, but you're going to have a quiz on the last four chapters on Friday before that happens."

He expected the collective groan and didn't faze him.

"It'll be 20 questions and as soon as you're done, you can leave. If you've read what you need to, you should be out of here in 10 minutes. No essays, just multiple choice. Maybe you can squeeze three-and-a-half days out of this brief break."

The mood lightened a little.

"Happy studying. See you Friday."

As the students started to walk out, Professor Cort raised his palm toward Mia.

"Mia, can you stay for a few minutes, please?"

That startled her. The professor had complimented her a few times during class and had only once asked her how she was so good at the experiments. He didn't press when she told him that she simply didn't know. She had never had much success raising plants, or anything for that matter, when she was younger.

The professor waited until the stream of students filed out, and once the last one was gone, he asked Mia to close the door.

Mia felt sweat on her brow.

Why would he want to close the door and talk to her privately? Maybe he knew she had helped Sarah and she was about to flunk out.

"Am I in trouble?" she asked.

The professor smiled. "No, nothing like that. I'm sorry, please have a seat."

He motioned for her to sit at the desk nearest his.

"I'm just passing along some information."

"What about?"

"A colleague at the University of North Florida in Jacksonville contacted me yesterday. We graduated together, actually."

"What about?"

"He said he has someone in an odd situation. Something that was hard to explain. Something science can't explain. It's an unusual case, but based on the talents you've already shown in class, I think you may be able to help him."

"Help how?"

"The person needing the help is already on campus. I haven't met him, but after my colleague told me a little about his predicament, I suggested I might know someone worth talking to. It just so happened this man's next stop was to see me if that meeting didn't pan out. I don't know all the details, but I wasn't expecting him to be here so soon."

"How do you think I can help?"

"It's your aptitude in this class. What I've seen you do sometimes defies explanation and natural talent. Maybe even defies science. It's not exactly normal and nothing I, nor the few colleagues I've trusted to visit this class, can explain or have ever seen."

"What does that mean?"

"We don't know. I didn't want to tell my colleague too many details about you simply because he hasn't seen you in action. He's one of my closest friends, but I'm still not comfortable telling him all the details, since any man of science would have to see to believe. I also don't want to use you as my own experiment. Not yet, at least. I can tell you're not comfortable with the attention and completely understand. However, I do have to ask."

"Wait, is he coming here right now?"

"No, I wasn't going to blindside you. I told him I wouldn't give your name or allow any interaction until I spoke with you and you agreed to it."

Mia thought about it. She was being asked to meet a stranger with an unusual situation and for some reason, her favorite professor thought she might be able to help. Did this mean she was unusual? Or maybe unusually broken?

Stop, Mia. You're spiraling.

"I'm not sure, Professor. This is a little unexpected."

"No worries, Mia. I'll let him know to forget it."

"I'm not saying that. Will you be here for another hour or so?"

"Yes, I brought my lunch and don't have class for another two hours. I was going to go over some research I was doing. Why?"

"Let me take a walk and think about it. I'm going to grab something to eat in the SUB."

He smiled. "Of course. Take all the time you need. If you don't return before my next class, I'll assume you don't want to do it."

She nodded. "Thank you."

Mia walked out and down the stairs to the first floor. She thought about the request on her way to the Student Union Building and almost walked into two people as she contemplated. How could she help anyone? What was this mystery man needing?

She got to the food court and got herself a slice of pizza and some soup. She didn't feel like being inside on another nice day and took her lunch outdoors.

Mia went to her favorite spot when she wanted to be alone or study. It was a bench that stood between two big trees. Students didn't usually use this particular bench since it was on a corner of the large quad. Most flocked to the center area, where there was more activity and people.

She sat on the bench and opened her lunch, working on her soup first.

Mia's head snapped to the left and she was overcome with a sense of sadness. She wasn't sure why. Her head then filled with the image of a baby, suffering and lost. The baby was a little girl, and Mia got a sense that she was missing something that was making her sick.

Mia shook her head, trying to dismiss the random thought.

A student walked by wearing a cast on one foot and struggling with a single crutch. Mia's first thought was of the student turning, lifting her crutch, and attacking Mia with it.

Where did that come from?

As she tried to ask herself why her thoughts so often went to the first dark place she could imagine, another image filled her head.

She pictured the same experiment scene from a few days before. The odd feeling of seeing something near the window returned. Then the dull headache started, but this time it formed at the back of her head and neck. Instead of feeling like something was at a window, she felt a presence behind her. Not like someone breathing down her neck, but someone nearby standing and watching. This time, she didn't hesitate and turned around. There were a few students walking to and from classes, but she saw a man sitting on a bench about twenty yards behind her. He wore a hat and a long coat and was turned to his side. He was feeding a squirrel. He was too far away for her to see his face, but the uneasy feeling strengthened as she watched him.

He didn't do anything out of the ordinary. He didn't glance at her or make any unusual movements. He just seemed to be enjoying feeding the squirrel.

Mia turned back around. The throbbing eased but was still there.

She picked up her pizza and wanted to finish it, but realized she wasn't hungry anymore. Her mind filled with thoughts of the professor's request, and she realized she had decided what she was going to do only a few moments after the professor asked. She had spent all the time since trying to find something to change her mind.

She had to know. She knew she had to know.

Mia got up and returned to Professors Cort's room. He was looking at some papers and eating a sandwich when she opened the door and walked in.

"Mia? I take it you decided. Again, don't worry about it. I know it was an odd request to begin with."

"I want to hear him out," she blurted, not letting him continue.

His mouth stayed open for a few seconds. "Oh, okay. I was almost sure you wouldn't do it."

"What made you think that?"

"You just seem guarded and to yourself most of the time in class. I've had other students who couldn't hold a candle to you get pretty full of themselves when others were in awe of them. You're easily the most gifted student I've ever had, and your ego is still in check. Are you sure about this?"

She nodded. "Yes. How long will it take him to get here?"

"I'm not sure. My friend Carl left me a phone number and asked me to text him once you decided."

He texted out a quick message.

"Okay, sent. Do you mind waiting? If he's on campus, I figure it would only be fifteen minutes at most once he…"

His phone beeped.

"That was fast. He's on his way."

Mia sat down at one of the desks near her.

"Your colleague didn't give you any details about this man?"

"No, just about the situation and that he felt the man

could be trusted, although he did purposely leave out some details. Said it would be best if I heard it from the man directly. He also told me to keep my mind open. So, I guess my advice to you is to do the same."

There was a knock at the door.

Professor Cort went to open it. Through the small door window, she only saw dark clothing.

The professor greeted the unseen person and, before he took a step in, Mia knew who it was. She'd felt the same presence in the quad.

The man was in a nice suit, wearing a long black jacket over it and a brown fedora on his head. He was pasty white but had a gentle look. He wore rimless glasses, black gloves, and a nervous smile as he turned to Mia.

"Mia," Professor Cort said. "This is Mr. Soren Strand."

He removed his gloves and reached out a hand. "It is my pleasure to meet you, Mia Morales."

She felt the beginning of that tingling sense, but his voice was soft and calm. Her guard came down immediately.

"Hello," Mia said. "So, how can I help you?"

Mr. Strand looked back at the professor.

"Oh, of course," Professor Cort said. Although he was as interested in knowing the full story as Mia was, he knew he was just a middleman. Still, he hoped to get answers afterwards.

"I'll give you some privacy," the professor added. "I'll be down the hall in the breakroom. Just let me know when you're done."

He smiled and walked out. Mia felt a little nervous being alone with a man she had just met in an empty class-room, but there was enough activity in the hallway to hear her scream in case he was a secret killer who wanted her as his next victim.

"May I sit?" he asked.

"Yes, of course."

He looked at the desks and instead pulled up Professor Cort's chair. "What did the professor tell you?"

"Just that someone needed help with an unusual request, but he didn't give me any details."

"I apologize for the way you were informed. I'm sure you must think it odd. It is a delicate matter, and I must be cautious."

"Why?"

"Most would not believe what I'm about to tell you. However, if your professor recommended you as a possible candidate to aid my plight, you may be able to relate."

"It's okay. Just tell me."

"I must begin by telling you the gravity of the situation. The life of a child, an infant, in fact, is in the balance."

"A baby?"

"Yes, my granddaughter. Her life is in danger, and I'm not sure we can find a way to cure her under the current circumstances."

"What do you mean? Why not take her to a doctor?"

"Oh, this is beyond science and medical professionals. There is something going on with my granddaughter that is unexplainable. We have taken her to several doctors, and none can tell us what is wrong with her."

Mia was intrigued. She thought of her younger cousins. "Tell me everything."

"My daughter was young when she had her. A teen mother. The baby exhibited unusual behavior at birth."

"Unusual how?"

He took in a deep breath. "It's my understanding you

exhibit characteristics that are beyond normal explanation. Is this something you realize?"

Mia's concentration broke. "What do you mean?"

"The abilities you have with these plants. You understand if a professor who has studied this for years says you are defying explanation, that means something. I'm wondering if you realize what you're doing when you do it. Or when you aren't. Some sense that you feel that goes beyond plant experimentation."

"Professor Cort told you? He said he hadn't given that many details to his friend."

"No, your professor did not divulge your secrets. You see, I also have senses that cannot be explained. The details are hazy, but with both of you in the room together, I was able to pick up visions of your memories. Based on your reaction, I take it I am correct?"

Mia looked down. She had sensed him earlier at the bench but didn't know how. She'd experienced odd feelings throughout her entire life, but they were infrequent enough that she didn't think much about them.

"I just figure it's what I'm good at. Everyone has something, right?"

"Yes, but very rarely do they defy science. Have you had other things you knew or were told you were extraordinarily good at doing?"

She thought. "Yes, when I was younger and my grandmother was alive. She helped teach me how to cook and make things."

"Spells and cures, maybe?" he asked. He had no judgment in his voice.

She remembered her grandmother teaching her how to make concoctions when she was younger.

"Yes, I guess so. She told me I had done a good job, but I figured she was just being a nice grandma."

"As family should. I wonder how deep that goes," he said. "Anything else?"

Her eyes slowly rose toward him, but she didn't want to make contact.

"I sensed you today. Also, a few days ago in class, I sensed something else. I don't think it was you. It was different, but I felt something. Why are you asking me about this?"

"I need you to keep an open mind. My grandchild. She's not sick in the standard sense. She went through something, and now a part of her is missing."

"Like a body part?"

"Not exactly. Her soul has been … corrupted."

"Corrupted?" Mia thought about a computer getting a virus.

"I'm not sure that is the best word to describe it. Something supernatural invaded her life. Something that may have been part of her mother's world. I do not know. The doctors can see there is something wrong, but they cannot identify what it is. Her vitals are weak, but not critical. They wanted to keep her and fill her with needles and experimentation, but that only confirmed what I already knew. They could not help her and would just use her as a test subject, so I took her home. I've been seeking an alternate solution ever since. If you look into her eyes, you will see something is missing. Her soul is weak. Like it is somehow disconnected from her body. I believe, but cannot prove, it was taken from her. Stolen."

"Stolen how? What could have done this to her? A person?"

"Possibly. A person gifted in something dark, or maybe a dark presence."

Mia shook her head. "So what brought you to me? I'm

good with plants. How does that translate to helping a corrupted or stolen soul?"

The words came out of her mouth without thinking. She surprised herself that she even asked, but she kept thinking about her cousins and what she would do if this was happening to one of them.

"A sense," Mr. Strand said. "In addition to sensing memories and images of others, I am also in touch with the supernatural world. That connection expands the things I can see in others."

"Things like what?"

"The aura of a person. I can sense if someone is sick and dying. Little, subtle things that can tell me more about a person in a few seconds than if I'd known them for years. I've been traveling around hospitals and colleges, where there are many people who are stressed or sick, hoping I could pick up something that might help my granddaughter. When the professor and I spoke, he mentioned his friend's student. I sensed this could be something."

"From a conversation with a professor in another city?"

"Sometimes thoughts and conversations leave imprints I can pick up on. It was something in his words. Maybe his trust for your Professor Cort. Before I realized you were sitting on a bench near me as I fed the squirrel earlier, I sensed you. I felt that you sensed me, but wanted to know if you even realized what was happening. Up until the moment I walked into this room, I wasn't sure if I was going to tell you all that I already have or just bid you a good day and leave. The strength and aura you exude is more powerful than you realize. I don't know if that means you can help my granddaughter, but I think it is worth pursuing."

"Pursuing how?"

"Testing whether these abilities you have can be honed

27

and sharpened. Possibly enough to help my grand-daughter."

"Aren't you able to help with your abilities?"

"No, my gifts are different. Being able to empathize and sense the auras and memories of someone's being only helps me realize something is seriously wrong with my granddaughter. It won't help me cure her. If you are able, you have a much better chance than I do to save her. She is my world. My daughter has been unable to cope and is also a shadow of herself. She was a wild child, and this hasn't necessarily calmed her wild ways, but it has been difficult for her. She wants to help also, but her default reaction to pain or conflict is to run away. To be brutally honest, I am surprised she is still around."

Mia sat and pictured the baby with a missing or damaged soul. What would that even be like?

"So, Mia Morales, do you require more information from me?"

Mia looked at him and said, "I don't know. This is so much to take in. What is it you're asking of me? If I could help, how would I even start? I have no idea what to do."

"That you may leave to me. I know some things we can try, even though I cannot perform them. I understand this is much to take in. All I ask is that you go home, think about it, and if you get a chance, ask a family member about what we discussed and about your relationship with your grandmother. Someone who was around her. They may help give you clarity and allow you to see that there is more to you than you realize."

He reached into his coat pocket and pulled out a wallet. He handed her a card.

"Here is my number. Call me when you decide. If you decline, that is fine. I can continue searching and will bear no hard feelings. Although I do hope you will consider it. I just ask that you get back to me within the next two days."

Mia took the card and nodded. "Okay, I'll do that."

Mr. Strand stood up and offered his hand again. She shook it and he walked out.

"I will let your professor know he may have his domain back. Thank you for your time and for keeping an open mind."

She looked down at his card.

It read, "Soren Strand, Spiritual Advisor," with a phone number below it.

Mia wasn't sure what she was going to do, but she felt like her entire life was about to change.

Chapter Four

PROFESSOR CORT RETURNED to the room as Mia stared at the card, thinking about the stranger's offer. The professor didn't pry, but she knew he was curious.

"Thank you, Professor. Interesting conversation and an interesting man. I'm going to think about it. Seriously."

Mia's classes were done for the day. She called her Aunt Grace to check if she was home. Grace was an accountant and was able to work remotely, but sometimes worked out of coffee shops or while out running errands when time allowed. She was divorced with four kids: Bianca, a college freshman only two years younger than 20-year-old Mia; Omar, a high school senior; Brenda, a high school sophomore and cheerleader; and Brian in 6th grade. It was still mid-afternoon, so the kids should have all been in school, and Mia needed to talk to her aunt.

After three rings, Grace answered and told Mia to head over.

Mia walked into the house about fifteen minutes later to find her aunt folding clothes on the living room couch.

"Hi, Mia. You're here early."

Aunt Grace knew Mia's routine. She usually studied in the afternoon after classes, would usually see her boyfriend Tino after he got out of work at six, then return to her apartment to study more and get ready for the next day. At least twice a week, she would come by Grace's house until it was time to see Tino. Coming by this early wasn't typical, and Mia loved to keep to her routine.

"Are you okay?" her aunt said once she looked at her face.

"I am," Mia said. "Something strange happened today, and I need to ask you something related to it."

Grace's head tilted as she put down the clothes she was folding.

"Sit down, Mia. You know you can ask me anything."

Mia moved to the loveseat opposite the couch.

"What's going on?" Grace asked.

"I'll tell you why I'm asking after I ask it, but please don't think I'm losing it."

"Okay, go ahead."

"You know how I've told you about odd things that happened in my botany class and how for some reason, I was really good at it?"

Grace nodded.

"I just figured it was something I was naturally gifted with, but things have gotten weirder the last few weeks, things that I haven't told you about. It's almost like I can feel an energy in the water running through the plants, and I'm doing things I don't think should be possible. It's like I'm cooking something I don't understand, and it made me think of Grandma."

"Grandma? Why?"

"When I was younger and Grandma was still alive, do you remember her wanting me to help her with her herbs and mixes to help you or Mom when you were sick? Or the kids?"

Her aunt's forehead wrinkled. "Yes, I remember."

"She always told me I had a special knack for it. I know she used some herbs for our *medicinas*. Even though she would never talk about it in detail, she said some people would roll their eyes if they knew about our beliefs and call it crazy folk medicine. But if I remember right, they usually worked."

"How old were you when Grandma died? Ten? Eleven?"

Mia thought about it. "I was ten. I remember because she died exactly a month before my birthday."

"You never talked about this with your mom?"

"No, I mean, she and Dad died three years later. It never really came up."

"Yes, you were too young, I suppose. Here's the thing. You know what a *curandera* is, right?"

Mia always pictured her grandmother as a *curandera*. Using herbs and natural cures to fix ailments.

"Yes, that's what Grandma did. Like a healer."

"The thing is, she was more than a *curandera*. When we were little, we would hear people call her a *bruja*. A witch. The first time I heard someone call her that, I told the lady off. She was in our house and called my mother a witch. I was so angry."

"What happened?"

"I got my butt whipped, is what happened. Your grandma got so mad at me for being rude to her friend. What I didn't know was that she meant the term in a good way. The woman was in awe. I didn't realize until I was a teenager that your grandma could heal not just a cold, but she knew spells and methods of helping with someone's soul. The insides of their being."

"Did she teach this to you and Mom?"

"Hah! Mia, you know how sometimes colored eyes or a special talent skips a generation?"

Mia nodded.

"Well, it skipped me and your mother. She tried to teach us some basic things about healing herbs. Your mom burned stuff when she tried, and I'd usually cut myself if I used anything sharp. I once sat there and did everything right, step by step, and your grandma just looked down and threw everything in the trash. That's when she knew. We had zero of her talents."

"Did you feel bad?"

"No, not at all. I saw what she did, but it was never something I really wanted to do. When you were about four or five, you once saw her doing something in the kitchen and ran up and asked her about it. She made you pull up a footstool and you stood there, watching everything she did. Eventually, you were helping her mix things, and you paid attention. You were completely fascinated, and Mom had this gleam in her eye that we never saw when we tried. Eventually, she had you helping with more advanced mixes."

"What does that mean? I don't remember that at all. Not until I was older."

"What kind of memories do you have?"

"I remember it being like helping her cook. It just felt natural. I never thought any more than that."

"It was definitely more than that," Grace said.

"What do you mean?"

"When she said you were special, she wasn't just being nice. You have a talent for it. I think you would be knee deep in it if she and your mom hadn't died so close to each other. Now I feel bad that I didn't pursue it when you moved in with us."

"No, Aunt Grace. Don't even try to feel guilty. You had to take in another kid to go with your four."

She smiled. "I still should have, but then again, not sure how I would have helped since I was so bad at it. What brought this on, Mia?"

Mia took in a breath. She promised she would explain, so she did. She didn't give every detail, but she knew her aunt wouldn't think it was crazy. Not with a mother like hers.

When she was done, Aunt Grace sighed. "This brings up old memories. And you're saying this man just knew?"

Mia nodded. "Yes, I'm not sure how, but he's pretty special, too, from what I can tell."

"And there's a baby at stake?"

"Yes."

"What do you think you're going to do?" she asked.

"It's a baby's soul. I know Brian and Brenda are in middle school now, but I still sometimes picture them as toddlers that Bianca and I used to babysit. What if it was one of them? I think I have to at least try."

Grace sighed. "That's what your grandmother would do. I would have told him to piss off and figured he was a perv, to tell you the truth, but I don't have the sense that you do. Are you sure?"

"Not 100%, but knowing myself, how can I say no if something happens to that baby and I might have been able to help?"

"I understand. You have more of your grandmother in you than her own daughters did. I mean that in a good way. Mom was always trying to help strangers and people in need. It's just who she was. Your mom and I wanted none of it."

"Thank you."

Grace bit her lip before speaking. "So, are you going to tell Tino?"

She hadn't thought about it but knew she couldn't keep it to herself.

"Yes, I should see him tonight. I'll tell him."

"What do you think he'll say?"

"I'm not sure. He knows a little about Grandma, but not many details. I haven't told him anything about what's been happening at school."

"Why not?"

"I don't know how he'll react to something like that. What if it scares him off?"

"Look, I know he's got that old macho thing going on, and I'm not going to tell you again how I think you should have moved on a long time ago—"

"Yet you just did," Mia said, smiling.

"I'm sorry, Mia. I just think you have to be comfortable enough to talk to him about almost anything."

"He gets it from his dad," Mia said. "You know that."

"Doesn't matter. He's in a modern world and should be man enough to make his own decisions."

"Easy to say, but not reality. I don't know. If I'm going to do this, I have to at least let him know. I just don't want to freak him out."

"Trust your instincts. Do what you have to do. You've been together for what, three years now?"

"Three and a half, but who's counting?" Mia said.

"Good luck with that. I think you're doing a good thing. If you want to do it, don't let him change your mind."

"Thank you, Aunt Grace. I'm glad I talked to you. Good memories of Grandma today."

Grace smiled. "Yes, I miss her and your mom every day.

You'd make them both proud. Go ahead and grab something to eat. I take it you're going to study until you go see Tino? I have to go get Brian and Brenda soon. Why don't you just study here if you don't want to go back to your apartment?"

"Thank you. I'll do that."

She tried her best to study but was distracted. Her cousins were happy to see her, but they had their own homework to do before dinner.

Mia's phone dinged about ten minutes before six. Tino told her he was heading home, and she wasn't sure if she was dreading it or looking forward to it.

Chapter Five

Mia drove to Tino's house. They'd grown up a few blocks from each until Tino moved with his dad halfway across town, but it was only twenty minutes by car. Tino was in the shower when she arrived. His dad let her in, gave her a nod, and then went back to his room like he usually did. She pulled out a textbook and read until Tino finally came out.

He smiled when he saw her and gave her a quick kiss.

"We staying in tonight?" he asked.

"You want to get something fast to eat?" she asked. "Just some pizza down at Roots would work."

He looked at her. "Something wrong?"

"No, just need to talk to you about something that happened at school today."

"What? Somebody hit on you? Do I need to go down there tomorrow and kick some ass?"

His first reaction was always the most outlandish one. No one had hit on her. Not today, at least. She usually kept her head down but still received an occasional offer to lunch or a movie. She would politely tell them no thank

37

you and that she had a boyfriend. Most of them were fine with that. If anyone went overboard, she just ignored them until they quit.

"No, nothing like that. Let's just go, okay?"

He nodded but held her gaze for a few seconds. "Okay."

They drove three blocks to an outdoor shopping center. Roots had been there for over twenty years and was locally owned by the parents of one of their high school classmates.

They ordered and said hello to the owners, who they had known most of their lives. They ate an appetizer of mozzarella sticks and talked until the pizza arrived. Tino didn't push, but he didn't hide his impatience.

They each had a couple of slices, and as Tino picked up the third, she saw his anxiousness. His thoughts would get more paranoid if she waited any longer.

She took a sip of her drink and then inhaled a deep breath.

"Okay, so you know my grandmother was a *curandera*."

He nodded. "Yeah, you mentioned that a long time ago. What does that have to do with school?"

"Be patient. It's been a strange day. It turns out her skills went way beyond a normal *curandera*. According to my Aunt Grace, I may have the same type of skills she did."

Tino just nodded.

"I've been having some weird things happen in class. Things that are hard to explain."

"Are you failing?"

She frowned at him. "That's your first conclusion?"

"Sorry. Keep going."

She proceeded to tell him about what had been happening with her experiments and how she had even freaked her professor out. She explained in more detail than she needed to, since she was avoiding getting to Mr. Strand as long as she could. But it was time.

"My professor stopped me today and told me about a man who wanted to talk to me."

She told him every detail. How the man was able to sense her and how she had felt and sensed him when she was eating and when he was in the room with her.

"So, what does he want from you?"

"To help him with his granddaughter. He thinks she's missing her soul and that I might be able to help."

"Why would you help him? What if he's some kind of serial killer?"

That thought had crossed her mind about 30 seconds after learning the stranger was asking about her, but after their conversation, she didn't think he was out for murder.

"He knows my professor's friend, who said he trusted the man. So I don't have any reason to be scared."

"You told him you'd help him?"

"No, Tino. That's why I'm talking to you. I spoke to my aunt when I got home and after she told me more about my Grandma, I decided I need to at least give him a call and hear him out. I just wanted to tell you first."

"That's why you shouldn't be at school and exposed to these weirdos. You should let me take care of you. It's my job."

She shook her head.

Not this bullshit again.

In the time they'd been together, his outdated attitude hadn't changed. She thought maybe after a few years in college he would let up, but it had just gotten worse.

"You already know how I feel. We have a better chance at a future if we both work. I'm not going to stop going to school because of your outdated attitude."

"It's the man's job to take care of his girl."

She wanted to get up and smack him with the cheese shaker and tell him the blunt truth he always seemed to ignore. He couldn't support her on his own, and her idea of being taken care of didn't involve living with his father. But she held her tongue.

Mia had accepted his attitude wasn't completely his fault, and he had never commanded her to do anything. Not yet, at least. She didn't want to get into a fight, so she took another bite of her pizza before speaking again.

"Tino, I'm just letting you know. I'm not asking permission."

"I don't think you should do it. Not unless I go with you."

"Like your dad's going to give you a day off for that."

"He will!" Tino stiffened up. "He might. If I tell him it's important."

Her eyebrows rose as Tino continued. "Can you meet this stranger after I get out of work?"

"I don't know. It's not the point. If you're there, you're going to find something to say since you can't contain yourself."

"I'm a passionate guy. That's why you love me."

"No, it is because I love you that I put up with it more than I should. Let me just meet with him alone. If I can't help, this will be over soon. It's a baby, Tino. How can I say no?"

He didn't answer for over a minute and looked down. He was breathing hard, the air whistling out of his nostrils. He thought college was a waste of time, but he knew nothing he said would change Mia's mind.

"Whenever you do go, you need to call or text me before you get in and we're gonna set a limit. I need to know where you'll be, and if I don't hear from you every 10 minutes, I'm going in."

"Every 20 minutes," Mia said.

He looked at her and finally blinked. "Okay."

They both took a few minutes to eat another slice of pizza and calm themselves before they said another word. There was still a hint of anger and frustration in his voice when he did speak. She had already made her decision.

Mia was going to at least try, and as much as she didn't want to stir the pot with Tino, he wasn't going to stop her. Not this time.

Chapter Six

Mia's first class the next day started at 10 a.m. and she arrived on campus by 9:30.

She sat on the same bench where she had been the day before. She didn't have Professor Cort's botany class today, but planned to wait until the next class to drop by and tell him about her decision and how it went with Strand. She pulled out the stranger's card and dialed the number.

"Yes?" his voice answered in a monotone.

"Mr. Strand? This is Mia. We met yesterday."

"Yes, Mia, I remember your voice. You have made a decision."

"How do you know?"

"I can sense it. You are also anxious to tell me. I am unsure if that is a good or bad omen."

"Yes, I have. I thought about it and I'm willing to meet your granddaughter to see if there's a way I can help. I still don't see how, but I'd like to try."

"That is wonderful news, Mia. When is a convenient time?"

"When's good for you?"

"I will work around your schedule. You just inform me when you have an hour or two to spare."

Mia would be in class late today and had a test tomorrow.

"It's already Thursday. Is Saturday good? I have classes in between."

"I would like to meet sooner, but a two-day wait is fine. I will meet you on Saturday. Give me a good time and I will send you the information on where to meet. I cannot thank you enough. I hope we will have success with you."

"Okay," Mia said.

She wasn't sure what she'd just agreed to, but she felt good about it.

Mia got through her classes and aced her quiz on Friday, then called Soren Strand to set up the time and location as soon as she was out.

"Greetings, Mia. Are you still available for tomorrow?"

"I can meet any time after 10:30."

She figured it would give her a chance to eat breakfast and be alert for whatever might happen.

"I will send you the address of the house we are renting."

They hung up, and she received the text a minute later.

Going to his house, she thought. *What if it was an elaborate cage where he'll keep me forever?*

That couldn't happen. Tino wanted her to check in every 20 minutes and he would come for her if she didn't do it.

Mia got up the next morning and already had a text from Tino, who had gone into work extra early. After a week of studying and homework, Mia liked to sleep in an extra two or three hours on the weekend, but today would be cut short. She was up by nine and Tino made her promise she'd call him before she left. He wanted her to go by the worksite, but he knew his father would be upset if she came by unless it was during lunch or a break.

She called Tino, but it went straight to voicemail. She knew he had rejected the call. Ten seconds later, her phone dinged.

"Sorry, can't talk," Tino texted. "Working. Just text me before you go and when you get there. Then every twenty minutes like we said, okay?"

"I will."

"Promise?"

"Promise."

"Okay, be careful. I'll be worried the whole time you're gone. And if anything seems wrong, leave. I'll talk to you during my lunch break. Love you."

As overly macho as he tried to be sometimes, he didn't hesitate telling her how he felt. The problem was, he also thought that justified his behavior.

"Love you, too."

She stopped texting and called her aunt. "Any plans today, Aunt Grace?"

"Bianca and I are going shopping a little later. You getting ready to go meet that man with the grandbaby?"

"Yes, we'll see how it goes."

"Just be smart. I know I don't have to tell you that. Now your cousin Bianca, I have to remind every five minutes. But you? You I don't have to worry too much about."

"Thanks Auntie. I'm just nervous."

"I get it. I'd be nervous, too. We don't know what this man sees in you. This may not mean anything, or it may open a whole new world. Keep your mind open, but know your limits. If you can't help, don't force it."

"I know. I'm nervous, but excited. I'm afraid I'll be disappointed if it's nothing, but also afraid if it turns out to be something real."

"I understand. You call me if anything happens, okay? I'll be back in a few hours when you should be right in the middle of your meeting. I'll take off and slice that man's throat if I have to."

Aunt Grace probably wouldn't kill the man unless he truly tried to hurt Mia, but she was a mama lion. Even if she didn't kill him, Mia believed she'd at least put him in the hospital.

After hanging up, Mia put the address on her phone's GPS and took off.

Tino had already texted her a few times. She messaged him when she left, but he knew she wouldn't read or reply if she was driving.

When she was five minutes away, she turned off the highway into a neighborhood with houses bigger than she was used to seeing. They weren't mansions, but two-story, older, and beautiful.

She was several blocks in and went through a maze of unfamiliar roads and finally reached the right street. She slowed down and rolled down her window, checking on the addresses that were hard to see on the houses. She never fully trusted her GPS, but knew she was close.

Finally, she reached her destination and pulled in front of a house with a semi-circle driveway.

She read her texts from Tino after she parked and sent him a message that she had arrived and was about to head in. He didn't reply right away, but she felt confident he'd start counting the minutes as soon as he read the text receipt time.

She parked and got out of the car. Mr. Strand was waiting in the doorway.

The door was partially open behind him. He was wearing the same coat and hat he had on the day he met her.

"Greetings, Mia. Thank you for coming."

"Were you leaving, Mr. Strand?"

"Please, feel free to call me Soren or just Strand. And no, I'm not going anywhere just yet. I'm naturally averse to low temperatures, but the baby seems to prefer the cold, so we have the AC running low in the house. It is a minor inconvenience compared to what my granddaughter is going through. Please come in."

He pulled the door open a little wider and a younger girl stood by the stairs.

"This is my daughter, Anna," he said. "I wanted you to meet her before meeting my granddaughter."

He leaned in towards Mia and whispered, "She's a bit of a germaphobe, so please take no offense if she doesn't shake your hand or allow you to touch her. She means no disrespect."

Mia walked in and nodded towards his daughter.

"Anna, this is Mia."

Anna nodded her head and gave a weak smile. She motioned for them to follow and started up the stairs.

Strand extended his arm.

"The baby is on the second floor. Please go ahead."

They went up the stairs, which led into a small open area in the center and two hallways on either side. They walked into the left hallway, and Anna entered the second room on the right.

Mia followed. The walls were decorated with pink balloons and teddy bears. The crib was made out of natural wood. Anna stood at the crib and looked down.

Mia eased forward and got her first look at the baby. She realized Strand had never told her the baby's name.

Mia looked down. The baby was pale, and her eyes were closed. The veins in her head were easily visible, and she had her hands balled into fists. Her lips were dry and chapped.

"This is my granddaughter, Annika," Mr. Strand said. "She will wake soon. She never sleeps more than two hours consecutively."

Mia whispered. "When she is up, what is it you want me to do?"

Strand smiled. "Just look into her eyes. Pick her up. I need to see the interaction between the two of you. I need to sense some kind of connection. If there isn't one, then I will thank you and we will move on. If there is a connection, I may ask you to do a little more. Just remember to keep your mind open."

"My mind's been more open the last few days than it's ever been in my whole life."

"That is good. Extremely good."

As if on cue, the baby stirred. Anna put her hand on the baby's chest.

Strand gestured Mia forward. "Please, take a look at her face."

Anna moved back. The baby didn't cry but was making noises in her own language.

Mia looked over the crib. The baby's eyes were open and gazing right at her, but she didn't react to the stranger staring at her. She didn't cry or get fussy. She just stared.

Mia looked closer.

"You may lift her up," Mr. Strand said.

Mia instinctively turned to Anna. She knew better than to touch a baby without the mother's consent. As she stared at the baby's mother, she realized Anna could have passed for 14 or 19. She still looked so young.

As Mia studied her, Anna's eyes diverted to her father. She looked back at Mia and nodded.

"It's okay," she mumbled.

Mia looked back and reached into the crib, gently putting her hands underneath the baby and lifting her up with care.

She was so small and light. She pulled her up vertically, so that the baby's face looked straight at Mia's.

Mia couldn't stop staring at Annika's big, blue eyes. She got lost in them for a few seconds. Mia got a sense that Annika was gazing into her, too. She thought maybe it was Mr. Strand trying to read them, but that wasn't it. It was something else.

Something was missing. Mia had an odd feeling she'd never experienced before. She focused deeper into Annika's eyes, and the baby held the gaze. Neither one blinked nor moved for the next several moments.

An unfamiliar sensation overcame Mia. It wasn't like the headache that Mr. Strand had given her at the university quad. It wasn't happy, and it wasn't sad. Empty was the best way to describe it. It was like Mia had a part of her insides pulled out that left a gaping void inside her.

Then a sense of sadness washed over her. Mia pulled Annika in close, resting the baby's cheek against her own. She felt a tear stream down unexpectedly, followed by another. She didn't start bawling, but the tears continued. She rubbed her face against the baby's. Annika cooed, but just barely. Mia kissed her cheek. Annika breathed a little harder and then gave Mia a strong embrace before gently resting her face on Mia's shoulders.

Annika didn't make a sound. She just seemed like she was calm and comfortable in Mia's arms.

Mia had no way of understanding what it was she was feeling, but the sense of emptiness was undeniable.

She needs me.

If her soul was truly missing, Mia already knew she would do whatever was in her power to save this child and get it back, even though she had no idea how.

Mia turned back to Strand.

"What did you see? Or feel?" Mia asked. "Or whatever it is you are able to do?"

Mr. Strand had his eyes closed, then eased them open.

"I believe you are what I have been searching for. She responded to you. There is definitely a connection. Are you willing to step in all the way?"

Mia's eyes watered and she hugged the baby a little closer.

"I want to, but how do you know that I can help?"

"That is what will come next. The connection is one thing. The ability to affect a change is quite another. There is a place where I want us all to travel to. It's in a remote location and you may find it uncomfortable to go to with a stranger, and the place is ... strange, to say the least."

"This entire week has been strange," Mia said. "What could possibly shock me now?"

"Then shall we proceed?"

Mia nodded. "Yes, I have to know."

"Please, bring her down with you. Let us begin now."

He led the way downstairs. Anna started to put her baby bag together and made no effort to take Annika back from Mia.

"Do you wish to travel with me, or would you prefer to follow? It will be a thirty to forty-minute drive to reach our destination."

Mia knew she should follow them, but that would

mean separating from the baby, which she didn't want to do.

"It's okay. I'll go with you."

"Excellent. Please, follow me."

They headed into the garage. There were two vehicles, a black Cadillac Escalade and a smaller sports car.

They entered the SUV. The car seat was already set up.

"Mia, please feel free to stay in the back with Annika. It will give you more time to bond as we travel."

Her phone started to beep. It was her reminder to text Tino.

She texted as Anna and Mr. Strand strapped the baby into the car seat.

I'm okay, Tino. Baby and daughter were here. Story is legit. Still checking a few things, but I'm okay.

This time, he replied almost instantly. *Don't stay any longer than you have to.*

Mia wasn't about to tell him she'd already done something dangerous. She'd gotten into a vehicle with a stranger. She knew it was stupid and a Safety 101 common sense mistake, but all she could think about was the sadness she felt for Annika and how badly she wanted to help her.

Everything else was secondary.

Yet the thought of this entire thing being a ruse to take her to the woods to kill and torture her filled her mind.

One way or another, she was about to find out.

Chapter Seven

ANNA STAYED in the front seat as they traveled. They were soon out of the city limits and heading into the countryside.

Mia looked at Annika and couldn't understand why she had no reaction to the drive. Every baby she'd ever been in a car with would either cry, laugh, or at least look around when traveling. But Annika just sat there. She did look at Mia a few times but didn't try to reach for her. She seemed comfortable and docile. That was it.

"Where are we going?" Mia finally asked.

"Don't be alarmed," Mr. Strand said. "It is an area that has a strong connection to the spiritual world. It will help me determine if there is any hope of you having the power to help Annika.

They traveled the rest of the way in silence.

Finally, they were close. Mia had already messaged Tino again as the second twenty-minute deadline passed.

"We are almost there," Mr. Strand said. "You may want to message your person that you may miss the next deadline."

Mia's face reddened. "How did you know?"

"Your phone dinged almost exactly 20 minutes ago with what I assume is a reminder. You've then sent a message on your phone almost immediately. You are in a car with strangers in a situation that would be difficult to explain to those close to you. I would be concerned if you did not have a safety plan in place."

"It's just … my boyfriend worries about me."

"As he should. It's a good sign that he is worrying. We are only a few minutes away now. Please let him know you may miss the next curfew. It is difficult to get a phone signal at the place we are going to."

She nodded and texted Tino to give her up to an hour before freaking out since they had limited reception.

Strand pulled off the two-lane road, and they passed acres of tall corn crops. This time Mia was looking ahead, curious about where they might be going.

The car slowed. There were no houses or businesses, just the endless cornfields.

Strand pulled into an area where several large, thick trees appeared and stopped.

"What is this place?" Mia asked.

"We call it Hollow Rock," Mr. Strand said. "It will make more sense once you see it."

He started to unstrap Annika as Anna waited outside the car.

Mia held the baby as she followed Mr. Strand. As they moved past the trees, Mr. Strand stopped and reached down, moving loose grass and leaves that were covering up something.

Underneath the leaves, just a few feet off the ground, was a set of doors, similar to a tornado bunker. Mr. Strand removed more vegetation, pulled the storm doors open, and entered.

Anna motioned for Mia to follow and went in herself.

Mia got to the doors and looked in. There was a staircase leading down. She started walking and noticed faint lighting that increased the more she approached. She didn't see any light bulbs, but a glow was emanating from somewhere ahead.

She went down several more feet and then walked into a wider opening that lit up with blue light and saw Mr. Strand and Anna standing in wait. She looked around and couldn't believe what she was seeing.

One side of the room contained a stream of water running through it that was about two feet wide. The blue light was coming from the water, and the reflection of the light sparkled along the walls. The room looked more like a cave.

"What is this?" Mia asked.

"It's a natural cavern that connects to a caved-in tunnel further to the south. I suspect this was used at one point to smuggle people and illegal contraband, but it seems the cave-in stopped any criminal activity."

She looked closer. There was a marble table set up in the center of the room, about twenty feet from the stream.

"What is that table for?"

"For the baby," Strand said. "This table is important. If there is any chance of saving Annika, it will have to happen within this cave. With the table and the stream."

"I don't understand. What's so special about this cave?"

"Please, let us try this. If it works, I shall provide additional details about this location. There is no point in delving into them if this will not possible. Please place Annika here."

Strand pointed to the table as he moved toward it. Mia

joined him, as her instinct to protect Annika was replaced with concern.

Anna reached into her baby bag. She pulled out a thick blanket and placed it on the table.

"Please place her on the blanket," Strand said. "She will be okay, I assure you."

Mia looked at him, then back to Anna. They didn't look like they had anything sinister planned, although it looked a bit like they were setting Annika up to be sacrificed.

She placed Annika on the blanket. Mia was afraid she might roll off, but other than her feet and hands flexing, the baby didn't move much. She just took turns staring at Mia and Anna.

"What now?" Mia asked.

"Now we check if you are able to make a connection with this place. It is unique. The water in this stream has remained pure over the years. This one is special, but requires a conduit."

"A conduit?"

"Someone or something that can channel the power that comes through the water. This is a spiritual place. There are many areas in the world that border the different planes of existence. The Underworld, Heavens, and all other planes that exist. There are more than you would ever expect. Places such as this one where the borders between these worlds are thinner make those planes easier to reach. If there is any chance of reconnecting her soul, a sacred place such as this one is key."

"What do you need me to do?" Mia asked.

"Just place your hands on Annika, please."

Mia nodded and put a hand on the baby's chest and the other on her head. The baby reached up for the hand on her head, and Mia extended her free index finger without removing her entire hand. The baby gripped the finger gently. Her facial expression didn't change, but Mia felt a calmness within her.

Mr. Strand walked to the stream and gently reached down and scooped up water in his cupped hand. He fixated on the water and stood up, then turned to the table and let the water drip gently on the hand that Mia had placed on Annika's chest.

The water was cold at first, but Mia felt her hands warm. Then she felt a small jolt between the center of her palm and Annika's skin. Another jolt coursed through the finger that Annika was holding. The baby gripped her finger tighter and twitched as another surge of energy hit. It wasn't painful, just unexpected. It felt stronger than being zapped with static electricity, but not enough to hurt. Mr. Strand reached back down into the stream to gather more water, but this time he let it drop on his granddaughter's head.

More jolts followed, but they were less powerful and more steady. They didn't hurt, and Mia was able to remain calm now that she knew what was coming. The baby's head moved left and right like she was trying to figure out what was happening. It was the most Mia had seen her react to anything so far.

Strand put his hands over Mia's and then held his palm on Annika's head as well. He closed his eyes and then slowly opened them.

He motioned to Anna, who pulled a small towel from the bag.

"You may let go now," he said.

Mia lifted her hands, but the baby didn't want to let go of her finger. Mia lifted her hand higher, but let Annika keep her grip.

Strand took the towel and gently dried off the baby's

hands and head, then dabbed every part that had gotten wet.

Anna handed Mia a towel. She dried off her hands, never letting go of Annika's grip.

"You may take her," Strand said.

Mia picked up Annika, and the baby wrapped her arms around Mia's neck with gentle force.

"What just happened?"

"There is already some power here. The spiritual power that comes from being between worlds. I poured the water to see what would happen, and you made a connection. This is something I cannot do and no one we have encountered so far can do, either. If we are able to retrieve her soul, we need to be able to return it to her body. This is where it can happen. You are the one, Mia Morales. You are who we've been looking for. Will you please help us? Will you help Annika?"

She knew what her answer would be before he asked it. She held Annika closer.

"Yes, of course. I'll do whatever I must to save her."

"I cannot thank you enough, young Mia," Mr. Strand said. "I will be forever in your debt if you are able to help save my granddaughter."

"I'll do my best," Mia said as she held Annika.

"Now, I'm sure you're wondering what comes next."

"Saying I'll help and not understanding exactly how is a little terrifying," Mia said.

She had committed to do what she could, but she didn't have any idea what that meant.

"I believe that in order to truly save Annika, you will require much more power, and I do not just mean from you. Power for this type of magic not only needs someone as talented as yourself, but it must be at the right time under the right circumstances. In truth, as strong as you are, you require more focus. What you have now are raw, natural abilities. You need to enhance them in whatever way possible, both within and around you."

"How do I do that? I'm not even sure what I'm supposed to do."

"For the next few days, I ask that you return here. Call me, and I will meet you at any time of the day or evening. You may even reach a point where you can come on your own. We will work on tasks to help you concentrate and refine your abilities. When the time is right, we will perform the first step of what I think is necessary to heal Annika."

"So I just show up?"

"For now. After what I just witnessed, I have confidence we will succeed. When will you be able to meet again?"

Annika held on a little tighter.

"I have some studying to do the rest of the weekend, but I'll call you tomorrow and arrange something for Monday," Mia said. "I have a three-hour gap in classes and should be able to meet you sometime between."

"That will be fine. I am at your mercy, and you have my eternal gratitude."

Mia smiled. "I just want to help save her."

They walked out of the underground cave and back into the car. Tino had already texted her three times. The messages all popped up as soon as they exited. Definitely no reception down there.

Once they got Annika in the car, she texted him back. *I'm okay. Took a little long, but heading back. I'll call you once I'm on my way.*

Can you come over?

She thought for a moment. *No, I have too much homework and have a quiz Monday morning. Let me get it all done tonight and hopefully tomorrow night will be better.*

He didn't text for another couple of minutes, then *OK* was all he sent. She knew that meant he wasn't happy, but right now, she felt saving this baby's life was more important than anything else in her life. She needed to clear out as much of her schoolwork as possible to dedicate the proper time.

They arrived back at Strand's rental house, and she left after giving Annika a kiss on the cheek. Annika didn't react, but it made Mia feel better. She had planned to call Tino once she got on the road, but her thoughts kept racing to what had just happened.

Could I possibly save this child's soul?

Chapter Eight

GABBY STOOD with her gun drawn, aiming at the animal writhing on the ground.

"*Imeanza roho. Umefukuzwa! Imeanza roho. Dunia inakuamuru!*" Ricky said softly.

This was the first time he had spoken the Swahili incantation correctly since Dr. Jackie had taught it to him when trying to save his mother not so long ago.

Imeanza roho. Begone spirit.

Umefukuzwa! You are banished!

Imeanza roho. Begone spirit.

Dunia inakuamuru! The Earth commands you.

It took three encounters to get it right and fully memorized. He found he was able to gain his focus much easier once it became second nature.

Ricky and Gabby were in an abandoned house without electricity. It was just after midnight.

Ricky continued, his voice gradually rising. "*Imeanza roho. Umefukuzwa! Imeanza roho. Dunia inakuamuru!*"

The huge rat's foot-long tail whipped as it spun and jumped on its hind legs. Its eyes were red. It hissed, but it didn't move. Gabby raised her gun and was about to pull the trigger when something moved on her right. Gabby turned her gun in the direction, but before she could see anything, the rat was dead on the floor. The black feral cat that had been hiding in the shadows had snapped its prey's neck.

"The case of the spirit-killing cat," Ricky sighed.

"We got some practice out of it," Gabby said as she lowered her gun. "One less piece of evil in the world."

"That wasn't even a challenge," Ricky said, shaking his head. "Not our demons. It was a weak spirit at best."

"We'll get there, Ricky. We just need to find a better way. I still can't believe how many dark incidents are out there."

"At least we know the intel was good and this wasn't a total waste."

"This spirit could have hurt others, and I'm glad we stopped it, but I don't know how much time Ally has left. We need to do something else. Fast."

"Something like what?" Ricky said. "I'm not sure what else to do."

"Your contacts in these chatrooms. How much do you tell them about what we're really doing and looking for? Still not everything?"

"No, not everything."

"Maybe it's time to tell them."

"That's the problem. The people out there who do tell everything sound crazy. Some get removed right away."

"Maybe don't tell everyone. Maybe share more details with the few you think you can trust. Send them pics of this demon rat to show them you listened. What about the new guy that sent us here?"

Ricky hesitated. "That's not a bad idea. There are only

a small number of people that I might be willing to trust, anyway. Maybe I'll include the new guy, too."

"Tell them the way you're telling me. Tell them a little more of what we've seen and what we've gone through. If they don't turn on you, then offer a little more. Just keep them from knowing who we really are."

"So I shouldn't mention that I was tried and acquitted of murder based on how crazy my story was?"

"No, if they know who you are, they may turn against you with preconceived notions. If you can just reach a few legitimate resources that believe your story, I think they'll sympathize."

"I guess that's a solid approach. Let's get back to the hotel and you can help me put a good message together."

They watched the cat finish off its kill. Ricky stepped near it to be sure it hadn't gotten possessed, but it looked at him and stood its ground, guarding its only meal of the day. Gabby was snapping pictures, just in case.

"Kitty is clean," Ricky said. "Just hungry. Enjoy the Spirit Special, wildcat."

They left and returned to their hotel. They had only been in Huntsville one night. The intel that led them to the possessed rat house was solid, but they detected the creature without much effort. They had it beaten in less than half an hour, even with the feline assist.

They initially rented separate rooms when they were able to stay at hotels, but over the months, they had grown comfortable enough to book a single room with double beds. Their shared trauma had made them close, like siblings brought together by fate.

Ricky was on his laptop when Gabby finished washing up and came out of the bathroom.

"Gabby, I'm in," he said. "Let me know if you think this is too much info or not enough."

Ricky pointed to his draft.

"Found and destroyed a minor spirit tonight in an abandoned house in Huntsville. Easy kill. Used small exorcism and spirit shifted into a rat, which was then killed by a hungry cat. A little embarrassing, but the truth. Pics attached. The problem is that this is our tenth encounter, but we have a much larger goal and we're limited on time. We need someone who can point us in the right direction. I'm hoping that someone is in this smaller group, so I'm sharing the rest of this with caution."

Ricky sighed. "And this is where I'm letting loose. I questioned if this was a good idea with every word I typed."

Gabby read the rest out loud. "We're looking for two powerful demons. What we encountered tonight doesn't come close to the type of power these demons exhibit. I don't want to give too much more information away just yet. I need to know who I can trust. All I will say now is the demons are strong. One lives and travels in reflections. The other feeds on fear. If any of this sounds like something you can help with and you don't think I'm nuts, please send some feedback and I'll decide if I can share more. Serious replies only, and thank you in advance to anyone who might be able to help."

Gabby put her hand on Ricky's shoulder. "That sounds good, Ricky. Maybe mention some of our other legitimate encounters. Something they might be able to verify."

Ricky added the additional details. Once he was done and she reviewed it, he added one last note.

"I hope this is enough to prove our worth, and if you are able to filter the truth in this message, please contact me via DM. We will continue to move on, but we can't afford any more distractions."

He posted the message. He stared at it for a few

seconds, half expecting he'd get a quick reply, but he knew there wouldn't be. Someone who truly believed them would take the time to validate their story.

Ricky left the laptop on and took his turn to wash up. They had driven without much sleep and were going to take advantage of an early ending to the night.

"If we don't hear back, where are we heading tomorrow? Arkansas or Louisiana?"

Ricky shrugged. "If you have no preference, we'll flip for it. We're flying half-blind anyway."

She nodded. "You know Halloween is just a few weeks away and whenever I see anything related, I picture the bodies I worked with in my head. I know you don't say much about it, but do you still think about your sugar skull, or is it just the demons?"

"I see both. The skull is still the most unnerving."

"Why?"

"It just all reminds me of losing Ellie. That skull ties everything together."

He reached into his backpack and pulled out the skull. "I can't believe I still can't break this thing, even though I know it's no longer possessed. I still remember when my sister Myra handed it to me, saying it appeared in her room while I was still in jail. Then there are the skull designs that appeared on the faces of your dead body displays. After all this time, I still don't know what it all means."

"I understand," Gabby said. "I dream of those bodies almost every day, and I don't think it'll stop until we save Ally."

Ricky put the skull back in his pack and they went to sleep.

It was still dark when Ricky jumped up, startled by another sugar skull dream. It had been his grandmother again, speaking through the skull. She told him she understood why he was doing what he was doing, but she wanted him to get back to his sister and to his life as soon as he defeated the demons. Then the skull exploded and jolted him awake, but instead of hearing an explosion, it was a ding.

He walked over to his laptop. He had a message.

He clicked the notification. It was from "Dead-Blogger."

"SkullBrother, I read your message last night and spent a few hours doing some research, which I finished this morning. I believe you. More importantly, I think I can help you. If you're truly serious, reply with an encrypted message."

"Gabby!" Ricky yelled. "Wake up!"

Gabby was a light sleeper, especially since Ally had been born. She leapt out of bed.

"Did you hear back?"

"Yes, the new guy, DeadBlogger, says he can help us. He didn't provide details, which makes me think he might be a fraud after all, but he wants to discuss over a secure line."

"Is he available now?"

"I just got the message, so I would hope so."

She pulled up next to him on the small table and grabbed a chair.

"Let's do it," she said as she rubbed her eyes. They tried to avoid speaking directly to each other since both needed a good teeth-brushing. This was more important.

Ricky opened a private session and turned on the end-to-end encryption to increase security.

He typed, "Thank you for replying, DeadBlogger. Hoping you are serious as we are trying to determine our next steps. Ready to talk."

They both stared at the screen as Ricky sent the message. Nothing happened for the next minute.

"Watch this, please," Ricky said. "I need to wake up."

He ran to the bathroom, splashed cold water on his face, and started to brush his teeth.

The laptop dinged.

Ricky rushed to the bed and jumped into his spot with the toothbrush still in his mouth.

DeadBlogger had replied.

"I am serious. I think I can narrow down your choices of where your demons may be. I just need a little more information."

Ricky's heart sank. One of the warning signs was someone asking for information without providing anything to justify why. A typical red flag for a fishing expedition.

"You'll forgive me if I'm hesitant to provide more info without some type of verification of why you believe us. We have much to protect."

The reply was almost immediate.

"I understand. You mentioned you were hunting two demons. One with reflective characteristics, correct?"

"Yes."

"These must be higher-level demons compared to what I know you've already faced. What you stated was bold, and we both know over 95% of the people here won't believe you and why I think you targeted a much smaller audience. That final 5%, though, those are the true warriors who are invested in what we do. It's difficult to weed that out, but I have some special connections that may help."

"What type of special connections?"

"Those are mostly my secrets, but let's just say, along

with other people, I have some gifts. Sometimes they are stirred by special circumstances. Even an online post."

Gabby and Ricky looked at each other. "You buy this?" Ricky asked her.

"Sounds like bullshit, but if he believes our bullshit, what have we got to lose? Keep going."

"Okay, I'll bite for now."

Ricky typed. "Small steps until we determine if we can or can't trust each other."

"Then let's start by telling me something private that you haven't shared on these boards. I will do the same."

Ricky thought for a moment.

"The demons I seek possessed me. They made me do things I couldn't control."

There was a long pause.

"I sense and see things I can't really explain. I think the demons you are looking for have been in my thoughts and dreams."

"How?" Ricky typed.

"Follow the rules."

Ricky turned to Gabby. "All in?"

"All in," she said.

"My situation was public. Extremely public. My life was destroyed, and I went on trial. I was acquitted since the judge felt there was no way to legally prove what everyone in that courtroom saw, but refused to believe was true. That unseen supernatural forces, witnessed by over a hundred people and caught on camera, were actually responsible for what I was accused of. There was no way to link it legally."

"Ricky Luna," DeadBlogger typed. "I suspected, and I followed your case. I truly believe you were taken over by these demons. You lost your girlfriend, didn't you?"

"Yes. I lost her."

Ricky's fingers trembled as he continued to type. "I killed her."

"You did no such thing. Whatever it was did this to you. I didn't track them further myself since I thought they had disappeared, but a few months ago I read about some disturbances and started to sense something strong. I didn't link it to you until last night when I read your post."

"Are you a medium or psychic of some kind?"

"Something like that. I honestly can't explain it, but I do sense things and sometimes they turn into patterns. It's rare, but it happens. And it's happening now."

"I shared a couple of my deepest secrets. One that I knew might make you walk away. What is yours?"

"I am much younger than I allow myself to be perceived. I have to look up some of these words before I type so I don't sound my age. I believe I have some kind of connection to other planes where spirits and darkness exist."

Ricky started to breathe faster and turned to Gabby.

"Do you still believe him?"

"Yes," she replied. "It's too batshit crazy not to be somewhat true. At least he believes it."

"We choose to believe you," Ricky typed. "For now."

"I have not asked about your partner, but were they involved, too? Your best friend, maybe?"

"No, not my best friend. The woman with me was also affected by the demons after what happened to me. She has more at stake than I do. If you can get us more information, I will share details of her story if she agrees. For now, I can tell you that the stronger demon fed on my fears. Fears that it created in my head, making me question reality. It took over my drug-addict mother and then me. It terrorized us."

"That is enough for now. I'll stick with calling you

SkullBrother instead of your real name just for additional safety. SkullBrother, you want to protect your sister, don't you?"

Ricky smiled as he thought of Myra.

"My confidence in you just went up a few points," Ricky typed.

"I'll see what I can find and will get back to you soon."

DeadBlogger disconnected.

Gabby closed the laptop cover and turned to Ricky with a smile. "Progress."

Ricky nodded. "Progress."

Chapter Nine

AFTER LEAVING STRAND'S HOUSE, Mia got to her apartment and studied until almost 3 a.m. She was distracted initially, but she had a keen ability to shut out almost everything when she was focused.

Mia spent Sunday studying some more and preparing for her quiz. She read a few additional chapters for one class and wanted to set up an early Monday dinner with Tino, but she kept seeing images of Annika in her head. She decided to contact Mr. Strand instead.

She texted him and told him she'd contact him as soon as her last class was done on Monday.

Mia aced her Monday morning quiz with thirty minutes to spare. Once her final class was over, she went straight into the hall and called Mr. Strand.

"I was hoping you would be available, Miss Morales," he said. "Would you like to meet at the house, or can you go directly to Hollow Rock?"

She thought about it. "Hollow Rock is fine."

"Do you recall how to get there?"

"No, I was paying attention to the baby and didn't really think about where we were going."

"I will send the directions to your phone. It should take you under 30 minutes to get there from the university."

"I'm leaving in the next five minutes."

She let her GPS lead her. As she neared her destination, she thought only of Annika and what might happen today. She was the only car on the road the last few miles and finally reached the group of trees in the nearly hidden location.

Mr. Strand's SUV was already there.

She got out of her car, but no one was outside. She walked toward the shut doors and saw a note.

"We are inside. Did not wish to keep the doors open and invite any unwelcome animals, but they are unlocked. Please come in - Strand."

She pulled on the thick metal handles. The doors were surprisingly light and she closed them behind her before she started down. She got to the sparkling room where Mr. Strand, Anna, and baby Annika were there to greet her. Annika's head turned slightly as her mother held her, acknowledging Mia's presence.

"So glad you are here, Mia." Strand said.

"Will I be doing anything with the baby?"

"No, not today, but I want her to be present so that you can get accustomed to each other's energy."

"How exactly am I going to practice?" Mia asked.

"Just be patient. I may not be able to fully explain everything you will experience, but my hope is it will make sense to you in time. I need to monitor you more than anything. Be aware that things can be deceptive. Your mind may require a way to cope with what you do not understand. I must also give you a warning."

"Warning?"

"You may hear or see things that try to discourage you from what you are about to do. You are dealing with a power that is beyond this plane, and no matter what someone or something may try to do in order to distract or confuse you, remember the larger task we are hoping to accomplish."

"Why would someone do that?"

"Because we are dealing with powerful forces, and your abilities could increase that energy three-fold. Others may fear that and try to use it for their own purposes. Just remember the why."

Mia tried to process the information as a feeling of dread came over her. She tried to shake it off.

"I'll try to keep that in mind. What do we do first?"

"For today, we will start small."

Strand reached into his jacket pocket and pulled out a pouch about the size of a fist. It was green with a red drawstring. He pulled the pouch open and removed a stone. It was a little larger than a golf ball and made of some type of translucent material.

He placed it on the center of the table.

"A rock?" Mia asked.

"Not a normal rock," Mr. Strand said. "This is a special type of geode crystal. It has a partially hollow center and is sometimes used in spells to hold items that enhance power. Magicians and false fortune tellers some-times used modified versions to generate a glow that makes it look more sinister or to falsely indicate they are in touch with the other realms. Today, however, it will serve as your first true test."

"What am I going to do with that?"

He pulled out another item from the pouch.

He moved toward the stream and reached down. He held a small ceramic cup and scooped up some water. He placed the cup on the edge of the table.

"Is that a mystical cup of some kind?"

"No, just something I took from my cabinet at home. I bought it in Japan many years ago, but it is otherwise an ordinary ceramic cup."

"What do I need to do?"

"The water. I want you to try to move that water from the cup to the hollow center of the stone."

Mia didn't blink as she repeated his words in her head. "This is beginner level? How am I going to do that?"

"The same way you can make a plant grow. Whatever it is you do or feel in your classroom. At some point, you are connected with the plant and can manipulate it and the water that runs through it, correct?"

"But the plant is a living thing," Mia said. "It has water running through it like blood and the sun to make it bloom. These are inanimate objects."

"You must view them as having no difference. On a plane or other world, this water is like blood. Imagine that the stone cannot live without the water coursing and pulsating in its center."

Mia tried to picture it in her head but knew she couldn't hide her confusion.

"I understand your doubt," Mr. Strand said. "Just concentrate and try to become a part of the water, as you do with the plants.

Mia thought of her classroom experiments, then looked at Annika. She turned back to the cup of water and the hollowed stone.

She moved closer to the cup until her eyes were directly over it and looked down its center. She stared at the still water but felt nothing.

Maybe I can feel for it.

She placed her index finger inside the water and stirred it around, then eased it out and focused on the wet drip. She let the water ease down her finger and palm by raising it and felt a slight tingle as drops landed back into the cup. She looked at the water again and concentrated on the ripples she caused.

Mia couldn't feel the same connection as with the plants, but her nose filled with the smell of fresh rain. She could sense wetness splashing on her face. She could almost taste it. She looked back down, and the water had settled. She tried to relax and saw one small ripple start from the center of the cup, but that was it. She tried again and this time, three waves of ripples moved.

Then everything went dark.

She sensed a blackness around her and felt like she might lose her balance. She looked down and the water filled with something yellow.

What is that?

An eye. Yellow with black specks mixed in like a cat's, wide open and staring back at her. She gasped and her hand instinctively tapped the cup, almost causing it to fly off the table, but Mr. Strand pulled his hand out and stopped it before it could fall. The eye rippled with the water before fading away.

Mia realized she was holding her breath and let it out in one big release.

"Did you see that?"

"See what?"

"In the reflection. It looked like the yellow eye of a cat."

"I saw nothing of the sort, but I did not have the same viewing angle as you did. Remember what I told you. You may see things you will not be able to explain, but it may be the forces of nature fighting back. What did you sense?"

"I was just starting to feel a connection with the water. I made it move, but just when it felt like I might have a grip on it, that eye appeared. I lost whatever sensation it was."

"What about the rock?" Strand asked.

"I was only able to concentrate on the water. I didn't even try with the rock. It's like I have to understand how the water feels before I can do anything else with it."

"Understandable for your first time. Unfortunately, I will have to make the situation more complicated. There are no cracks or holes in the crystal that will allow the water to seep into its center."

"Then how am I supposed to get it in there?"

"That I cannot answer, but I hope you will be able to at some point. What I can tell you is you must let go of the earthly, three-dimensional vision of the water physically filling in through the rock. The rules are no longer the same. The water must appear inside the hollowness."

"I don't understand what that means."

"It is just a matter of trial and error for now. I would not expect anyone to understand. Not yet, at least. If all goes well, you will. It does appear you made some progress and that is all we can hope for. It is a solid first step. That is why you must practice. Even on your own with something seemingly unrelated. In your classroom, at home, or wherever an opportunity may present itself. Your abilities are not limited to this underground cave of Hollow Rock."

"I feel like I failed you. Like I failed Annika."

"Make no mistake, there was tremendous success just now. It may seem like you accomplished nothing, but no one else has been able to do what you already have. It all starts with a connection, no matter how insignificant it may seem to you. A psychic connection is one thing, but what you have is more than that. You will get stronger. Hopefully sooner than later."

This seems impossible.

"I just hope you do not let this discourage you," Strand said. "Will you return?"

"I'm not giving up yet. I'll be back."

Chapter Ten

RICKY AND GABBY only had to wait a day before another message appeared in the dark chatroom.

"I have some information," DeadBlogger said. "I believe I've found two or three incidents that tie to the demons that terrorized you and your partner. Check them and see if anything sounds familiar."

DeadBlogger pasted screenshots of two newspaper articles and some social media conversations. The articles were from local newspapers in Macon, Georgia and Andalusia, Alabama.

Ricky pulled up the first article from the *Macon Telegraph*. It was only three short paragraphs under the police blotter section of the paper describing suspected vandalism on the 3000 block of Mulberry Street. Ricky realized on the second to last line what had piqued DeadBlogger to look deeper.

"It is reported a teenage party got out of hand. Glass from broken mirrors caused minor injuries."

Ricky opened the *Andalusia Star-News* article that

mentioned two teenagers being arrested for destruction of property.

"The 16-year-old, whose name is being withheld due to his age, claimed that he was defending himself from an attack by a tall man in black."

The article went on to say no evidence of an additional assailant was found.

"Those could mean anything," Gabby said. "What are the other items?"

There were three additional screenshots that appeared to be from private chat groups and social media photos. There were at least four comments stating how the party was "...one of the best ever!" and "Can't believe what happened!" And finally, the last comment said, "I'm gonna have nightmares. No one better narc!"

The last item was a photo that showed the outline of a cracked mirror with dull yellow eyes in several parts of the broken glass.

Ricky opened the next few labeled "Andalusia." The discussion in this chat group was more serious.

"What do we do? We all know Bobby and Wes didn't do anything. Whatever that was tried to attack us all. Bobby and Wes might have saved our lives."

"No one say anything. They've never been in trouble. I'm sure they'll be fine."

"We owe them a beer."

There was only one accompanying picture. It was a blur of color, but DeadBlogger had circled an area in red. It was something both Ricky and Gabby recognized.

A shadowy figure was looking down with red eyes and a hint of snarling teeth.

DeadBlogger was right. He was also a gifted hacker, apparently.

"Do these look familiar?" DeadBlogger posted while they were looking them over.

Ricky looked at Gabby before typing. "Yes. Too familiar."

"I hope this is enough to help figure out what path they're on."

"Yes, I think so," Ricky typed. "The problem is, we need to know where they're going, but this is promising."

"Where were you headed next?"

"From the boards, we were heading to Shreveport, Louisiana, or somewhere in Arkansas. Some activity in both that might be worth a trip."

"I saw those posts, too. Let me do some checking, but I can tell you the one in Arkansas is a wash based on some discussions last night. I'd suggest heading toward Louisiana, and maybe I can point you in a more specific direction by the time you get close. I'm hoping I can find something more recent than what happened in Shreveport and tie it to these previous events."

Ricky and Gabby glanced at each other and shrugged.

"As good a plan as any right now," Gabby said.

The pair got ready and stopped for breakfast before getting on the road again. They had at least an eight-hour trip ahead of them if they didn't stop.

Ricky drove the first four hours before Gabby took over. They were an hour past Mississippi when Ricky's laptop dinged.

"I checked news outlets in Louisiana and found more areas they may have hit in Lafayette and New Orleans. There was some type of incident in both locations. Lafayette two days ago, and the one in New Orleans just happened last night."

"Which one do you think is more likely to be legit?" Ricky typed.

"I'm seeing a lot of chatter about an incident at the Zombie Bones Voodoo Shop in the New Orleans French Quarter. And it's coming from a few different sources. If I had to choose one, that would be it."

Ricky read DeadBlogger's messages as more links popped up.

"What is it?" Gabby asked.

"There was an actual interview with people from the voodoo shop. They claimed it was vandalism and the damage was minor, but there's another discussion in a private group. It says the shop was attacked by dark spirits and the voodoo shop would handle it on their own. The person saying this claim to have been in the shop and over-heard the conversation."

"So, what do you think?" Gabby asked Ricky. "How much further out of the way is it?"

"If we cut back and catch IH 55 now, it'll only take another hour or so."

"You think we should?"

"I think he's worth trusting," Ricky said. "At least so far. I can't think of a reason for anyone to give us solid intel and then purposely lead us in the wrong direction. Since this New Orleans thing just happened last night, maybe we'll get lucky."

"Yeah, I understand," Gabby said. "We've had so many disappointments, it's hard not to be skeptical. But what other options do we have?"

"Okay," Ricky said. "Then let's go check out some zombies and voodoo."

Chapter Eleven

MIA WENT BACK to Hollow Rock the next day after her classes but made no significant progress. She made the water ripple and yelled in frustration a few times, but she left angry and feeling lost.

She got home that evening and tried to distract herself with her studies, vowing to keep trying.

Mia arrived at her botany class the following day and sat by her lab partner, Laura, as usual. The day's experiment required comparing various chemicals in the soil to see how they affect plant growth.

Mia sighed. She was frustrated and wanted to get back to Hollow Rock. She didn't need great soil. She was pretty sure she could get full growth in any compound so long as it had enough water and life to manipulate.

She watched the transparent pot that was holding her plant and spent the first ten minutes helping Laura more than doing her own work.

Mia had her partner up and running in about fifteen minutes before she looked at her own plant. She rubbed her hands on the stem and leaves and let the nutrients and water flow through it. She felt its growth surge in a way she hadn't before. It was sharper. Up until now, Mia could always sense a plant or leaf growing and push it to grow faster without really understanding how. But something had changed. She could actually feel the relief of the individual leaves as they soaked in the treated water.

She thought about her failures at Hollow Rock. The plant here in her class was being fed through the soil below and was one united piece. In her experiment in the cavern, there were two separate components.

She stood up and walked toward the professor's desk.

"Everything okay, Mia?" Professor Cort asked.

"Yes, just wondering if you have any extra plants that you weren't going to use today?"

He nodded. "Yes, there are always extra. I set aside the plants that are already dying in the blue bin in the back room. You're welcome to them."

"Thank you," she said as she walked into the rear storage room.

The room was filled with portable potted bins with overhead lights to keep the plants as fresh as possible. Mia grabbed two plants from the blue bin and pulled them from the soil they shared with the others in the weak batch. She put both plants together in one smaller pot.

She returned and set the new pot about six inches from her class experiment.

She looked down and felt Laura staring at her, wondering what she was doing. Mia ignored her and concentrated on her dying plants.

She tried to harness the same feeling from Hollow Rock and concentrated on one plant. She felt the insides of the plant moving and pulsing. Although she sensed something, she couldn't do anything with it.

She breathed in and out, trying to calm herself. The dying plant was still dying.

Finally, she balled her fists and felt as if she was gripping the dying leaves. She imagined herself squeezing the roots and pulling water up through the stems. She sensed leaves wanting to burst and squeezed her hands together tighter.

Small streams of water jumped from the leaves and water splashed outward and into Laura's face as it threw drops around the desk.

Laura gasped but didn't yell. The rest of the students and the professor turned to see her pull off her goggles and wipe them dry, along with her wet cheeks and forehead.

"Everything okay?" Laura whispered.

"Accident," Mia said. "Sorry, my fault. Added a little too much."

"How did you do that?"

Mia shrugged. Another failure. She got the water to move, but that wasn't going to help her. She needed it to somehow jump into the other plant and fill it. That rock in the cave had no way in. The water had to penetrate it or shift from one piece to another.

How am I going to work with different planes of existence if I can't even deal with water from a friendly classroom plant? I'm never going to be ready.

She stifled her frustrations and returned to her dying greenery. Within five minutes, the two nearly dead plants were healthier than all but her original experiment. But to Mia, that wasn't enough.

As class finished, Professor Cort asked her to stay. She had been expecting this. She wasn't sure how much he knew.

"Mia, I've been curious about how it went with Mr.

Strand. My colleague told me you were helping him with a family issue."

"Yes," she replied, nodding slightly. "I'm doing what I can."

"I don't mean to pry, but was it as mysterious as my colleague made it sound, or was he just trying to mess with me?"

"No, he was right. What Mr. Strand proposed is kind of out there. He thinks whatever talents I have here in class may help his granddaughter in some weird way."

"It's not dangerous, is it?"

She shook her head. "It's strange, but no, I don't think it's dangerous at all. I'm hoping I might be able to help, but still not sure if I will. I'll let you know how it goes."

"Thank you. Just be careful."

"I will."

She smiled and left.

Later that afternoon, she was back at her aunt's house. Grace was making enchiladas for dinner, which was one of Mia's favorite meals. Whatever Aunt Grace lacked in learning spells and cures from her mother, she more than made up for it with her culinary skills.

"Hey, Aunt Grace. How's it going?"

"Everything's looking good. I was afraid I was going to overcook the rice after I almost broke the handle on that pan last week, but it seems to be holding up."

An awkward silence followed.

"So, are you going to tell me what happened with your mysterious friend?"

Mia had planned to tell her almost everything, but wasn't sure where to start, so she blurted out the first thing that popped in her head. "We met at this hidden cave. He said it's an area that's highly sensitive. A place where our world is closer to other planes of existence."

"Like heaven and hell?"

"Maybe. I'm not sure. He just said other planes, although I'd figure heaven and hell would have a lot more between them."

"Yes, you're right. Mom always said there were other places in the universe we can't see. We just didn't know how to get to them. She said she knew there could be spirits around any corner. I always thought she was joking, but as I got older, I realized she meant every word. She didn't talk about that kind of thing often, sticking more with the herbs and potions, but it was obvious she believed it."

"Yes, I think she was right. I'm just starting, but I don't have a reason to doubt him yet."

Grace tasted the enchilada sauce and then took a long look at Mia.

"Mia, I want you to be careful. There's a reason Mom only stuck with the basic healing potions and spells. She didn't say much about it, probably because she knew your mother and I would never have to worry about it since we were so bad, but one night, she told us a story about when she was younger. I'm not even sure if I should repeat it."

"Go ahead. I want to know. Maybe I need to know."

Grace paused and took in a deep breath before beginning.

"She said when she was in her early twenties and pregnant with your mother, she went through a period of sickness and was having a hard time sleeping. On one particular night, she started having crazy thoughts. She said she started getting paranoid and her mind filled with images of the baby jumping out of her stomach and ripping her apart. She pictured the baby crawling out of her, leaving her insides spread everywhere. Horror movie type stuff. Like a cheap version of *Aliens*."

Mia realized she was holding her breath.

"She said she tried to stop it but couldn't control her emotions, and she went from being scared to crying. She just couldn't get a grip. Then she felt darkness. She said the best way she could describe it wasn't fear, but more like this horrible feeling of dread and sorrow. She saw something in the corner of the house. It was a shape, maybe five feet tall, and it was just staring at her. She felt its dark thoughts and understood it was trying to survive, stuck in its world but wanting to live. It was attracted to the light of our world that is beyond the darkness of its own."

"Light beyond darkness?" Mia asked.

"The living have a light. Mom said it was our souls, and that's what these spirits are attracted to. Something pure, especially love. But this thing was jealous and angry and wanted to destroy Mom's light since it couldn't have it."

"What did she do?" Mia asked, her voice shaking.

"She thought about throwing it across the room, then the baby moved in her stomach. She stood up and said she felt like she had drunk an entire pitcher of coffee and was filled with a jolt of energy. She ran at the spirit and startled it since it didn't realize she could sense it. It then turned and jumped out of the house. As far as she knew, it never returned again. She said she got a few more feelings like that during her pregnancy, but nothing that real or intense. It scared her, though. She wanted no part of it, and whatever she had dabbled in before, she decided to never do it again unless she had no other choice."

"That's terrifying, Aunt Grace."

"It should be, and why I think she told us when we were in our teens. Scared the hell out of us at the time, too. She never told us what it was she had tried or done in the past, at least not in detail, but we knew she had at least

experimented. She said that darker magic was too dangerous. I just want you to be careful. You're new to this and I
want you to take her advice, even though it's passed down
a generation. Be sure that what you're doing is done the
right way. Don't get too caught up in it."

Mia took in a few big breaths until her heartbeat
returned to normal. "I understand."

"I have something for you."

She walked away into her bedroom and came back a
few seconds later. "I have this. It was Mom's."

It was a worn, leather-bound book.

"What is this?"

"Mom did almost everything by memory, but one day,
she started forgetting some of the details of herbs or
potions she hadn't mixed in a while. She realized she was
getting older and wanted to write down what she knew, just
in case someone ever needed it. This is her book. Her
collection. I've only glanced over it since I never had a
need to use it, plus it's not like I would have been able to
make any of it work. Most of it's basic stuff, like how to
cure fright and unexplained fevers, but I'm sure there's
more. More that was beyond what your mother and I
could ever understand."

"Shouldn't you keep it?"

"I have no use for it. No matter how well I follow these
recipes, I'll never get them right. That's why I stick to the
kitchen. You're the first of her descendants to show any
kind of ability. Maybe you can find something to help
you."

"You've had it all these years?"

"Actually, your mom was the one that kept it safe. I got
it after."

Mia understood.

"Thank you, Aunt Grace."

"Just be careful, okay? Promise me."

"I promise."

Chapter Twelve

Tino texted Mia three times while she was at her Aunt Grace's house. She replied after the third one. He wanted to see her. She had already postponed dinner plans twice and knew she couldn't push it back anymore. She was hesitant, since she wasn't sure how he would react to everything that had happened.

Two minutes after six, he called.

"Hey, Tino. Out of work?"

"Yes, you wanna meet at my house or go somewhere?"

Mia knew the conversation might not go her way. She had originally planned on telling him everything, but now she wasn't so sure. She didn't want to risk a public scene, but also didn't want to be at his house. His father was pretty good at giving them their space, though. She wasn't sure which option was better.

"Let me meet you at your house. I'll make something."

She wasn't a great cook like her aunt, but she had a few meals everyone seemed to like.

After they hung up, Aunt Grace put some wrapped enchiladas in front of her.

"I didn't mean to overhear, but you *are* right in front of me. You can eat these now or save them for leftovers later."

Mia kissed her aunt, then headed straight to Tino's house. She started cooking while he was in the shower. She was making beef tacos with rice, which was the quickest thing she could think of based on what Tino's father had in the kitchen.

Tino came out in a t-shirt, shorts, and sandals. He hugged her from behind and gave her a kiss on the cheek. She turned to her side, trying not to take her eyes off the food, and gave him a peck on the lips.

"Be careful," Mia said. "You might burn yourself."

"You're worth it."

She smiled and forgot about the apprehension she was feeling just for a moment. Tino sat on the couch with the TV on. His dad was already in his room. Unless he had a good reason, he wouldn't come out until it was time to eat.

About fifteen more minutes passed and the cooking was done. Mia started getting their plates ready for the table, then turned to Tino.

"Is your dad coming out?"

"Nah, I'll just take it to his room. He's watching something."

Tino got up, grabbed a beer and the plate, and took them to his dad. Mia was relieved he wouldn't be joining them, but some part of her wanted him there to help postpone the inevitable conversation.

"He said thank you. Already took a bite and said it was *delicioso.*"

She nodded, and they sat at the small dinner table together.

Tino took a few bites and looked at her. That was his impatient look. She knew it might get worse if she didn't start speaking right away. She tried to start but held back.

"So you going to tell me what happened now or not until after I eat seconds?"

"Just keep an open mind, okay?"

He took in a breath, bracing for bad news.

"I met Mr. Strand and the baby back at the same place. It was just to practice. I tried to make water jump from a cup on one side of the table into a hollow stone that didn't have any cracks or way to the center."

"How are you supposed to do that?"

"I'm not sure, but Mr. Strand seems to think I can. He said it will be important when it comes time to try to save the baby."

"Sounds like bullshit to me. You sure he's not some crazy, perverted magician?"

"Yes, I'm sure. Anyway, I tried but just couldn't do it. I tried everything to get some kind of hold of both things at the same time, but it still doesn't make sense. I can move the water some, but I don't have a lot of confidence yet."

"Does he think you're some kind of witch?"

She tried to maintain her smile.

"No, he just thinks whatever I have is special enough that I can help."

"Since you couldn't do it, does that mean this is over and we can go back to normal?"

His words were short and staccato.

She shook her head.

"I just need to keep trying. I went to my class today and tried to do something similar with water and plants."

"And how did that go?"

"A little better. I still can't do what I need to and got frustrated, but I was definitely more focused—"

"Did you finish your experiment?" he cut in.

"Yes, I did. I even helped my lab partner. I feel stronger, but it also felt—"

"Why don't you just quit already? How many times have I told you I want to be the one to take care of you? I don't want you doing this anymore. It sounds crazy, and I don't trust this guy. It doesn't sound like you'll be able to help him anyway."

"You don't seem to trust anybody. Ever. You just need to trust *me*. If anything happens or anyone tries to mess with me, you think I'm going to let that happen? He's had several chances. First at the school, then at his house, and now twice in the underground cave. We've never been alone and he's depending on me to save his granddaughter. That's it."

"I'll bet he's depending on you."

She felt her ears burn as heat rose from her neck. She couldn't stand when he got like this. He was no longer listening and instead jumped right into his agenda.

Mia was about to snap back, but then she thought of Annika. Tino was almost a grown man and could fend for himself. This poor child couldn't. Mia's face tingled with heat, but she took in short breaths until she calmed down.

"Anyway, I still failed. But I'm going to keep trying."

"That's everything?" Tino asked.

She thought about mentioning more about her conversation with her Aunt Grace, but her decision was made. She wasn't going to give him another opportunity to shoot her down.

"Yeah, that's it."

Tino looked at her, then resumed eating. She was ready to leave but didn't want to make things worse or give him a reason to bring any of it up again.

"So, how was your work today?"

He swallowed the food in his mouth and then started talking about his day. Within a couple of minutes, he was so into his story about how one of the carpenters accidentally shot a nail into his foot that his attitude changed. They laughed and seemed to enjoy the rest of their evening, but Mia was doing everything she could to fake it.

As Mia headed back to her apartment, she realized she was getting better at hiding her emotions. Tino would have been able to see through her a week ago, but her focus had changed. Nothing was going to keep her from trying to save Annika.

Mia got home and had some reading to do. She grabbed a cup of water and started studying on her couch. After twenty minutes, she realized she had been reading the same page for fifteen minutes. She set her cup down on her coffee table and walked into the kitchen.

Mia returned to the couch with an apple in her hand. She set it on one side of the coffee table, then placed her cup of water on the other and set her book between them.

For the next hour, she tried to move the water toward the apple. She wasn't trying to make it fly into the apple's skin, but just splash against it. Anything.

Like the classroom, she was able to get some water to jump across her book and hit the apple, but it was only a few drops. Nothing that would penetrate with significant force.

It was almost midnight when she realized she had been in a frustrated trance. She bit hard into the apple.

You have to do better to have any chance of saving her.

Chapter Thirteen

RICKY AND GABBY continued their drive and were a few minutes from New Orleans.

"Have you ever been there?" Gabby asked.

"I had never left Texas before we were relocated and I started chasing these demons," Ricky said. "Even though my grandmother traveled all over the world, I didn't get to go with her. I had planned to travel once I could do it on my own, but that wasn't my path. I guess these demons chose my path. How about you?"

"Yes, before I was married. Took a trip with some friends for a bachelorette party. We did pretty much what you'd expect the first night. We drank and gambled and listened to the musicians on the street. The bride-to-be spent the last two hours of the night puking on the street. We ended up taking her to the ER, but fortunately, we were there a week before the wedding, so she had plenty of time to get better."

"So a big party city?"

"Yes, but it was more than that. With the bride laid out the next day, a couple of us saw the more interesting sides of the city. Some I didn't even know about. There's the World War II museum, street artists, the food, and the historical markers. Oh, and the haunted history. A lot to appreciate."

"Sounds like it was a memorable trip. Was the wedding a success?"

"The groom ended up passing out at the altar from partying too hard the night before the wedding. The marriage was over within 18 months. So a hard no."

"Encouraging," Ricky said.

When they finally reached the French Quarter, Ricky was caught off guard at how narrow the streets were. It was an interesting sight to see for the first time. So many restaurants, some with lines of people trying to get in even though it was the mid-afternoon on a weekday.

"The food is that good," Gabby said. "Really."

Ricky had his GPS on, and they passed by the voodoo shop. Gabby found an expensive parking spot about two blocks down. As they approached the shop, they passed several food places and bars before arriving. It was a small place, but almost every inch was filled with something.

The young woman at the register greeted them. "Welcome to Zombie Bones. Can I help you with anything?"

Ricky looked around. There were voodoo dolls, skulls, and all types of voodoo and occult related artifacts on the walls and shelves.

"Yes," he said. "We heard that something strange just happened here. Do you know the details?"

The girl scowled. "Why would you be asking about that? You reporters or something? Or just people trying to dabble in voodoo?"

"We have a common interest, is all."

The girl stared at him. "Nothing really happened," she said in a flat voice. "Just some broken windows. Vandals."

She stared at Ricky without blinking.

There was one other customer in the store, but she had just walked out.

Gabby leaned on the counter, realizing the young woman had probably been inundated with people asking about what happened. She thought of trying a different approach.

"I'm going to be straight with you," Gabby said, staring directly into the eyes of the young woman. "Two demons stole my baby's soul and killed people close to my friend here. We are trying to find these demons and retrieve my daughter's soul before it's too late. She's a shell of herself and her physical body is with my family and friends. If we fail, she'll probably die. We have reason to believe the same two demons, one that feeds on fear and another that travels through reflections, may be the same ones that were here in your shop. Now you'd have to be completely out there to believe this, but that's why I'm looking you in the eyes. I'm hoping you'll see how serious I am."

The young girl blinked as Gabby paused for a moment, then continued.

"We're running out of time. We need help. And if there is any chance you think what happened here might have involved the same creatures we're looking for, any type of information you give us will stay with us. Any confirmation might help us find them. Please, for the sake of my daughter, consider it."

The girl's eyes were watering.

"Give me a minute," she whispered.

The young woman walked to the back of the store.

They heard voices as Ricky turned to Gabby.

"I wasn't expecting that."

"We can't lose any more time. I was just hoping I could

find a way to connect with her. I didn't realize how much I was going to say until it just started spewing out. It's like I couldn't stop myself."

Ricky nodded as he looked over the voodoo dolls and totems on the walls. "This definitely seems like a place that's more open-minded."

The girl returned after a few minutes. An older lady was behind her. She was dressed in an elegant black halter jumpsuit and looked like she was returning from a business meeting.

She looked back and forth at Gabby and Ricky, as if she was summing them up.

"My granddaughter tells me you have a story about demons. She said it was too crazy not to be true, but she is young. You will tell me your story, but you will tell it my way. Is this something you are willing to do?"

Gabby and Ricky nodded without looking at each other for acknowledgement. They both knew what was riding on this.

"Come with me," she said as she started walking back towards the door she came through.

They followed her, and the room they entered was filled with shelves of items. The room wasn't large, so everything felt cramped. One corner contained a small nook with a desk, some chairs, and a desk lamp.

She motioned for them to sit. There were three chairs on one side of the desk. Ricky and Gabby sat down as the woman moved toward one of her shelves.

She returned, looked at them, and didn't break her gaze as she pulled the chair back and took her seat.

She raised her hands and put a box on the desk. She opened it slowly and pulled some items out, including a long needle, a few small bottles, and some cloth.

"What is that?" Ricky asked.

"If your story is true, I need to prove it. What I am about to do won't kill you. However, if you are telling a tall tale, it will hurt. If your mind is trying to hide the truth, you will feel a moment of fierce pain. And I must look into your eyes to know if you can be trusted. Is this acceptable?"

"Both of us?" Ricky said.

She pointed the needle at Gabby. "No, only you."

"I can do it," Ricky said.

"No, it must be her."

"Why?"

"She claims to have the soul of her child at stake. She has more to lose. Young man, if this woman's story is to be believed, you have already lost your loved one, correct?"

Ricky started to say something, but thought about Ellie and looked down. "Yes."

"The one with the most to lose will be the one with the most emotion. The most desperation. I can sense that, but I need to enhance the process."

"Do whatever you have to," Gabby said.

"But you don't know what she's going to do," Ricky objected.

"Does it matter? Unless it kills me, I'm going to do whatever it takes. If it was for your sister, would you do it?"

Ricky thought of Myra, then nodded.

The woman looked at them both and then proceeded to reach into the box.

"My name is Carlotta James. I am not some small-time swindler claiming to tell your future. This is our business, and I only help those who truly need it. And if my instincts are correct, you do."

She took a bottle and opened it. She popped off the lid and put a finger inside. When she pulled it back out, it was covered with a thick red oil. She opened her free hand with her palm up, beckoning for Gabby's hand.

Gabby didn't hesitate.

Carlotta gently held Gabby's wrist, then rubbed the oil lightly around Gabby's forearm and top of her elbow.

Carlotta lifted the needle and clanged it on the table. Ricky jumped a little when she did, but Gabby didn't move. She only thought of Ally.

"Tell me again what you told my granddaughter. No need for every detail, just the highlights."

"My daughter," Gabby started. "My daughter's soul was taken by two beings. Demons. They killed Ricky's girl-friend and took my daughter's soul. My baby's body is with my sister's family, but she isn't right. I believe her soul is gone and all that remains is a barely breathing shell. I want to retrieve her soul and save her."

Carlotta looked straight at her and didn't blink. She raised the four-inch needle and laid it on the top of the red spot on Gabby's forearm.

"I am going to insert this needle into your arm. There will be some minor discomfort at first, but if you are telling a falsehood, the discomfort will spread to your mind and squeeze as much pain as it can from you."

Fear of the needle crept up on Gabby and she stared at it, but she let her mind fill with Ally's face and it subsided.

"Do what you must," Gabby said.

The woman nodded. She pushed the tip of the needle in gently, then started to recite an incantation. It was in French, but her eyes didn't roll back or change colors. There was no show. She just moved the needle around gently, then pressed it in a little deeper.

Ricky stared at the needle and saw something he hadn't seen before. The needle was hollow, and a clear substance was flowing through it.

"Are you drugging her?" he asked.

"No," Carlotta said. "I am giving her a potion that will tell me if she is worthy of my trust."

That's drugging, Ricky thought to himself.

Gabby winced but didn't fight it. She felt the cold liquid flow into her as her free arm's fist tightened. There was a burst of heated pain near the needle, but it wasn't unbearable.

Gabby twitched as her back arched in the chair. She let out a deep grunt.

Carlotta held her wrist tightly and didn't let go. Gabby felt a sharp pain up her spine and tried to stifle a scream.

Ricky stood up. "What are you doing to her?"

Carlotta didn't react. He reached for Gabby's arm and just before he got a grip, her free hand flipped over to block him.

"Okay," she muttered. "I'm okay."

She sat up straight and was overcome with a feeling of calmness. The cold she felt quickly warmed, and she relaxed.

Carlotta stared into her. Gabby stared right back.

A moment later, and only for a second, Gabby saw Carlotta's eyes turn yellow and then back to their normal dark brown. It caught her off guard, but she kept her composure.

Carlotta pulled out the needle and let go of Gabby's wrist.

It was over.

She handed Gabby a small cloth and Gabby wiped the oil off her arm and elbow.

"Well?" Gabby asked.

Carlotta didn't answer right away. She poured some alcohol on a cloth and cleaned the needle, then got up and returned her items to their places on the shelves.

She came back and sat down, not giving away her thoughts.

"You can be trusted," she finally said. "And I know why you are here. I expected someone might come asking about them. I could sense they were here searching for something. Or someone."

"So what does this mean? Are we talking about the same demons?"

"What happened here was an abomination," Carlotta said. "This shop is old, and I guarantee you my grandmother was a woman of incredible spiritual power. She could talk to the other world, to those good and bad, and it almost drove her insane when she was younger. However, once she realized that she could use her abilities to help others in some capacity, she became a trusted resource for this city and those experiencing evil in their lives."

"Please, give us the details," Ricky said.

"We came in yesterday and I noticed a bad aura in the shop. We deal in good and sometimes bad forces and everything associated with voodoo, but understand it is our spiritual way of life. The propaganda you see with voodoo priests and priestesses dressed in skeleton paint and wearing a tall black hat is not all that we are. That may have been relevant at some point, but now it's just for show."

Ricky nodded. "I understand."

"So the bad mojo. I noticed some of the voodoo dolls on the floor, but more importantly, that the back door was open. We have an alarm system, but I received no notifications or alerts. The doors weren't broken or kicked in. So whatever got in either had the key or someone let them in. I knew right away it wasn't the latter. Something had been in the store. I looked up and saw some of the long room mirrors we sell. Two of them weren't in their place.

They were on opposites sides of the room facing each other."

"What happened?" Ricky asked.

"I only felt a shadow of something that had been here, but that was all. Nothing unusual happened the rest of the morning except for one customer. It was a man who came to me and asked why some of our crosses were broken. I had no idea what he was talking about until I followed him to the source. We have a basket of wood and metal crosses that have various prayers connected to them. There were maybe forty total crosses in the basket and more than ten were broken from the bottom, making them appear as square crosses. I picked one up and felt an instant jolt. A cloud of darkness came over me, and I thought of hurting myself and anyone nearby. It passed after a moment, but when I looked up, the customer was looking back at me, clearly afraid. I tried to calm him, but the man left. He was quite angry, thinking I was ridiculing him."

"And then?" Gabby asked.

"At first, the afternoon and early evening went without incident. I was in the back, and we were a few minutes from closing when I heard my granddaughter gasp. She sounded panicked, and I ran out to the main area. There was only one other customer here. I didn't want to scare him, too, so I walked casually to my granddaughter and asked her what had happened."

"What was it?" Ricky asked.

"I looked at the voodoo masks on the wall and one was out of place. It was in the same spot, but flipped around and upside down. I thought maybe my granddaughter was just spooked from the break-in and her imagination was running wild, but I did sense something was off. Once that final customer walked out, I locked the door and my granddaughter yelled from behind me. I turned and saw her screaming and holding her mouth, yet I did not see anything near her. So I looked up and saw her facing the group of items we have hanging from the ceiling. She was shaking and when I got closer, I realized why. One of the shrunken heads was bleeding from its eyes."

"What did you do?"

"I ran to the back to gather items to fight whatever was present. It had terrified my granddaughter and needed to be gone."

"How?" Gabby asked.

"I planned to draw them out and banish them from my shop and from this world. I grabbed candles and some herbs to burn while my granddaughter was still screaming. I started the ceremony and said my prayers, and every mask in the store turned to face me. The entire room filled with fear. I could smell it. There were two beings of similar strength here. One of them was feeding off that fear. I lit a wooden stick to generate smoke to reveal and repel them, and as I waved it, the mirrors and glass pictures in the room all flashed at once."

Ricky and Gabby looked around. There were four big mirrors throughout the store, and some of the walls held reflective metal and frames.

"You saw a face in the mirrors and on anything with a reflection," Ricky said. "With yellow eyes like a cat, right?"

Carlotta nodded. "Yes, eyes from the other side. Eyes looking into the world it so wants to be a part of but finding it just out of reach."

"What kind of spirit did you sense?" Gabby asked.

"I realized then it was no ordinary pair of spirits. These are the remnants of true demons. Demons that want to be part of this world and know they have no place here. They were ancient, yet they smelled of new strength and new life. And a desire for more. The fear they took from this room and the power of the items here, especially my personal collection in the back, gave them additional strength. They are driven to build on that power, and this was just a stop along their path."

"What did the mirror one do?"

"Once all the mirrors were filled with its face, its eyes glowed brighter and it shattered two mirrors. As it did, my granddaughter and I turned to see it, and the reflective being pulled the stick from my hands. It needed it for something, but I don't understand how it did so without the ability to cross over. They possess a power that may be the strongest I've ever encountered. The energy it took just to wretch if from my hand was enough to shatter two mirrors and crack glass."

"What happened after that?" Ricky asked.

"The stick fell to the floor, then my sense of them was gone almost immediately. The fear along with it."

Gabby pressed. "Was there anything else?"

"Yes," she said. "They have a plan. An incomplete one, but they are no longer alone. They are using an outside presence to aid them."

"What kind of outside presence?"

"I am not sure. It could be another being or a human. Am I to assume this all sounds familiar?"

Gabby and Ricky both nodded.

"You've been very helpful," Gabby said. "I'm glad they're gone."

"Yes, it sounds like we encountered the same creatures. One demon feeding off fear and the other using its reflection."

"Any chance you were able to sense my daughter or her soul?" Gabby asked.

"No, but I did sense their hope. For all the fear and evil

that gripped us for such a short time, the hope was unmistakable."

"Everything that's happened to us started in Texas," Ricky said. "Did you get any sense of where they may be headed next?"

"They left no trace of what direction they were headed. I wish you good luck. They will not be easy to defeat. I have something that may help you, but as strong as they are, it may not matter. Wait here."

She walked to the back and returned with a box. She handed it to Gabby.

"Take this."

Gabby opened the box. It was a leather necklace with a flat oval ruby the size of a quarter.

"This amulet will protect your soul," Carlotta said. "It is powerful, and these creatures must not be allowed to cross over. I only hope that it helps."

"Thank you," Gabby said. "You've helped rekindle our own hope."

"Just succeed in your endeavor, both of you. I fear to think what would happen if they were able to make it completely into our world. Two powerful demons let loose in the streets."

Ricky and Gabby thanked her and took their leave.

"What do you think?" Ricky asked.

"Our DeadBlogger was right. He came through here."

"I agree."

"Then we go all the way. We trust him with the next step."

They sat in the car and Gabby opened the box with the amulet. She took it out and handed it to Ricky.

"What are you doing? She gave that to you."

"It's to protect my soul, Ricky. I'm here to save my daughter's soul, not mine. I'm willing to give my life for her, and the demons know that. I'm more of a threat to them. I need you to survive in case they stop me."

Ricky wanted to protest, but knew it was pointless. She was right.

"At least we know we're on the right path," Ricky said.

"Yeah, even though that path may lead us to our doom," Gabby said without smiling.

"Then doom it is."

Chapter Fourteen

Mia woke up at 3:24 a.m. on the couch. She didn't remember falling asleep, but her neck twinged as she straightened her head. The almost finished apple was still on her coffee table and bruised to a dark brown. As her eyes focused on the apple, only one thought came to her.

A rotting apple. A perfect reminder of my failure.

She rubbed her eyes and decided it was time to move to her bed.

Something crunched.

Mia leapt to her feet and looked around her living room, illuminated only by the end table lamp by her couch.

The apple. It was on its side with a piece missing.

I must have knocked it down when I jumped up.

As she stared, there was another crunch, and jagged marks cut off another piece of the apple down the middle, spilling seeds onto the coffee table.

Something unseen had bitten into it.

Mia rubbed her eyes and wondered if she was really awake.

The sink's water faucet turned on. It was at its max flow and a hard stream splashed against a dirty plate and dishes she hadn't washed yet. Mia ran to the sink. The water was bouncing off the plate and splashing on one side of the counter.

She shut off the valve, but the water didn't stop. Had the handle broken?

She opened the cabinet under the sink and found the main water valve. It wasn't leaking. She turned it until it stopped, but the water from the sink kept flowing.

Mia had helped her aunt replace her faucets and knew that was the main valve and should have cut the flow.

She stood up and removed the dishes from the sink, which stopped the ricochet, and then grabbed some paper towels to clean up the counter as the water continued to run.

Save her.

Mia flipped around. The voice was deep and resonated in her head. Someone was in her apartment.

Mia instinctively pulled her largest kitchen knife from the wooden block on the counter.

Her phone. She needed her phone. It was sitting on the armrest of her couch.

"Who's there? I have a gun!"

She did have a gun, but it was tucked away in a drawer in her bedroom. She hoped the intruder didn't see her hands shaking as she gripped the knife so tightly it made her hands turn white.

One of the kitchen wall cabinets flew open and several plastic food containers fell onto the counter below. One of the smaller containers bounced off the counter and landed cleanly on the center of her kitchen table.

Save her.

Mia flipped around. The voice wasn't coming from any

specific direction. It seemed to be surrounding her. A dull pain hit her sharply on her forehead.

She looked up and the steel refrigerator door was flashing. She looked closer and colors of orange, yellow, and red shimmered in a flashing strobe of small square reflections, like a bunch of tiny disco ball mirrors. There was some kind of shape in the middle of all the colors.

You must grow stronger.

Then it hit her. Strand said her mind might mess with her as she tried to improve. He also said there might be things she didn't understand trying to discourage her. Could there also be things trying to encourage her? This voice said "Save her." Unless it was her subconscious mind overworking on how to improve.

Save her.

Mia now understood the voice was in her head and no one was in her apartment. Water. The container on the table. The voice or her mind or whatever it was wanted her to try again.

She put the knife down and looked at the faucet and back to the covered storage container.

She let herself calm down and concentrated on the flow of water. She was able to get a firm grasp on the flow and shot a small stream toward the container. The water hit it on the side but only made the container slide a few inches.

She exhaled as the stream stopped.

Must try. Harder.

She closed her eyes and focused. A thicker stream shot out and hit the container, but this time, she was able to slow it down as it struck so it didn't knock the container over. The water flew with force but eased into an embracing pool around the container, trying to find a way in or through. She eased the water around the sides and top of the container but couldn't penetrate it. She stopped the flow again.

The cabinets in the kitchen flew open and banged shut.

Then again. Every cabinet opened and slammed closed over and over again in a steady rhythm.

Mia yelled as the wooden knife block fell to the floor and every knife inside it levitated out and suspended in the air, facing her.

Must try harder.

The voice wasn't gentle. It made her wince as it overpowered her senses.

Three knives flew towards her, and as she threw her head back, the knives stopped in mid-air, only inches from her face. The shimmering lights that were on the refrigerator door spread, covering every reflective appliance, filling the entire room with light.

Then something grabbed her shoulder.

Again.

Mia's breath was coming in short bursts as she stared at the tips of the knives that were close enough to smell. Whatever had grabbed her tightened its grip. It felt like a hand, but not human. She looked down and saw shadows of long fingers gripping her. She tried to look back but only saw darkness.

"I'm going to try harder," Mia said, her voice shaking. "I promise."

She didn't think. She turned to look at the flow, and the entire stream coming from the faucet flew out toward the container. The lid eased off to one side and the water flew into it until it filled. She stopped the stream, and the container's lid closed.

She had no idea how she had done it. The knives fell and the strobing lights stopped.

Better.

She felt whatever presence was in the house. She stood there for a few more seconds and held her breath until she couldn't anymore. As she exhaled, she regained her composure enough to release some of the fear. Her face and neck were dripping with sweat, and her shirt was damp with it.

Mia bolted to the bathroom and washed her face. She broke into deep sobs once she finally settled down. She stared at the bathroom mirror, afraid to look behind her, but she knew somehow that the voices and reflections were gone.

Whatever had been in her apartment had forced her hand. She didn't penetrate the storage container, but she still found a way in. It wasn't a complete success, but without a doubt, an improvement. One that she thought she could repeat.

"I guess scaring the shit out of me is one form a motivation," she said to her reflection.

She wanted to call Strand, but it was a quarter to 4. She needed time to settle down and process.

Mia jumped in the shower for a quick rinse and changed into dry clothes. She jumped under her bedroom covers, leaving the mess in her kitchen. She stayed up until exhaustion took over and at some point after 5 a.m., she fell asleep.

The price of progress.

Chapter Fifteen

MIA'S ALARM buzzed at 7:30 a.m. She jumped up and rushed to the kitchen.

The table and counters were still wet. The knives and storage containers were strewn across the floor.

It had all been real.

She cleaned up the kitchen, bathed, and changed before calling Strand. He answered on the first ring, and Mia explained what had happened. She was talking so fast Strand didn't get a word in until minutes later when Mia had finished her tale.

"This is unfortunate."

"Why would something out there want me to help your granddaughter?"

"It is difficult to say. Beings from the other side have many reasons to loathe the living. Jealousy, power, or for no reason at all. Maybe whatever it was fed off the fear or anxiousness you have about possibly not being able to help Annika."

"How did it get to me? My apartment?"

"As I told you, there may be unexpected events that

occur when dabbling with other planes. However, I never expected this. I am truly sorry it did."

"What do you think that was, Mr. Strand?"

"A bad spirit. A lost soul. Maybe if you are able to harness this power to save Annika's soul, this invader thinks you can do something that will benefit it as well."

"How?"

"I do not know. I am just glad you are safe. I must confess, I am happy that you found a way to progress, although I am not happy with the method used or the unpleasantness it caused."

Mia didn't say anything for a moment. She had made progress, but still wasn't exactly sure how she did it. However, now she knew she could.

"Mia, I must ask. Does this alter your commitment to my granddaughter?"

"No," Mia said softly.

After the night's events, she didn't think bailing out was even an option. If this spirit or spirits or whatever it was didn't get what it wanted, it might come after her. And next time, the knives might not stop in midair.

Mia thought she may no longer have the choice that Mr. Strand seemed to think still existed.

MIA WAS at school an hour later. She didn't have botany today and was in her General Ecology class with Professor Diaz. The course was popular due to the inclusion of field trips that were always enjoyable, but today was a lecture on the dynamics of population growth, which even a seasoned comedian would struggle to make interesting. Even so, Mia would typically be fully engaged, but she hadn't heard more than a few words of the lecture.

She was still thinking about the night before. The last time she'd been terrified like that was when she still had full-on nightmares after her parents died in the car crash, but this was different. She wanted to return to Hollow Rock that afternoon, but she needed additional time to refine and repeat what she had been able to do under pressure, or it would be a pointless endeavor.

A spasm kicked Mia's shoulder forward. She reached back to grab it as heat emanated from her shoulder blade.

It spasmed again. She got up as quietly as she could. Most of the class turned to see her walk out, although the professor didn't miss a beat.

Mia rushed to the bathroom. The heat on her shoulder blade was getting worse, and the spasms continued. She moved to the center of the three sinks, then turned around and lifted her shirt. She looked back at the mirror and saw something dark on her shoulder blade. She lifted her shirt a little more, revealing a bruise in the shape of a palm with long marks that looked like skinny, misshapen fingers.

Not fingers. Claws.

The black claw marks moved. This was impossible. The marks twisted and curved on her shoulder blade as they broke into smaller pieces and formed something.

Free her.

Mia screamed.

Someone yelled.

"Who's there?" said a voice from a stall behind her.

"I'm sorry," Mia said. "I … slipped and almost fell."

"You almost gave me a heart attack. I dropped my phone and almost ran out of here with my pants down."

"I'm so sorry."

"As long as you're okay."

She looked back at her shoulder. The words were gone, but the claw-shaped bruises were still there. The shadow figure had grabbed her shoulder the night before. Her waking nightmare.

But nightmares don't leave bruises.

Mia realized how fast she was breathing and saw the sweat on her forehead. The bruise was real. The message had to be her tired mind playing tricks on her, but it said to free her. Was it her own subconscious elevated by her desperation to help the baby, or the same voices from the night before she wasn't sure she actually heard?

She splashed her face a few times and took in some deep breaths until she calmed down.

"You're not going to get anything done staring in the mirror," she whispered to her reflection.

She walked out of the bathroom as a man in a uniform approached. She had screamed louder than she thought. Someone passing by had alerted campus security. Mia apologized and gave the same slip excuse. The guard didn't push any further.

Mia returned to the classroom and looked down as she felt all eyes on her interruption. She sat in her seat and her mind was racing. She looked around the classroom to see if there was something she could practice on, but nothing seemed to fit.

Then she felt something flash in her head. It was a sensation of water flowing, but it was muffled compared to what she'd experienced before.

She tried to concentrate on it and the muffled sounds sharpened.

Professor Cort's botany class was in the next room over. It was a different section, and Mia knew a few of the students taking it. They were working on a plant experiment. She sensed it.

Water. Plants.

Her shoulder blade started to heat up again. It felt like the fingers of the shadow were there, pressing gently.

Mia felt a shiver rise from her shoulder through the back of her neck. More plant leaves. She could sense the soil beneath the leaves. The water coursing through them.

Another soft push on her back.

She felt the entire room next door. She didn't sense any students or the professor, but she felt the room pulsing as the leaves inhaled the light and fed off the soil.

There was no empty rock for her to attempt to send the water to.

It's okay, just work on your control.

The sounds of the professor speaking and movement in her classroom melted away. She only felt the flow of the water in the adjoining room. She sensed each individual plant leaf. She closed her eyes.

Move.

A jolt snapped Mia's head back. She had a firm grasp of the plant leaves, but she had no idea what to do with them. Her head spun as she tried to work out her next step, but her mental grip tightened. There were seventeen, each with a unique feel. A unique signature. She tried to tug at each one.

Someone gasped, breaking her concentration. Then someone yelled.

Mia's eyes opened. She saw a few students standing with shocked looks on their faces.

A few classmates were pointing toward the door. Water was seeping underneath it as the edge of a leaf eased through. Another followed.

"The window!" a male voice yelled.

She turned to the windows and two leaves were on the outside glass, sliding across, trying to find a way in. Some still had soil attached to them.

"Mia, are you doing this?"

It was her lab partner, Laura, who sat a few desks behind her.

Mia ignored her. The strength she felt was too strong to stop.

Push harder.

Mia thought about her own lab experiment a few days before. This must have been the same or similar experiment. She remembered the feeling when the water penetrated into the soil.

She focused on several of the plant leaves that were now coming through the bottom of the door and some that snuck through a partially opened window.

A fast stream of water flew from one of the door leaves across the room and hit the window.

The classmates who hadn't noticed the invading plant life all turned as the water struck the glass.

Mia didn't flinch as some of her classmates yelled.

"Control, Mia," she whispered to herself.

Mia looked at the leaves that had connected pieces of soil. She pictured the dirt as the hollow rock. What if she could penetrate the soil that led into the plant?

Another stream flew from one of the plants across the room and landed on the glass, seeped through the thin window opening, and moved to one of the window leaves. The stream penetrated the small amount of soil and up its stem with enough force that the ends of the plants popped as the water shot through.

It has to be more than the plants.

She looked up at the classroom windows. The glass.

Glass was made of sand. She thought of the tiny granules that would need to be heated and treated to become glass. It was still porous sand. If water hit a patch of sand, it would penetrate the tiny gaps between each piece of individual sand and seep through.

She pulled two new plant streams. They hit one of the glass windows, but just splashed back, hitting a few students in the face. She thought of the glass being filled with tiny pores.

It's just sand in disguise, Mia. You can do this. It's just sand.

The glass only looked solid, but she knew that could be changed and manipulated. Three hard lines of water shot out of three leaves, but this time, the window absorbed it. There was no splash and she could feel it inside the glass, but it didn't come out the other side. It was like the water was trapped between the glass.

She tried again, picturing larger craters. This time, the shots were harder and when they landed, she pushed more forcefully.

Mia squeezed her hands together and more streams shot across the room. The water slammed into the windows this time, but without pause, and went through the glass.

One of the students ran up to the window.

"It's dripping on the outside!" she yelled. "I don't see any cracks. How is this possible?"

Mia felt a final surge as she let out a huge breath and let go.

When she did, the window shattered. Fortunately, it blew outwards, so no one was hurt.

More classmates yelled and leapt out of their seats, unable to process what they were seeing. Streams of water were shooting across the room, and Mia had a crazed look in her eyes. She hadn't heard or noticed what was happening around her.

Joey, another classmate, turned toward her.

"Mia, did you do that?"

She looked at him as she noticed the streams falling. Several students had wet hair, and there were at least ten leaves scattered throughout the room with soil everywhere.

The door opened and Professor Cort came running in. He closed the door behind him to keep his students that followed from entering. The professor stared at Mia, who still appeared dazed. Then he looked at the mayhem in the room.

"Mia, are you okay?" he asked once he had regained his composure.

The professor showed no fear, but the curiosity that forged his desire to be a scientist had overcome him. He was trying, like the others, to process what had happened in his classroom and what he was seeing now.

Mia stared back but didn't answer.

Professor Cort turned to Professor Diaz. "What happened?"

"I'm... I'm not sure," she said. Professor Diaz was trembling.

Mia shook her head as her mind cleared and she came back to her senses. She looked up at Professor Cort.

"I'm sorry," she whispered, feeling the surrounding fear. "I don't know what happened. Or what came over me."

"Class, please put your things away," Professor Cort said. "If it's okay with Professor Diaz, maybe we should dismiss early for today."

No one moved.

Professor Diaz turned to Cort.

"Yes, that's a good idea. Class, you can leave now. Don't worry about the mess."

The students were all focused on Mia. They didn't move.

"Class, leave now," Professor Diaz said, raising her voice but trying her best not to yell.

This time, everyone grabbed their things. Mia was still in her seat.

Laura turned to her. "Mia, I'm not sure what's going on. I consider you a friend and I don't know how you do what you do, but it doesn't change the fact you just scared the crap out of everybody. Even so, I do hope you're okay."

Laura put a hand on Mia's arm, then grabbed her backpack and rushed out. As she did, another student ran back in. She was so rattled she had left all of her things on her desk.

Professor Cort turned to Professor Diaz. "Professor, can you give me a private moment with Mia?"

Professor Diaz shook her head and walked out. Her hands were still shaking.

Once Professor Cort and Mia were alone, he sat at the desk next to her. "Mia, is this related to whatever is going on with our visitor the other day?"

Mia stared at him, then nodded slowly. "Professor, I didn't mean for that to happen. I didn't even know I could do what I just did."

"Mia, I don't think anyone can do what you just did. Are you safe? Are they doing anything to you?"

She shook her head. "No, Professor. I'll tell you. I'm trying to help save a child. I can't explain scientifically how I can do what I can do or how I can help, but I'm learning something new every day."

"Mia, I'm a scientist, 100%, but I do accept there are things we can't explain. Yet, I think in the end everything will have an explanation, but there may be other forms of science we don't know about or that just haven't been classified yet. Something considered supernatural today may turn out to simply be another plane or dimension that we just haven't learned how to prove. The problem with the unknown is that we sometimes put ourselves and others at risk when we don't know enough about it. I just want to be sure you're not in danger."

"Yes, I'm safe. If all this helps me accomplish what I'm trying to do, it will be worth it. It's a life we'd save."

"I'll talk to Professor Diaz. I won't give anything away but will try to get her to agree to give the same message to our students. My class saw their experiments fly out of the room while this class saw everything invade. I'm sure they're freaked out. I'll tell them you're working on a science experiment with a colleague and that was a side effect. I don't want you to feel fear or hinder your development, but I also don't want you to leave school or harm your bright future because of what's going on. Maybe I can give you a knowing glance that might keep you grounded if things get out of hand in class again. Thoughts?"

Mia nodded. "Yes, thank you, Professor. Right now, though, I need to go. I had some type of breakthrough and I need to see if it will help me do what I need to do. But I want to help you and Professor Diaz clean up first. This is all my fault."

"No, whatever you're doing is more important. A child's life has more weight than a mess in science class. Please, go."

She sighed. He could have had her expelled or been as terrified as her classmates had been, but instead, he was doing his best to be supportive. Her respect for her favorite professor had just doubled. He was helping her more than he could possibly know.

She left, and as soon as she was out of the building, she called Mr. Strand. He answered on the first ring.

"Can you meet me there?"

"Of course. Your voice sounds hopeful."

"It is. Something else happened today in class. I think whatever scared the life out of me last night and today must have jump started something. I hope it makes today a better one."

"I will see you in thirty minutes."

She rushed to her car and sped off, hoping almost destroying her classroom and making herself an outcast was worth it.

Chapter Sixteen

Mia normally never drove more than 2 or 3 miles over the speed limit, but she was going 70 on a 55 mile per hour road. She had to get there and test herself while everything was fresh.

She arrived almost ten minutes faster than normal, and Strand's vehicle wasn't there yet.

She got down and walked to the storm doors. There was no lock, and she looked out toward the open fields to see if there was a vehicle coming yet.

Mia couldn't wait. She pulled open the doors and headed down.

The room looked like it hadn't been disturbed since the last time she'd been there. The soft blue glow of the water was the same, and the small bag where Strand kept the stone was on the table. She reached in, hoping he hadn't removed anything, but it was all there. She put the stone on one side of the table and then picked up the cup.

She walked to the stream and looked at the calm water. As she bent down to scoop some water out, she saw something flash in the stream. It was yellow. She wondered if something had fallen in.

Then she saw it again. It was yellow and round.

Mia dropped the cup as a chill ran up her neck and fell on her bottom. She got lightheaded and sensed a darkness in the room.

She turned slowly, thinking something was behind her and that maybe Mr. Strand had come in, but no one was there.

She shook her head and got back up. She reached into the stream to get the cup she'd dropped. Something brushed by her wrist. She pulled her hand out fast and water splashed all over her.

She looked closer into the water and only saw the cup. It was a wild stream. Of course, there could be some small bug or fish swimming around, but the events since the night before had her on edge.

"Just freaking out since you're here alone," she said aloud.

Mia reached back in and pulled out the cup, now filled with water, then stood up and placed it on the side of the table opposite the stone.

She moved a few steps away and then turned to her right. Something was there. She saw a shadow. A movement. Something. It was distracting, and it seemed to be coming from deeper in the tunnel.

Maybe the serial killer she always imagined would show up at her place one day had finally caught her at an unexpected location. A killer that had been following her for days, learning her routine. Serial killers were notorious for that. She'd never get to help Annika, as Strand would find chopped up pieces of her body in the stream. Or maybe just her decapitated torso, with her head destined to sit in a jar of formaldehyde as a serial killer's trophy with her eyes removed. The killer would never be found and her head would sit there for decades until the killer died of natural causes and the police found his body and collection.

Stop it, Mia. You always go too far. Stay in check, mind. We have work to do.

She turned back to the table and tried to shut everything else out. She looked at the cup and the stone. She moved closer to the table, shifting her gaze solely to the stone. With all the practice she'd had in the last few days, she had an easy grasp of the water. It was the destination that was the problem. She had to get that water into the rock.

She tried to remember the fear she felt the night before. The focus in her earlier class. She stared at the stone like it was an enemy. She wanted to rip it apart but couldn't. It was just a destination.

She picked up the rock and felt all around it, imagining the rock's smooth sides filling with dents, like dimples on a golf ball. Then she pictured each dimple opening like the sand she pictured for the glass windows in her classroom. The stone was a different feel, though. She couldn't picture gaping holes, but many small ones. She slowly guided the stream of water from the cup without even looking in the direction. She now owned that part of it.

The water stream came out gently, as much as she wanted to thrash it around. It hit the stone, which she had placed back down, but she let the water just kiss its edge. She had the water stream move around the stone, encircling it like it was feeling and testing it out, just like the storage container at her apartment. She pictured the holes, and then gently pushed the water into them. The water entered without hesitation. She felt it flow through and then let more soak in. She pushed a little harder, and the water moved in easier. She was able to make the water slow as it neared the hollow core.

The core was full. Finally, the water was there.

Then it wasn't.

The water surrounded the core and entered, but just as slowly as the water had entered and seemingly filled the rock's core, it escaped on the opposite side. The water went directly through and back out, slowly, and she couldn't keep it contained.

Footsteps filled the room as Mr. Strand, Anna, and Annika entered.

Strand saw her concentrating and directed his daughter to move behind Mia and out of her line of sight.

"Just act as if we are not here," he said. "I sense you are close. Keep going. Pay us no mind."

Mia started a new stream but held it. It was all about the stone.

She pictured the holes again, but she needed to separate the holes she imagined on the outside of the stone to let the water in while somehow making the rock solidify once all the water reached the center so it couldn't escape. She tried to get some kind of feel for it but couldn't. She tried over and over, but the water kept seeping through. Then she felt the darkness again.

The new stream she'd started fell before she was able to get a full grasp on it. The darkness was distracting. It was like eyes were staring at her, hidden in the depths of the tunnel. Maybe it was the spirits that had visited her the night before. Or a serial killer. It didn't matter. The darkness she felt was real.

Mia returned to the stream to refill the cup. She didn't acknowledge anyone else in the room and tried again.

The stream was up. It hit the stone and again started to penetrate. She got it to the core a little faster and it filled. It started to come through again, and she tried to imagine a solid shell within the stone, but she couldn't focus. The darkness hit her again and made her jump and turn. Something was with her, and it wasn't good.

"What is it, Mia?" Strand asked.

"There's something in here. Something in the water. Something in the tunnel. I'm so close, but I feel a presence. A distracting presence. I thought it might be my visitor from last night, but that one seemed to want to help me. What I feel now is something that doesn't want me to do this or is trying to hurt me."

"Please try once more. I will see if I am able to sense anything."

Mia turned, her concentration totally broken and remembering her dread from the night before.

The fear. She felt it swell in her throat and her stomach.

"I'll try," she said.

There was still water left in the cup. Before starting the stream, she picked up the stone again. She had to figure this out to succeed. Strand was right. She was close.

Mia lifted the stone to her nose and sniffed it. Didn't smell like anything familiar. She continued to move both her hands around it and placed it back.

She stared at the stone and ignored the water. Right now, the water meant nothing. If she couldn't hold it inside the rock, it wouldn't matter. Failing by 1 point or almost succeeding is still a failure. The baby's soul was the difference. That's what she was doing this for, right? She forgot about the baby. She was just concentrating and pushing herself. The baby was somewhere behind her. She could save her. She knew she could. Such a small creature, born from sperm and an egg, but now a small human. A helpless one. One that needed her to survive.

An egg. She pictured the stone, then an egg.

Yes. The baby came from an egg. An egg like the ones from a chicken, with a thin, yet strong layer on the outside to protect its precious contents.

She closed her eyes and pictured the stone and its hollow center.

The stream rose again, coming faster this time. It encircled the stone and penetrated. This time, before it reached the center, she pictured a white eggshell, and had the water dance around it. She allowed the water to caress the surface but lost her grip. The darkness was there again.

She heard Strand moving around the cave. He walked toward the stream. Mia tried to focus on her cup of water, but Strand was making distracting noises with his steps. No, not his steps. There was a different noise. It overcame her senses and broke her concentration.

It was his voice. He was saying something. She couldn't make it out, but the darkness started to subside. It was still there, but in the background, like a distant whisper.

Strand returned. Whatever it was, he had pushed it away.

Mia went back to her stream and shot out another burst of water. It penetrated and surrounded the center, and she focused on filling the center of the imaginary eggshell. The water was smooth and needed a way in. She thought of tiny craters in the eggshell, but only on one side. The water started to enter. She was almost there, then felt herself run out of breath. She sucked in a deep gulp of air and her head went black.

Her eyes focused. She looked up to see Strand and Anna were standing over her. Baby Annika, in Anna's arms, was staring, too. Her eyes were big, and she was pointing at Mia.

That's when she realized she was on the ground and on her back.

"What happened?"

"You exerted yourself too much," Strand said as he reached for her hand and helped her up.

She almost lost her balance. She was still foggy.

"You passed out," he continued. "You were close. So close."

"Yes, I think I might have figured it out, but I feel so tired."

"You are at power levels you've never experienced before. You said something else happened at school when you called me. What was it? You sounded overly excited."

"Yes, in my class. I made plant leaves flow from another classroom into mine and even got some water through window glass. It was like the entire room was one large container and I was able to fill it once I brought in the plants from the other room. I scared everyone and made a mess, but it was progress. I wanted to test myself as soon as I could. I'm not sure exactly how I did it, but that was power. I just have to figure out how to use it."

"You are almost there. There is nothing more you can do today, Mia. You've overexerted yourself and need to give your body and your mind time to rest."

"But I didn't do anything!" she protested. "It's still not done."

"You have gone beyond where I thought you would be by now. It will not happen all at once. I never expected you to exhibit even half of the skills that you already have. We may not have an infinite amount of time, but we still have a few more days for you to practice and refine."

"Days?" she asked. "Why days?"

"I'm getting the sense that the child will take a turn for the worse. I can sense her strength, but I also am able to sense when someone is on the brink of death. She is close, but she hasn't taken that final turn. Not yet, at least. This cannot be rushed, because without you at top form, it will be pointless. Panic mode will be a few days from now, but not today. If you can eliminate any negativity or distractions and get some rest, you will be more prepared than you were even today. You are improving at an exponential rate."

"What about that darkness I felt?" she asked. "What happened last night? Last night was helpful, but today it was a distraction."

"They will not interfere again."

"They?"

"Spirits are everywhere. The power you showed piqued their curiosity. I suspect these spirits engaged you last night to frighten you into action, but today I think they were curious and simply delved too close."

"What kind of spirits? Evil ones?"

"What you are attempting could attract good and evil, but they would all be curious as to what you can do for them before hurting you."

"Will they harm me or the baby?"

"No, so long as you continue following this path, they will stay away. You are no use to them otherwise. I tried to communicate with them. I told them you would never succeed and help them if they could not leave you alone."

"Help them? How?"

"Just a stretch of the truth to let you work in peace. Recall that this place was chosen due to its thin veil between spiritual planes. It has stood for thousands of years and will continue to attract those on the edge after we are long gone."

"You talked to them. What did they say?"

"I think they agreed. I assured them your power would be even greater if they stepped back."

"You really think I can do this?"

"Don't you? You felt how close you were. Imagine what you can do tomorrow with some rest and no distractions."

"No distractions," she said. "I'm going to have to deal with that tonight if I'm going to get any kind of rest or have any chance of saving Annika. I have to. I just hope no more helpful spirits show up to help by almost killing me."

Chapter Seventeen

As soon as Mia walked out of Hollow Rock, her phone vibrated several times. She knew it was Tino but didn't look at her screen. She got in her car and sat there. She looked at the trees and then at her surroundings. Everything felt so peaceful in this hidden anomaly located in the middle of open fields of nothing.

But underneath this inviting land was Hollow Rock, where she was trying to perform some kind of magic to reach another plane of existence. She also sensed the evil within it. Strand said forces in these planes, good and bad, might be attracted to her and what she was doing. He was right. Whatever it was that had come for her at her apartment may have had good intentions by using fear to fuel her, but what if she hadn't succeeded? Would those knives have finished their job? What kind of danger had she opened herself up to?

It took a few minutes before her mind started to settle. Her phone dinged twice more. Strand and Anna hadn't come out yet, and Mia wondered if they were discussing what she had just done or if Strand was communicating with whatever curious beings had almost killed her.

She could still feel the adrenaline coursing through her.

Stop it, Mia. Settle down. Process.

She set her forehead against the steering wheel, closed her eyes, and tried to clear her mind. After a few moments, there was another ding, so she opened her eyes and reached for her phone. Twelve missed texts and several missed calls, one from Aunt Grace and the rest from Tino.

She looked at the texts.

Call me.

Hurry.

What's taking so long? Aren't you in class?

Then more of the same.

The one text from Aunt Grace read, *How are you doing?*

She replied to her aunt first. *I'm okay. I'll be by later tonight. A lot more stuff to tell you.*

She knew a text wouldn't be enough for Tino and she needed to keep their dinner date. She punched his contact and he answered on the first ring.

"Hey, where are you? I was getting worried."

"I had class."

"Is that all?"

She hesitated. She didn't want to lie to him, but his tone was short and she sensed he was angry.

"I was still practicing over at the underground cave."

He didn't say anything as she felt the heat in her chest, wondering if he could sense the partial lie.

"What's so important, Tino?"

"I got off early. We got a quick side job today and got a little extra pay. Wanted to go somewhere nice. Can you do a late lunch instead of dinner, or are you going to cancel on me again?"

"Where?" She wasn't in the mood to go, but she didn't want to deal with any more friction.

"How about a good steak? Have you eaten?"

In all the excitement, she had forgotten to grab lunch and her stomach growled, answering the question for her.

"As long as it's not a place where we have to dress up. I don't have time to change."

"Okay. Want me to pick you up?"

"No, I'll meet you wherever you want to go."

"Let's go to the Longhorn. It's been a long time since we've been there."

She agreed and hung up. Of all the things she wanted to do right now, seeing Tino wasn't one of them. There'd been more tension than before, even during the phone call. She had been telling him everything before now but sensed his silent anger. Saving Annika was too important. Definitely more important than Tino and his judgment. The last thing she needed was another distraction.

Mia got to the restaurant and went straight to the bathroom. She washed her face and brushed her hair. The day had left her ragged, and as hungry as she was, she needed sleep. The events from the previous night and earlier at Hollow Rock had drained her even more than she realized. She wasn't about to tell Tino she passed out.

Mia sat at the table, ordered a couple of waters, and Tino arrived less than five minutes later. He was cleaned up from work and wearing dark jeans, boots, and a pressed, black collar polo shirt.

He kissed her and sat down. She felt him about to bombard her with questions, so she decided to take the offensive.

"So, tell me about the side job?"

"We hit a slowdown. The house we were working on didn't pass inspection, so the cement guy couldn't pour.

133

But we picked up a job that had been on standby. You know the cement will go bad if we don't use it fast enough, so we used it to build a small patio for someone. Once we were done, that was it. Nothing else scheduled."

His summary was short and to the point. Avoiding the coming conversation wasn't going to be an option.

"That's good, Tino. This afternoon lunch is an unexpected surprise."

He nodded.

"So how did school go today?" he asked. "Any new adventures?"

The tone in his voice was flat and monotone. He wasn't great at hiding his feelings.

Mia decided to mix in some truth now that her lie was out there.

"School was a little crazy. I made a mess with a water experiment."

"How'd you do that?"

She pointed to her head. "Special, remember? I don't know how to control it sometimes, but it was nothing."

It was something. She just couldn't bring herself to tell him the details.

"What about the freaky stream thing in the cave?"

"It was okay. Nothing special."

He looked down at his menu and she saw him shake his head.

"What?" she asked.

"You know what?" he said. "Just quit this already."

She imagined a steak flying across the room and smacking him on the head. Then a loud crash boomed behind them.

A waitress had dropped her plate and the steak that was on it fell to the floor.

"Are you okay?" the man at the table she was serving asked.

"Yes, I'm sorry. I don't know what happened!"

"It looked like the steak jumped off the plate," the customer said.

The waitress looked startled. "Don't worry, I'll get you a fresh one."

Mia had only thought about a steak flying. And only for a second.

Be careful, Mia.

"She's clumsy," Tino said. "So, what did happen in the cave?"

"Nothing," she said, defeated. "I made no significant progress, just practice. I'm not sure if it's going to work."

"I told you. You have no business there. You should be with me so we can live our lives."

What kind of life? she thought to herself. *If I don't finish school, I'll probably have to work twice as hard or be dependent on him. Which is what he wants.*

"I made a commitment. If I fail, I fail, but I'm not going to give up. And I'm not quitting school. I want to enjoy my meal. Please stop."

Her blood boiled. She felt the heat in her body rising.

Do not let him speak to you that way. You are powerful. You are greater than he.

The voice. The dark voice. It didn't sound menacing. It just sounded like it was stating a fact.

Ignore the voice, Mia. Distract yourself.

Mia thought of the experiment and her grip on the streams.

"It's not good when you can't admit you aren't good at something," Tino said. "You just need me. I'll take care of you. You don't need this stupid college degree or to be helping any strangers."

Just shut up, Tino. Please.

Mia closed her eyes. It took everything in her power not to think of a hundred forks flying at Tino's head.

He underestimates. He is weak. You do not deserve to be spoken to this way.

"One day we'll be married and all this nonsense will be pointless."

Focus on the streams, Mia. Ignore him. Ignore the voice.

"You won't have to work," Tino continued. "You should just be home waiting for me. I'll be working hard for you. For us. Your job will be waiting for your man."

She felt her blood pulsing. The streams she was trying to focus on turned red.

He wants control of you, the voice said. *No one should control you.*

The red stream was pulsing now. She squeezed it tight, then heard a loud thud.

She opened her eyes and Tino's face was filled with sweat. He had dropped his glass of water and the veins on his neck and arms were popped out and throbbing.

Mia sucked in a scared breath, and as she did, Tino's body stiffened.

The red stream. Tino's blood.

She realized she had a grip on the blood flowing through Tino's body. With a little more effort, she might be able to make it burst from his veins.

She gasped in fear and as she did, Tino's body eased and his veins retracted as he started to cough uncontrollably. He stood up, trying to catch his breath.

"Tino!" Mia yelled.

He held up his hand to stop her from getting up. He took in several long breaths and finally sat down. Mia handed him her water and he took a long sip. Their waiter rushed to the table.

"Everything okay?"

"Can you get him some more water?"

Tino finally caught his breath.

"Tino, are you okay?"

"Yes, I don't know what happened. It was like everything tightened up and I couldn't breathe. It felt like my chest was going to explode."

"Maybe you overdid it at work today," Mia said. "Do we need to go?"

He gulped down the rest of the water as the waiter quickly returned with two more glasses. Tino got up to go to the bathroom and returned a few minutes later.

"We should go," Mia said.

"No, no. I'm okay now. I washed my face. I'll just drink a little more water. Let's eat."

The rest of the customers went back to their conversations once they realized Tino was okay.

They ordered their food and Tino was too freaked out to ask any more about Mia's day or push her to quit what she was doing.

Mia's face went pale as she tried to make sense of what had just happened.

What did I just do?

Tino had made her angry. No, furious. He had a habit of telling her to quit school and maybe she had gotten used to it, but he pushed too hard today. The dark voice in her head may have frightened her, but it was correct. She didn't deserve for him to speak to her the way he did. He had no right to control her, even if he couldn't help it. It was all he knew after living with his father. His father who was alone because his mother finally left him after twenty years of his controlling attitude.

Is it time to break up?

"I love you," Tino said.

Mia softened and gave a weak smile. "I love you, too, Tino. But I'm not going to quit and I'm not going to stop."

She knew he wanted to protest, but he was still shaken, no matter how hard he was trying to hide it.

There would be no breakup today.

I still love him.

She did still love him, but also realized the power within her was stronger and more dangerous that she could have ever imagined.

But I could have killed him.

Chapter Eighteen

THE REST of their afternoon lunch was quick.

Mia wanted it to be over so she could go see Aunt Grace. She knew she could no longer have a conversation about this with Tino without getting angry enough to possibly kill him, and that was no longer a figurative expression.

She also needed some sleep. She wanted to tell someone about what had happened, and her aunt was the only viable audience.

Mia had lost her appetite and waited for Tino to finish his meal. He wolfed down his food as he rambled. Tino mentioned a few things about work, but he was rattled and didn't bring up any more about her school or helping Mr. Strand. Mia knew he was more concerned about how weak he must have looked in front of the restaurant customers and staff.

"Thank you for lunch, Tino, but I really need to go."

"Okay," he said without argument as the waitress returned with the receipt.

They walked outside and kissed each other goodbye.

The tension and lack of feeling in the kiss was obvious to both of them. She didn't want to invite a restart of their conversation now that they were away from prying eyes in the restaurant. Knowing the last thing he wanted was a reminder of what had just happened, Mia took advantage of it.

"Are you okay?"

Tino looked down. "I'm fine. I should have just had more water today."

He hesitated and was about to say something, but Mia cut in.

"I have to go study and get some sleep. Big test tomorrow. I don't want to talk any more about today or me quitting. I'll call or text you later."

She turned around without giving him an opportunity to respond to her partial lie. She felt the heat of his gaze on her, but as angry as she had been, she was more fearful for his life if he pushed her buttons again.

As badly as Mia wanted to see her aunt, she decided to go home instead and get herself together. She had a lot to process.

She spent half the evening replaying all that had happened in her head. The slightest noise spooked her. It wasn't a good night.

After her classes the next day, Mia got in her car and texted her Aunt Grace that she was on her way. She hoped there were no unexpected emergencies with the kids and her aunt would be free to talk privately. Her mind was racing so fast she deliberately concentrated on the speedometer to calm her mind.

She arrived shortly and when she walked in the house, her cousin Bianca was in the kitchen getting a snack. Omar and Brian were sitting in the living room, doing homework, sharing bowls of chips and junk food. Brenda wasn't home.

"Hey, guys," Mia said.

Bianca and Brian gave her a hug and Omar just waved, concentrating on his book while stuffing a handful of chips in his mouth.

"Where's your mom?"

"She's in her bedroom on her laptop," Bianca said. "We're trying to get all our stuff done so we can go see Brenda cheer at the game tonight."

Mia knocked on Aunt Grace's door.

"Come in!"

Mia entered as Grace was typing furiously on her laptop. Mia waited patiently and about a minute later, Grace stopped typing, then stood up and hugged her niece. Grace stayed staring at her face as they let go.

"You look tired, but you have something you're dying to tell me, don't you?"

Mia nodded and whispered. "I don't want the kids to hear, though. You want to go outside or get in the car?"

"Let's go outside."

Grace walked out of the room. Bianca was finishing her snack at the table.

"I'll be right back," Grace said. "Mia and I are going to take a walk."

"Okay, Mom," Bianca said.

Omar just grunted and a few chips fell out of his crunching mouth. Brian threw up a peace sign.

"Pick that up when you're done, Omar."

They walked outside. Aunt Grace used to take them on walks when they were all younger to the park that was about three blocks down. They headed the same way.

"What happened?" Grace asked as they reached the sidewalk.

"It was unbelievable," Mia said. "I have to start with my apartment."

Mia told her about the visitors and knives and how she had initially thought it was just a dream. She rushed through the dangerous parts and emphasized how that jolt led to progress in the classroom, although she had left it in shambles. Aunt Grace's eyes narrowed, but she let Mia finish.

Mia told her about the Hollow Rock. She got to the part about the darkness she had felt, but then slowed her speech down as she tried to read her aunt's face and determine whether it was too much.

"Oh, no. You tell me everything. Good or bad," Aunt Grace said.

Mia took in a breath and told her every detail. When she got to the end of her Hollow Rock portion, she hesitated.

"Is that it?"

"No, there's still something else with Tino."

Mia spared no detail, and as she brought up how she thought she had caused Tino's attack, she stopped for a moment before continuing.

"I just don't think I can tell him any more, Aunt Grace. He got me so angry and I can't say with 100% certainty that I did that to him, but I really think I did. He's just so negative about everything. And wanting to control me. I know this isn't anything new, but it's getting worse. I don't think he'll be truly happy until I quit school and let him take care of me."

"And live with his dad while you're having sex in the next room? I don't think so."

Aunt Grace tried to be tactful, but when she was angry or defending her kids or niece, she didn't hold back.

Mia laughed but didn't know what to say.

"Okay, Mia," Grace said. "I'm happy you made progress, but whatever this darkness is could have killed you. I mean, in the cave is one thing, but following you home and to your class?"

Mia stopped walking. "I hadn't even thought about it, Aunt Grace. What if something follows me to your house? I can't do that to you or the kids! I'm so sorry. I could be putting you all in danger. I need to go."

Grace put her hands on her niece's shoulders. "Oh, no, Mia. You can stop that talk right now. If this was happening to one of my children, I'd protect them at any cost. I may not have birthed you, but you are more than just my niece. You're part of my family. And we'll face this together if we have to. Staying away is not an option."

"But Aunt Grace…"

"Stop. End of discussion."

Mia's eyes started to tear up.

Aunt Grace hugged her. "You never expected having to deal with any kind of darkness like this, did you?"

Mia shook her head as she dried her eyes.

"It doesn't matter, though, does it?" Grace said. "You're going to keep trying to help this child even if there are beings out there that could kill you, aren't you?"

Grace knew the answer without Mia having to say a word.

"I understand why you have to do this, but you're going to have to be strong like your grandmother, Mia. You can't let yourself be harmed. And how much do you think you can trust this Strand? It bothers me that he didn't tell you this could happen."

"He kind of did. He just said I might attract things from the other side, but I didn't expect this. I don't think he did, either."

"This is getting dangerous, Mia. I don't like it, but I

also won't be Tino and tell you what you should or shouldn't do. You know the risks and I wish you weren't doing this, but I know if your grandmother was in your shoes, she wouldn't hesitate either. I just need you to promise you'll continue to tell me everything, even if you think I can't take it."

"Okay, Aunt Grace. I promise."

Now it was Grace's turn to hesitate.

"What is it, Aunt Grace?"

"Something I don't want to even suggest," Grace said. "But feel that I have to. The book."

"Grandma's book?"

"Yes, Grandma's book. I told you she dabbled in some of the darker parts of it, but she gave it up."

"Yes."

"I can't believe I'm saying this, but there is also something your grandmother told us once. She said sometimes you have to use darkness to fight darkness. She did it once out of necessity and said she prayed she never had to use it again."

"Are you saying you want me to use this darkness? Is it some kind of black magic?"

"I don't know if I'd go that far. The incantations Mom used were mostly prayers straight out of the Bible. Where these others come from, I never asked. Mom just told your mother and I to never use them unless we had no choice. But yes, I guess that's what I'm saying. Whatever visited you at your apartment and at school might decide to let the knives go if they don't get their way next time. I just want you to be prepared."

"Meaning to try these incantations?"

"No. I just think you should read through the book and if you absolutely must fight something evil, it would be good to be prepared. Maybe you won't find anything, but like your grandmother said, sometimes you have to fight darkness with darkness. Don't practice it, just learn it."

Mia's eyes were wide as she nodded.

"Now let's talk about Tino. His macho shit needs to stop. It's getting worse and I know you sometimes blow it off and won't tell me. It doesn't matter if it's his dad's influence, but there's a reason his father is still alone all this time after his wife left. I knew him in high school. He was nice on the outside but didn't think much of women. Thought we only existed for cooking, sex, and to do whatever a man commanded. Tino can't help inheriting some of that, but he's going too far. I'm glad you didn't kill him, but part of me is happy he got a warning."

"I could have really hurt him."

"But you didn't."

They kept walking and were already at the park. There were a few kids there, but it was mostly empty. They stayed on the edge and found a bench to sit on.

"I want to know more about how you felt with all this newfound power. Even *Mami* never showed us any way of moving things around."

"Maybe she didn't have a reason to. I still can't do what I need to, so I have to get better."

"My concern is your control. What if you hadn't been able to stop yourself? Or what if you were dealing with more dangerous material, like boiling water or acid or something like that? People could really get hurt in that crossfire."

Grace had a point.

"I learned better control, but I never considered my emotions. But what if I can save this baby's soul? Then what's next? What does it mean?"

"It means you can do a lot of good for people, and still get your degree. Don't lose focus. I'm glad your professor knows some of what's going on. You need to be extra cautious. Another professor could have kicked you out of school."

"Maybe that's why I let go," Mia said. "I know Professor Cort is curious about the situation and he's been positive about the things I could do before I started flinging water and making the windows bleed. It didn't seem to freak him out much."

"That's true, but he's not like most people. He knew something weird was going on before he ever asked you. Most people aren't going to be the same way."

"What are you saying?"

"It may sound hypocritical after I just said I'd support you and offered you Grandma's book, but I want you to be careful. I know in your head and in your heart you are doing your best to help this child, but my job as a mom and your aunt is to make sure you're safe."

Mia thought she sounded a little like Tino, but knew it wasn't the same. Aunt Grace wanted to protect her. Tino wanted to control her.

"Thank you, Aunt Grace."

"Do me a favor?"

"What?"

"Remember the drawer locks I used to have in the kitchen when the kids were little?"

Mia nodded.

"I think I still have some in the garage. Will you put all your knives inside your kitchen drawers and attach those locks?"

"I doubt it would stop whatever was in my apartment."

"I know, but it'll make me feel a little better."

"Okay, Aunt Grace. Learn dark spells, baby proof the drawers, and be careful. Got it."

Chapter Nineteen

RICKY SAT ON A BENCH, waiting for Gabby. With direction from DeadBlogger, their path had taken them from Louisiana to the small town of Fayetteville, Tennessee, where they found more evidence of their demons.

Now they were in Atlanta, Georgia, searching.

There were several potential hot spots throughout the city, but Atlanta was big and they spent almost two days chasing down each lead. Only one yielded something worthwhile, but the information was already old. They started this day before the sun rose but felt like it was already wasted.

Ricky sent a message to DeadBlogger: *This looks like a wash. The info was good, but looks like whatever it was moved on well before we got here.*

After another hour without progress, Ricky and Gabby found a place to eat breakfast. They took their time with their meal.

"It feels like we're stuck again," Gabby said.

"I know. We always seem to be just a little too late."

Gabby nodded. "What do you think they're looking for?"

Ricky shook his head. "I thought they were just searching for more power and fear to feed from after what they did to my family and your daughter, but after following this strange path they're on now, I don't know. Is the power just to terrorize? I worry about what their ultimate goal is, but at the same time, once they figure it out, I'm hoping they'll stay put long enough for us to find them."

Ricky's phone dinged. He'd set up an alert to let him know when he had a new message from anyone in the chat group. He cleaned his hands with a napkin and opened his laptop.

The message was a direct reply from DeadBlogger: *I think I have something. And it's recent. Are you away from prying eyes?*

Give me a minute.

Ricky nodded at Gabby and got up. They bagged what was left of their food and rushed back to Ricky's car. Ricky jumped into the passenger seat and fired up his secure hotspot.

He replied to DeadBlogger: *Ready.*

Florida State University in Tallahassee. I found chatter on some of the student sites that picked up a ton of search keywords. Check this out.

Screenshots started appearing from private student groups. The first one was a few weeks old.

How does she do that? It's like she can bring back these plants from the dead.

You think she's a witch? Or into some kind of occult stuff?

It's always the quiet ones.

The next screenshot was someone explaining in detail

how a student caused a mess in her classroom but was able to perform things that seemed impossible.

She's a nice girl. She helped me with my experiment. I still don't know how she does it, but it seems unnatural.

Ricky typed some more. *I don't understand. How do plants factor into the demons we're hunting?*

Then a few more screenshots came through. These were only a few days old.

Leaves and dirt crawled THROUGH THE WINDOW and under the door. And get this. We didn't have an experiment that day. They entered from the NEXT CLASSROOM!

Others in the chat detailed the same thing. Five different students describing water flying everywhere and the female student looking like she was in some kind of trance.

DeadBlogger replied: *I don't get the water and plant references, either, but sounds like a lot of unnatural abilities. Just like a certain kid who destroyed an entire downtown.*

DeadBlogger was right. Even if they didn't understand the connections, it sounded as far-fetched as what happened to Ricky as well as Gabby's big work showcase disaster.

Ricky turned to Gabby, who had been reading along. "These last posts are only a day old. What do you think?"

"I think we need to get to Florida."

Chapter Twenty

On her way home, Mia stopped at the closest superstore and bought a few packs of baby proofing drawer and cabinet locks. Deep down, she knew a few plastic latches wouldn't stop the darkness that visited her at home and in class, but she knew it would make Aunt Grace feel better.

She got to her apartment and installed the latches as soon as she arrived. She had some studying to do, but she could only think of Annika and what had happened with Tino.

She had power, but she knew it wouldn't be enough. Especially if this darkness turned angry if she failed.

Mia sat on her living room couch, opened her textbook, and tried to take notes, but she kept turning towards her bedroom, thinking about her grandmother's book.

This cycle repeated for almost twenty minutes.

You have to, Mia. It's only as a last resort. But you have to be prepared for anything. For Annika.

She closed her textbook and went into her room. She opened her nightstand where she'd kept her grandmother's book since the day Grace had given it to her. She had glanced through it a few times, enjoying reading her grandmother's writings, but hadn't looked past the first few recipes and healing prayers.

"I hope this is the right decision, Grandma."

Mia took the book and returned to her couch. She stared at the cover for a long moment before opening it. She thumbed through it. There were dividers in several sections, and when she opened the last divider, the first page was a note:

"For the one who has reached this section, before you continue, know that I prayed for a long time before deciding to include this. There are only a few incantations and I've listed their purpose, but the deciding factor that led me to record them is something I've never spoken about, not even to my own daughters.

A few years ago, I was asked to help the sick cousin of a dear friend. I didn't expect anything out of the ordinary and performed a healing prayer for fear, or curando de susto. *It didn't take me long to realize it was much more than what I expected. The cousin wasn't possessed, or I would have contacted the church for an exorcism, but she was being haunted by evil spirits. I sensed the darkness while I was in her room, and I saw cuts form throughout her body in the presence of my friend.*

I tried everything but wasn't having any success. I reached out to another curandera *who taught me a lot of what I knew when I was younger, and she asked me if I trusted her. I told her yes, and she took my hands and said I needed to understand what she was about to show me was dangerous but necessary if I truly wanted to help this person. She then showed me a few herbal combinations and incantations that didn't use prayers from any church or the Bible.*

There is no easy way to say this, but what she was teaching me involved black magic. The curandera *was sharing this with me because she felt it was the only way to get rid of the spirits. Then she told me something I never forgot and that I hope the person reading this will remember. When true evil is involved, sometimes you have to fight darkness with darkness.*

I used several of these words and potions to defeat what was haunting the cousin. I almost died in the process, but the darkness I used allowed me to save her. However, that darkness lingered inside me for many months and it took several cleansing rituals and prayers to finally get rid of it. Do I regret this? No. Had that darkness survived, it could have easily spread to my friend, her family, and others. The battle between good and evil is eternal, but there are some things so dark and dangerous that they must be destroyed before they can thrive.

I want whoever is reading this to understand without a doubt that this is black magic. It is a risk to you, your soul, and the people you love. These pages are to be used only as a last resort when a life is at stake and the risk of the darkness spreading is high. If you are only here out of curiosity, I beg you to stop. I did not make this decision lightly, and neither should you. Just be sure you are doing this for the right reasons.

Be careful, and may God protect you if you choose to continue."

MIA'S EYES were moist as she heard her grandmother's voice in each word she read.

She turned the page.

Mia wasn't sure how to classify what she read next. There were only five total spells, incantations, ceremonies, or whatever they should be called. Each had a title that terrified her and were only a few pages each.

Summoning, Power, Darkness, Evil Eye, and Fear.

Most of the materials required weren't too difficult to obtain. The list included effigies, jars, black candles, and more. She was pretty sure she could find all or most online, or maybe even locally.

As she read in more detail, three of the titles stood out:

Power, Darkness, and Fear. These three seemed like they could prove useful. She had power, but the darkness was stronger. And that darkness seemed to enjoy spreading fear. The Fear page materials included poppy seeds, ash, jars, and something called valerian root powder.

Mia jumped online but wasn't sure what to search for. She thought about it and tried "*curandera* supplies," "black candles," and "herbs" with mixed results, but one word she saw pop up repeatedly was "metaphysical stores."

Mia typed that in and got two local search results: Crystals and More and Alma's Alchemy.

Crystals and More looked like it sold mainly crystals and some of the items she needed, but Alma's Alchemy specified *curandera* supplies and also bore a neon sign with the word "Witchcraft." It was already closed, so Mia took the time to read and re-read the pages in more detail and planned to head to the shop early the following morning.

Mia arrived at Alma's Alchemy right when it opened. It was only twenty minutes away and located in a small shopping plaza between a video game store and a mobile phone carrier. An older couple was seated behind a counter in the back and a young woman was by the longer counter to her left.

"Can I help you?" the young woman asked.

"Yes, I need a few items that I hope you have in stock."

Mia handed her a list she had jotted down on a receipt in her car. The young girl looked at the list, smiled, and then walked to the back and handed the list to the older woman.

The woman looked at the list and back up at Mia. She stared at her for a moment, looked her up and down, then walked toward her.

"Hello, I'm Alma. We do have everything on your list in stock, but I must ask you something. I've never seen you before, but do you know what these materials are typically used for?"

Mia couldn't maintain eye contact. She wasn't expecting to be questioned.

"Yes, I do."

The woman stared, waiting for Mia to look at her, but Mia kept her eyes on the floor.

"What is your intention with these?"

Mia knew the lady wasn't going to help her unless she said something. She finally met the woman's gaze.

"I'm trying to save a soul. The soul of a child."

The woman blinked. She looked back at the list. "There are evil spirits around this child?"

Mia nodded.

"Where did you get this list from?"

"My grandmother. Well, her book. She's no longer with us."

"What was your grandmother's name?"

"Helena. Helena Beltran."

"You are Helena's granddaughter?"

"You knew my grandmother?"

"Yes, I did," Alma said. "She was a friend. Someone I trusted."

Alma handed the young woman the list and nodded. The girl started gathering the items.

"That is my granddaughter, Lorena," Alma said. "She knows enough to recognize some of the darker uses of some of the items we sell, which is why she knew to inform me."

"Then why do you sell them?"

The woman smiled. "Sometimes, as I am sure your grandmother explained to you, they are necessary."

Mia smiled. "Not directly, but she did."

"I would not have sold these to you had your answer

not been satisfactory to me," Alma said as Lorena handed her a couple of bags with the items. "I do not encourage their use, but I trusted your grandmother, so I will trust you. *Que Dios de bendiga.* May God bless you."

Mia paid and returned to her apartment. She laid out the items on her coffee table and looked at the black candles and other items before her. She let out a deep breath and opened the book to the "Power" section.

Just treat it like a cookbook, Mia. You may not need it. Just think of it as research.

"Research that might cost me my soul," Mia replied to herself. "Annika is worth it. Stopping this darkness is worth it. Grandma, please give me knowledge and strength."

Mia spent the rest of her weekend working on the spells and practicing at Hollow Rock. She didn't make any significant progress, but she was determined to improve and save this child she barely knew.

Chapter Twenty-One

RICKY AND GABBY gathered their items. It was a Sunday, so they would have to wait another day before going to the university. They used their time at the hotel researching the school, messaging with DeadBlogger, and figuring out a plan.

They started their university research with botany, which led them to plant sciences, then from plant sciences to the Department of Biological Science. Within this department were multiple classes dealing with plants, including Plant Molecular Biology, Plant Physiology, Plant Biology, Field Botany, Molecular Biology, and more.

"Where do we begin?" Ricky asked.

"We start with the building where the department is located."

"How many floors?"

"Wow," Gabby said. "The building looks pretty elaborate. Two five-story buildings connected by a two-story central lobby. Nothing in those chats indicated specific classes, did they?"

Ricky shook his head. "Central lobby sounds like a good place to start."

They ate dinner, updated DeadBlogger, and got a good night's sleep for the first time in weeks.

They drove to the university mid-morning, not wanting to arouse suspicion if they were there waiting.

They walked to the outside of the King Life Sciences Building on the FSU campus and tried to look inconspicuous as students were moving around them, some rushing to class. They immediately noticed a problem.

"They're using security access cards," Ricky said.

"We can just tailgate."

Ricky casually walked to the doors and stopped like he forgot something and returned.

"The signs say no tailgating or holding doors open since they're monitored by security cameras," Ricky said. "The last thing we want is to draw attention of campus security before we make it through the doors."

"What do we do?" Gabby asked.

"Give me a minute."

Gabby sat on an outdoor bench while Ricky left her line of sight.

He returned less than ten minutes later. He sat next to her on the bench and pulled out two student ID cards.

"How?"

"I've had to pick up some nontraditional skills to get into places. Students at a school rushing or studying are way too easy to pickpocket. When we're done, we'll just drop them at lost and found or somewhere they'll get returned to them."

They entered the building five minutes apart, then found a common area on the first floor where students were gathered, some eating and others studying.

Ricky pointed to some open chairs in a central area

where several students were studying, talking, or just killing time.

They took the open seats. They didn't have any books, so Ricky opened his laptop and handed it to Gabby while he pretended to go through his phone with one hand while holding an otherworldly tool in another. Ricky knew the Electromagnetic Field Detector, or EMF, wasn't foolproof and mostly used for low-cost ghost hunting. However, Gabby's experience with ghost hunters convinced him to give it a try. The EMF had proven useful on a few of the occasions where they had encountered stronger spirits. He figured it was worth a try.

They eavesdropped on the conversations around them and Gabby tried to engage the student nearest her, but nothing about the event came up and the EMF was quiet. As the time neared the top of the hour, students started to disperse.

"They're probably heading to class," Ricky said. "Let's blend in."

Gabby took out her own EMF as they moved with a group down a long hall. Ricky stopped as something moved on the EMF. He took a few steps in every direction, but the signal kept fading. He broke from the crowd and looked confused as Gabby approached.

"What's happening?" Gabby asked.

"I'm not sure. This pattern makes no sense."

Ricky stopped near a stairway as the signal strengthened. He took a step up.

"This is why. The signal's above us."

They moved up the stairs and Ricky went partially down one hall before moving to another. He found a solid signal right in front of a doorway. Gabby moved further down the hall but didn't pick up anything else. That doorway was the only source.

Ricky looked in. There were no students.

He reached for the doorknob, and it turned.

They walked in, almost tiptoeing to keep their steps silent. The room looked like some kind of science lab and smelled like a garden with a chemical spill.

"What class is this?" Gabby asked.

"It's General Ecology," a voice said.

A woman stood up from behind a table.

"I'm Professor Diaz," she said with a smile. "How can I help you?"

Ricky stumbled backward and started to say something. "Uh, no, we just, uh, walked into the wrong classroom…"

"Looking for a make-out room?" the professor asked.

Gabby and Ricky both looked at each other and grimaced. "No way!"

"He's way too young for me," Gabby said. "We're just colleagues."

"What can I help you with, then?"

"I was thinking about taking a plant class," Ricky said. "I really enjoy plants and gardening and … plant stuff."

"What he means is…" Gabby paused and thought about her approach before continuing. "Has anything odd happened in this building or in your classroom lately?"

Professor Diaz strained to maintain her smile.

"I take it you heard the rumors of the waterfest we had a few days ago?"

Gabby tried to hide her surprise and answered quickly. "Yes, we heard something about it."

Professor Diaz looked at Ricky and then back at Gabby.

"I don't recognize either of you. What are your majors?"

Gabby didn't hesitate. "Digital Media."

"Ah, so looking for a story to impress your professors?"

"Anything to get an A."

The professor studied their faces, going back and forth as if she was considering what to say.

"It was an unusual event. Are you sure you're just looking for a good grade?"

"We are also interested in odd happenings," Gabby said. "Things that kind of don't make sense. This one sounded like it fit."

"What did you hear exactly? And what do you plan to do with the information you gather?"

Shit, Ricky thought. *Dug too deep.*

"We just heard there was some phenomenon with water," Gabby said. "Sounded almost supernatural. We plan to use the information we gather to investigate and research, then add it to a project we're working on that we'll present at the end of the semester. We are also thinking about making an online video or podcast."

Professor Diaz smirked.

"Everything can be explained scientifically. We're pretty sure a magnetic experiment going on a few doors down and some metallic elements in our soil were the cause of our traveling zombie plants. It gave everyone a scare and generated some excitement, but I'm sure that's all that it was. Is there anything else?"

Gabby smiled back. "No. Thank you, Professor Diaz. We appreciate your time."

The professor kept her eyes on them as they walked out of the classroom. It wasn't until they were back on the first floor that Gabby finally spoke.

"First thoughts?"

"Other than she didn't believe a word of what you said?"

"A word of what I said? Not like you left me much of a

choice. I've never seen you babble before. Plant stuff? Really?"

"I know. She caught me off guard when she popped out from behind that table. She reminded of my high school algebra teacher who didn't let us get away with anything."

"Did you pick up anything unusual?"

"I only had a chance to glance at my EMF while you were talking to the professor. The signal was off the charts."

"So, what do we do now?" Gabby asked.

"Surveillance. Whatever happened in here, there's an entire class of students that were in the middle of it. I'll bet if we just spend enough time hanging out like we did in the lobby, we'll find someone who knows. The professor's reply sounded rehearsed, but with something this wild, there's no way the students wouldn't still be talking about it."

"Then we need to look more like students if we really want to blend in."

They left to get some supplies and returned with their stolen IDs about an hour later. Gabby wore a new backpack and Ricky had on a pair of headphones that weren't turned on to go along with his laptop bag. They had even stopped at a discount bookstore to get some cheap used books in the bag in case they were searched.

They also wanted to avoid Professor Diaz on the second floor, so they split up. Ricky stayed on the first floor and found a break room filled with students.

Gabby took the third floor and decided to start in a computer lab with over a dozen students and a lot of chatter.

Ricky got on his laptop and was looking through news sources while checking for any dark chatroom activity and keeping his ears open. DeadBlogger had asked for an update that Ricky hoped to answer with something significant soon, but otherwise the chatrooms were quiet.

Most of the students around him were alone and wore their own headphones as they studied. After about fifteen minutes, a larger group came in and grabbed snacks. They sat down and started multiple, animated discussions as they enjoyed their break.

Ricky waited a little longer. His social skills had been almost non-existent the last year or so, but he had to find a way in.

Gabby was having more luck. When she walked into the computer lab, she found groups talking. She heard a group mention the words "experiment" and "crazy" and walked up and introduced herself.

There were seven people in the group, and they all acknowledged her with a hello or a wave but continued their conversation. She waited for a break in the overlapping conversations before she broke in.

"So what is this experiment I hear you talking about? Sorry to eavesdrop, but it sounds interesting."

They turned to look at her. Two of them looked her up and down but didn't offer an answer.

"You don't look familiar," a friendlier face said. "Are you in this building often?"

"I only have one class here, usually first thing in the morning and work the rest of the day, but I was off and decided to come catch up on some studying while I had the chance."

Most of them nodded. The young student described the experiment at a high level, but it wasn't related to the incident.

Gabby wanted to interrupt to segue into her question, but the young woman spoke fast and didn't take a breath. Gabby waited, hoping to find the right moment.

Ricky was twiddling his fingers over the keyboard as he casually looked up at those around him. He kept searching for more details or something common to use.

He didn't have a solid reason to approach the group, but then, out of his left peripheral vision, he saw something that could prove useful.

A young man was sitting near Ricky with his backpack open, listening to music on his ear buds. A book on botany was partially visible. He prepared to get up and approach the student, but then realized he didn't know what to ask.

"Idiot," Ricky whispered to himself.

All the info he needed was resting on the keyboard beneath his fingers.

A quick search of botany told him more than he knew 10 seconds before.

"The study of plants," he read as he kept perusing. "How plants live and reproduce."

He kept on reading a few tidbits and realized other than the study of plants, he wasn't going to learn enough to have an intelligent conversation about it in the next few minutes.

Ricky studied the young man and tried to think of another way to reach him.

The headphones. Ricky realized his headphones, which were turned off, were muffling the sounds around him. He removed them and was close enough to the student to hear the song he was listening to.

Ricky stood up and walked over. The student looked up and popped one of his earbuds out.

"What's up?" the guy asked.

"80s much?" Ricky asked.

"Oh yeah. My mom and dad. That's all they listen to when we take family trips. Not my first choice, but when

I'm homesick, I go back to the 80s. I have to admit, I love that."

Ricky smiled, since he knew he didn't have to lie for his reply.

"I grew up with my mom and grandma, mostly," Ricky said. "My mom was the same way. She was kind of messed up, but she loved her 80s music. She had a pretty good voice and would sing Pat Benatar and Duran Duran at the top of her lungs. Every time she heard 'Open Arms' from Journey, she'd cry. Every. Single. Time."

The young man started laughing. "Oh, man. My mom did that a few times, too. Hell, I even caught my dad shedding a tear once."

They both laughed.

"I'm Ricky," he said, and offered his hand.

"Jason," the student said as he removed the other earbud.

"Haven't seen you around," Ricky said first.

"Ah, I keep to myself unless it's a study group. I don't remember seeing you, either. What are you taking?"

"Ah, well, I'm actually thinking about changing my major or maybe my minor. I saw your botany book in your bag and was wondering what that class was like. I was gonna ask you about it but then heard the music and that seemed to be a more important topic."

"Class is okay. Sometimes interesting and sometimes boring, but some of the experiments are cool."

Perfect.

"I heard there was some excitement in one of the classes a few days ago," Ricky said. "Some kind of freak water thing?"

"Oh, yeah. I have a friend in that class. She said it was crazy! Water started flying around everywhere, and even the windows were streaking with water from plants on the outside!"

"So what happened?"

"She said they were in the middle of the experiment and then water just started flying around the room. And then somehow, plants starting coming into the room from a different class. Hard to believe, but I've known my friend since high school and trust her, as crazy as the story sounds. Amy said that this girl is really good with the plants and always first to finish. She had a spaced-out look in her eyes as the water starting flying out of these moving plants. The professors told them it was magnetic interference from another class experiment, but I don't know. Science can do some crazy things, I guess. Magnets making stuff float and all."

"Wow. Who was the girl?"

"I don't know. It's like Maya or Mia or something like that. I've seen her before but don't know her. Heard she's the best student in a few classes."

Maya or Mia. That was big.

"I wish I'd been there to see that," Ricky said.

"Yeah, me, too. To be honest, I might have run out screaming if I saw plants invading the room and shooting water everywhere. Now, if it had been blood, I would have been knocking down the girls screaming on my way out the door. Without any shame, either. I don't mess with scary."

Ricky laughed. "Sounds like botany's way more fun than it sounds."

"That time I'm sure it was."

"It was good meeting you. I think I might just change my major after all. Glad to meet a fellow 80s music lover."

"Hope to see you around, Ricky."

They shook hands and Ricky walked out. He started up the stairs toward the 3rd floor to meet Gabby.

He was halfway up the first flight when he heard fast footsteps and then smelled Gabby's perfume.

She had an excited look on her face. She opened her mouth, then looked around. She motioned for them to head back down.

They followed each other to the ground floor, hoping Professor Diaz wasn't anywhere along their path.

They walked at a brisk pace outside the building, looking for a place to talk. They found a section of the building lined with bushes and a few benches and thick concrete barriers. Ricky pointed to an empty bench.

They did a fast check of their surroundings and were alone for the moment.

"What did you find out?" Gabby finally asked.

"I hit the jackpot," Ricky said. "Maya or Mia is the name of the girl in the class the chats mentioned. The guy I spoke to got the information secondhand, but he sounded reliable. He mentioned how the student he heard about seemed to make plants from another classroom travel into theirs and enter through the doors and windows, spraying water across the room. This has to be it. We have a name now. Well, two names."

"I got a little more," Gabby said excitedly. "I got myself in the middle of a conversation about some experiment and couldn't get a word in since this girl was talking and talking. Once they broke off, I asked a smaller group if they had heard about what had happened in that class. They aren't taking botany, but it seems like they all knew about it. They didn't know the name of the student, but one of them said she was in a nearby class in that same hall and saw something unusual a few days before. She said she saw a professor let a female student in his room alone while he walked out, and that's not something professors normally do."

A student walked by, and Gabby waited for him to pass out of earshot.

"So this girl said she got up to head to the bathroom but stopped after seeing a man in a hat and long coat talking to another professor. It wasn't Diaz, but someone named Professor Cort. So the man in the hat walked into the room and the professor walked off. She thought it was odd but left and did her business, and when she returned, the professor was kind of wandering the halls and on his phone. She peeked through the door's window and saw the man in the hat talking to that student. She was sure it was the same girl at the center of the whole water incident."

"So we have this Maya or Mia girl and a strange man that met with her alone before all this happened. I'll bet Diaz and this Professor Cort know more than Diaz let on."

Gabby laughed. "Would you have trusted sharing information about one of your students to a couple of people who walked into your room uninvited? Especially when one of them is a really bad liar?"

Ricky smiled.

"Good point. So what's next?"

"I'm worried. Time has gotten away from us, but this feels like we're close. We have two professors, the girl, and the strange man with the hat and coat."

"I could ask that same guy I spoke to if his friend has any more info, or maybe we can find this Professor Cort."

"No," Gabby said. "If we start asking too many questions and one of them tells this Maya Mia or one of the professors, we could lose any shot at finding out more. We have to stake it out since we don't know when the class is held."

"If that one botany class with Diaz is on the second floor and they're saying these plants migrated from a nearby class, that seems to be the hallway to stalk."

"Yeah, but odds are that Professor Diaz will see us. She may have even warned the other professors."

"It's a risk we're going to have to take," Ricky said. "The longer we wait, the more likely they'll be onto us."

Gabby thought for a moment. "Let me go back to the car and change my outfit and put my hair up in a ponytail. He'll never notice."

"You sure?"

"What color are your sister's eyes?"

"Uh … brownish, I think?"

"Exactly. Thanks for proving my point."

"What do I do?"

"You stay by the nearest stairway so you can make a break up or down the stairs if you're recognized."

Ricky nodded. Gabby took off and returned fifteen minutes later. He realized that had he not been looking out for her return, he would have thought she was one of the regular university students.

"How's this?" she asked.

"You were right. Thought you were somebody else at first."

"Let's go. Maybe we'll get lucky."

"Yeah, we could use a big break, but we're further along that when we got here. Let's go find this mystery girl. Maya Mia, we're coming for you."

Chapter Twenty-Two

RICKY AND GABBY got into position on the second floor. Ricky stood near the stairs with his laptop open to partially obscure his face. Students started to walk by, and he moved with them until he found one of the bench seats that lined the hallways and sat down.

Gabby faced a trickier situation. She couldn't hang by any classroom doors too long, but figured she could stand against the walls while holding an open book. The pair wasn't able to see each other, but they had the same goal: try to identify any botany classrooms.

Gabby was trying to get a peek at the books students were carrying, but most were hidden in backpacks or bags. As a group walked by, one student unintentionally smacked her with his backpack, knocking her book from her hands. As she reached down to pick it up, she noticed a male student with a book on botany. She moved slowly behind him and watched as he stopped and stood near a classroom door, waiting for the previous class to be released. Gabby slowed her pace as she walked by and glanced inside the room through the door's vertical window.

She texted Ricky. *I think I found one. Room 214. Next to Diaz's classroom. Did you bring any audio surveillance stuff from the car?*

Yes, he texted back. *What do you need?*

Just a small listening device. Nothing fancy.

Come walk by me casually, he replied. *I'm in a seat near the stairs with students all around me. I'm the one with the best hair.*

Gabby left her spot. She walked toward the stairs and saw Ricky wasn't exaggerating. Almost every chair was taken. Any one of the female students could be Maya Mia.

As Gabby got closer, Ricky tossed something across the hall and it smacked against the wall loud enough for every nearby student without headphones to turn, including Gabby. As soon as she glanced at the wall, something hit her in the face.

She looked down. The listening device was on the floor by her feet. She picked it up and scowled at Ricky. He was trying to hold in a laugh.

A female student found what Ricky had thrown against the wall and picked it up.

"Sorry, it slipped out of my hand," Ricky said to her and everyone that was still paying attention.

The student looked at the key fob and handed it back to him.

"Thank you," Ricky said. He started tapping on his phone as everyone resumed whatever they were doing before.

Gabby was heading back as her phone dinged.

That was supposed to be a distraction for everybody else. Ricky added a smiley emoji.

Some warning on the flying bug would have been nice, she typed back.

You all set?

Yes, I just need to find someone going into this class. Do you have the audio up to check it?

Way ahead of you. Flip it on so I can test.

He tightened his headphones. Gabby pushed the small button on the back of the device, then banged it hard against her shoe.

She didn't see Ricky cringe and grab his ear.

Why was that so loud? he texted.

Payback, she replied.

Then it's working fine.

A few more minutes passed as additional students gathered by the doors. The classes dismissed and the halls filled quickly. Some students started entering classrooms immediately, while others waited, hoping for a few extra minutes to review or mess with their phones. Gabby watched room 214's crowd as they passed each other while coming and going, then moved a little closer. A group was heading in and she found a potential target. She spotted a backpack with a side mesh drink holder. She popped the listening device in the mesh pocket, made sure the student found a seat in the class, and headed back down the hall. She was close enough to see Ricky but avoided getting too close.

Gabby sat on one of the chairs and picked up her phone to text.

We're set and just have to wait, she typed. *Just give me a signal. If this girl is as talented as they say, hopefully something will happen and a student will mention her.*

The hallway was almost empty, and only one student sat near Ricky now. They knew they might have to move fast and didn't want to depend on a text, so they each wore a Bluetooth earbud for their phones. Ricky adjusted the left headphone cup off his ear and put in an earbud. He would be listening to the bug from the laptop with his right ear while communicating with Gabby on his phone through the left.

Once he was ready, he whispered into his earbud. "If you can hear me, get up and go."

Gabby stood up and moved back down the hallway until she was out of Ricky's view.

They both waited as the class started.

Ricky turned up his laptop headphones. He heard bustling as the students settled in. It calmed down after a few seconds and the professor didn't waste time.

"Today's experiment is ready to go. We've been talking about how to get the best results when using organic versus chemical aids to grow various plants. Today, however, we're going to study how to help a plant that's dying. So we're going to play two distinct personalities. First, Mr. Hyde, who will poison the plants and cause them to degrade rapidly. Then, we become Dr. Jekyll and try to save our green victims before it's too late."

A few students mumbled to each other.

"If you veer too far off or are indecisive, your plant could die. In fact, I expect the majority will. That doesn't mean you fail, but the goal is to let your plant live long enough for the process to be measured and show your attempt gave it some sign of resurgence before succumbing to its end. The instructions are on the sheets in front of you. This is a full partner experiment. Only one set needs to be turned in per pair."

Then the room got loud again. No one was talking. Then the person they had bugged and her partner's voices took over.

"Jonathan, you want to split duties or just do everything together? I'll write it out as usual."

"How about a hybrid? I'll poison it and we work together to make it survive. Timing is going to be critical."

Ricky messed with some of the settings to try to increase the bug's coverage. He wasn't sure where or how the backpack was positioned, but he heard several more voices.

"Is that too much?"

"The mix doesn't look right."

"We'll kill it for sure."

All were talking about how to start the experiment. It went on for about ten minutes until several moved on to documenting the results and the sound level stabilized. Their plants were on their deathbeds. The voices started whispering for a long while. Ricky realized the students were hoping to be the first to succeed and didn't want to give away any strategy.

Gabby kept a steady rhythm. She passed Room 214, then continued walking almost all the way to the end of the hall before turning around and coming back. She shortened her route with each pass, trying to sneak in a glance each time she passed the room. She was anxious, hoping if anyone saw her, they would just think she was pacing nervously before a test.

Another few minutes passed, and the whispers got louder and more frustrated.

"This thing is a goner."

"Time to do CPR."

"You think we should wait?"

The voices all shifted into saving mode. They were mixing some type of chemicals and deciding on the time to implement.

Then panic filled the room.

"We waited too long!"

"I think you mixed that wrong."

"Now. Do it now!"

A few quiet seconds passed.

"It's not coming back."

"I told you to hurry! Now it's going to die."

"No one's going to pass this."

"You know Mia and Laura will."

"There!" Ricky said, stopping Gabby in her tracks.

The voices continued.

"How is Mia's table doing?"

"Looks like they're both happy."

"Figures. She's like a plant whisperer."

"I'll bet bringing a plant back to life is nothing to her."

"At least there aren't any moving zombie plants today. I would have killed to see that!"

"Go now," Ricky whispered.

Gabby headed toward the room and slowed her pace to try to sneak in a good look.

Gabby passed by but was facing the professor so kept her head down. The immediate hallway was empty except for one student with her head buried in a textbook. The student was so preoccupied she didn't notice when Gabby took two steps past the doorway and reversed so fast her shoes squeaked. Gabby soaked in a good view of the class with the professor out of her line of sight.

Three seconds was long enough.

She saw multiple students staring at one table on the back right from her view. A brunette held an intense stare at what was on her table while the redhead next to her looked lost.

She rushed out and returned to Ricky.

"Did you get a good look at her?"

"Cute. Intense. Looks like she hasn't slept much. She's a brunette, about your shade of brown."

"I get it. I'm more tanned than you," Ricky said, smiling.

They spent the remaining time figuring out what to do

now that they knew Maya Mia was just Mia and Gabby knew what she looked like. Ricky repositioned himself on the first floor near the stairs so he could follow Mia if she left, since they had no idea where her next class might be or if she was done for the day. Gabby would follow behind just in case she stayed on the same floor or went upstairs.

The classes released a short time later.

Gabby waited as the class let out. The girl she was sure was Mia didn't come out. Or maybe she had missed her. Something was wrong. Gabby had her image burned into her head and was sure she hadn't walked out.

She never came out of the room, she messaged Ricky, not wanting to risk talking out loud with so many students around.

How is that possible?

She made a quick walk toward the door and snuck in a side look.

Mia was there, talking to her professor.

The professor is talking to her alone at his desk. I'll bet Diaz told him about us and he's telling her about it.

Doesn't change anything.

What if he walks out with her?

We'll adjust. Just stick to the plan. Don't follow too close.

He probably described us to her.

Then let me tail her if she comes my way. Let's just hope the professor doesn't follow.

The door opened. Mia walked out and Gabby half-hid behind a few students standing nearby. Mia kept going in the direction of the stairs and headed down. No one was with her. Gabby started to text when the professor opened the door.

Gabby lowered her phone and pressed the back of her head against the wall. She could feel her breathing quicken.

The door closed as the professor went back inside his classroom.

Gabby exhaled as she texted. *On our way.*

She counted to the and then moved toward the stairs, looking away from the door in case the professor decided to come back out.

Gabby rushed down the stairs but didn't see Mia. She looked down and didn't see Ricky, either.

Her phone pinged: *Think she's leaving. Hurry, best to follow her in the car.*

Gabby suddenly felt panicked. *What if we lose her?*

We'll know she'll probably be back in this class in two days. Yeah, she's heading to the parking lot.

Two days is too long. We've already lost so much time. I need to save Ally. What if it's too late?

Just hurry.

Gabby broke into a run. She felt herself sweating and anxiety coming over her. Time was running short. Too short.

I'm starting the car, Ricky messaged. *I still see her. Let's go!*

Gabby reached the car and jumped in. "Did she see you?"

"No, she kept her head down like she didn't want to be seen," Ricky said. "Prof definitely told her."

"Wouldn't you?"

"Yes, so we just need to be extra careful since she's on alert."

Ricky pulled out and tried not to hit any students. A small crowd passed in front of them, and in the precious seconds he waited, they lost sight of her.

"What kind of car is she in?" Gabby asked.

"It's a light blue…" Ricky pointed. "There she is."

Mia drove a little fast, but nothing out of the ordinary.

"Not too close," Gabby said.

Ricky kept her in his sight. Mia left the campus and was heading down a city road. Ricky let cars pass between them and after about ten minutes, they passed a downtown area. Eventually, Mia turned toward a farm road and seemed to be driving out of the city. There were plenty of cars at first, but as they drove, the number dwindled. Mia made another turn onto a different farm road, but this time, she approached houses in the distance. Once they got past a few subdivisions, Mia pulled into a neighborhood. Mia gave no indication she thought she was being followed, but now there were no cars between them. Ricky slowed down and stopped by a curb in front of a random house.

"What are you doing?"

"I see her. Just pausing."

He waited until she was almost out of view and then resumed his tail.

Chapter Twenty-Three

MIA PULLED into her Aunt Grace's house and rushed inside. Fortunately, none of the kids were in the living room or the kitchen.

Grace was sitting at the table. She wasn't doing anything, just sitting there, staring at her as she walked in. That caused Mia, who was already sweating, to turn pale.

"What's going on Auntie? Is everything okay?"

"I was about to ask you the same," Grace said. "The kids are still in school and Bianca was here, but I sent her to do some shopping for me. It's just me and you here."

"Why?"

"For the first time since I was a teenager, I was overcome with something. I felt panic. Fear."

"Fear of what?"

"No, you don't understand. I felt *your* fear. Something scared you, and for whatever reason, I could sense it. At least I think that's what it was. I don't know what it is or why, but I knew you were on your way and that you needed me. That's why I asked Bianca to leave. I wasn't sure what you would tell me or what state you'd be in, but I was nervous. I can tell by your face I was right."

Grace lifted her hands. They were shaking. "These have been trembling the last twenty minutes. It's not my fear, but some type of anxiety coming through you. It's like I'm feeling what you're feeling."

Mia hadn't noticed, but now that she was aware of it, she could sense something emanating from Aunt Grace. Something she couldn't see but was definitely there.

"I feel it, too," Mia said. "It's like a loop of energy. Nervous energy, passing between us."

"I don't know if you're causing this or if it's some kind of blood link, but there's no denying it. What happened, Mia?"

Mia paced side to side, trying to figure out how to start.

Her aunt motioned to the seat across from her. "Sit. It may be easier." There was already a cup of ice water sitting there with two pieces of lemon. Grace had been expecting her.

"I went to class today," Mia started as she sat.

"More waterworks?"

"No, nothing. I kept to myself and just did my experiment. When I went to Hollow Rock a few days ago, I was completely drained and couldn't finish my last attempt. I even learned some of the darker spells from Grandma's book, just in case. I've made some progress and was planning on going back today, but I wanted to conserve my energy so I could give it everything. I know I'm close. Class ended, no one looked at me, and I didn't feel odd other than some resentment I sensed when my experiment worked and almost no one else's did. Some were jealous, some were angry, but most were in awe. Like they were looking up to me or wishing they were me. You don't know how strange that feels."

Grace smiled. "Meaning no one looks up to me?"

Mia smiled back. "You know that's not what I meant."

"I know. I was just trying to ease whatever this is."

Mia felt some of her tension subside. "Thank you. Anyway, you know your kids worship you, even if Bianca tries to hide it. But these are people I barely know."

Grace's hands stopped shaking as Mia continued.

"So I'm thinking everything's good, but then Professor Cort motions to me when class ends. I was thinking he was going to leave me a bill for the damage I caused the other day, but he had me sit down and told me that two people, a young man and woman, had snuck into Professor Diaz's class and were asking questions about me."

"What kind of questions?"

"About what happened with the plants."

"Who were they?"

"He didn't know. They gave Diaz a story about being some type of investigators. She said she almost believed them, but then they panicked and she didn't tell them any details. I figured this kind of thing would have gotten around school, but Professor Diaz didn't recognize either of them and said they were obviously lying. Professor Cort told me to be careful and they could just be paranormal wannabe investigators, but the fact they were willing to sneak on campus could mean they're dangerous."

"What do you mean, dangerous?"

"The other day, Mr. Strand told me that there may be other people or things noticing what I'm trying to do. Maybe something that's not human, or maybe humans attracted to places like the Hollow Rock. People or creatures willing to hurt or use me for my abilities. They could be evil people or spirits. He didn't say it straight out, but that could mean actual demons, if you can believe that."

"Oh, I believe. You can't believe in angels and heaven

without acknowledging demons and hell. If one exists, so does the other. It's part of the package."

Mia knew her aunt was right, but to hear it laid out like that made it no less scary now that she was so close to this plane crossing thing.

"This happened in my apartment, Aunt Grace! So it's possible a demon or evil spirits are watching me, and now these two people show up asking questions. The attack in my apartment scared me at first, but I was so happy I made progress I guess I didn't take it as serious as I should have. But now, the reality of people showing up at my school looking for me hit me hard. Fear just took me over. I kept my head down and got away from the university as fast as I could, but what if they were waiting for me? What if they come to my apartment?"

Aunt Grace tried to hide her own panic as she listened.

"Mia, when your mom and I were younger, I'm talking 9 or 10 years old, we could tell when the other was scared or in a high emotional state. I remember a night when there was a terrible thunderstorm, and the lightning was so close I was shaking under my sheets. Your mom ran into my bed and hugged me. She was scared, too, but she was a little braver than I was. Today was the first time I felt that since we were children, and it happened with you."

"What does that mean to you?"

"I'm not sure. Maybe a sign from your mother. Maybe just the universe showing us we can look out for each other. I think it just gave me some peace in the middle of the chaos I felt, if that makes sense."

"I think I understand. It is comforting to know you'll always be looking out for me. Or that Mom might still be. What do I do, Aunt Grace?"

"What do you want to do? Are you scared enough to quit this whole thing?"

"No. I won't quit. I'm doing whatever I can to save this baby and I won't change my mind on that. This spirit or demon already found me, and these new people got really close today. I kept thinking about what would happen to Annika if these people hurt me or took me away. And who would know? That's why I needed you to know. I don't think I can tell Tino much more. Not with him being back on his macho horse. You're the only person I feel I can count on."

"For now, how about you let me know where you're going to be and give me some kind of panic signal if I don't hear from you."

"I can do a little better than that. Give me your phone."

Aunt Grace had her phone by her on the table and handed it to Mia without hesitation.

Mia hit a few buttons and then started typing in some info. She went back to her phone for a few minutes and finished typing something on Grace's phone before handing it back.

"What did you do?"

"I installed a finder app to track my cell."

She pointed to a new icon on Grace's phone screen. "Just open this app. My username and password are already set. You'll be able to see my phone's location at all times. It may not track when I'm in Hollow Rock, but it should find my last location. I can also text you before I go in so you'll know I'm there. I've never been inside more than an hour or two, so if more time than that passes and I don't give you a heads up, it might be a sign to come find me."

Mia showed her aunt how to use the app and pointed out the general location for Hollow Rock.

"Mia, you're not planning on going today, are you?"

"I was. Why?"

"If these people are after you, do you think it's a good idea to go now?"

Aunt Grace had a point.

"Just stay here tonight to be sure, Mia. Please. You still have plenty of extra clothes in the closet."

"Okay," Mia said. "I'll go in the morning. My nerves are all over the place, anyway. I doubt I'd be able to make much progress in this state."

Mia spent a little time with her cousins that night, which helped settle her anxiety. She felt like she needed to enjoy her family time while she could.

Because everything in her being told her there was much more danger and darkness to come.

Chapter Twenty-Four

THE NEXT MORNING, Mia got to her car and didn't notice Gabby and Ricky, who had been in the neighborhood all night alternating sleep shifts as they kept an eye on her vehicle. They were currently staked out four houses down where they parked in an empty driveway after the owner left, hoping they'd left for work and wouldn't return anytime soon.

"There," Gabby said. "She's coming out."

The pair had already checked the address and made the connection that this wasn't where she currently lived but had sometime in the past. The house owner didn't have the same last name, but they figured it might be a relative.

Mia drove off, and Ricky and Gabby followed.

"How long do you think we should tail her before we risk her noticing?" Ricky asked.

"We don't know she hasn't. What if she's leading us to a bunch of cops or friends ready to pull us out of the car and interrogate us? Either way, I think we stick with her until the end. Something's gnawing at me and I think we have to hurry. We need to talk to her."

"I got the same feeling that the clock is ticking."

"Let's just see where she goes," Gabby said. "Keep the same distance."

Mia started heading past the neighborhoods and then turned down another farm road. She took several more turns until they were heading down one long road surrounded by fields and farms.

Gabby had her phone GPS on and was checking it closely.

"This road leads out of town. We're not going to get far without her noticing us if this traffic keeps dying down."

"I'll try to be careful," Ricky said.

Ricky kept following as the traffic died down. There were still a couple of cars in front of them.

"Ricky, pull up near her. Actually, get right behind her."

"You sure?"

Gabby nodded.

He passed the cars between them and was behind Mia's car before they reached the next light.

"Now what?"

"Bump her."

"What do you mean, bump her?"

"Hit her lightly. Nothing that will cause damage."

"I'm not a NASCAR driver," Ricky said. "I don't know how to control how hard I hit her."

"Wait until there's a stop sign or a red light. When she stops, just hit her gently. It should jerk the car enough to make her notice."

He shook his head but didn't argue anymore. They

moved down and he saw a light ahead that was still green, but quickly shifted to yellow.

"Here we go," Gabby said. "Hopefully she won't run this."

The light turned red. Mia slowed down and came to a stop. She was the first car at the light.

Ricky slowed down.

"You're going too slow! You have to hit her!" Gabby yelled.

"Not like I've done this before!" Ricky yelled back.

He let go of the brake pedal and the car moved forward. He resisted the urge to slam on the brakes and waited. At the moment the vehicle was about to make contact, he gently pushed down and heard a crunch as they jerked forward.

Both cars rocked and Mia looked back in her mirror, startled.

Gabby stuck her hand forward and pointed to the right. There was a dormant fireworks stand with dirt road parking.

Mia did as expected. She eased into the parking area and Ricky stopped right behind her. Mia got out of her car and moved to the back to check if there was any damage.

Gabby opened the door and started out.

"What are you going to say to her?" Ricky said.

She looked back. "We're both about to find out."

Gabby neared Mia, who was staring at the bumper.

"Are you okay?" Gabby asked.

"Yes," Mia replied, taking a moment before looking up.

"I'm so sorry. My boyfriend and I were talking and he just lost his concentration."

"It isn't so bad," Mia said. "Maybe a small bend on the license plate. I don't see any real damage."

Gabby pretended to look at the vehicles as well.

"Yeah, I don't see much. Let me get our insurance."

Mia finally took a good look at her. Then she glanced at the driver and immediately thought of the descriptions that Professor Cort had given her about the visitors searching for her. Her stomach turned.

"No, I think the car's okay and I'm fine," Mia said. "Thank you for stopping, but I really need to go."

Ricky saw the panic in her eyes. He'd seen enough fear in the last few years to recognize it. He got out of the car.

Mia backed up as he approached.

"Mia," Gabby said. "Please. We're not going to hurt you. We're trying to help you."

"How do you know my name?" Mia asked as she scanned for approaching cars. None were coming, so she screamed.

"Mia, please," Ricky said, stopping in his tracks. "We won't come any closer. We just need a minute or two of your time and ask that you listen. We mean you no harm. We just want to talk. That's all."

Mia looked back and forth at them. "Who are you and why are you asking about me? I know you gave Professor Diaz some bullshit story."

"Yes," Gabby said. "It was a bullshit story. We didn't know if we could trust the professor. I'm sorry about that."

"So what's the truth?"

Ricky and Gabby looked at each other.

The truth worked in New Orleans, Gabby thought.

"It's about my baby," Gabby said. "My name is Gabby, and this is Ricky. This is also about Ricky and how his life was torn apart by something. Something dark. Demons. Evil. We're just trying to save my baby, but we're running out of time."

Mia was confused. The baby belonged to Strand's daughter, Anna.

"What about your baby?"

"My daughter was stolen from me. Her soul, at least. She is back in Texas, but it's just her body. A body that's deteriorating every day. I don't think she'll survive much longer. But it wasn't people that stole her soul. It was a dark force. Demons. Two of them. We've been tracking these things and believe they're here now. And we think you're connected somehow."

"No, you're lying. He told me people might show up. I'm saving the baby's soul. Annika is here and I've seen her. She's not right, but she has a body. Her soul is missing. I'm not sure how you know that, but I know you're lying since I've seen her and held her body myself. You just want this power that I don't fully understand for something else."

"No," Gabby said. "That's not true. I don't know who you've been talking to or who Annika is, but after everything you just described, it sounds like that could be my baby. Her name is Ally. Maybe they're using another child's body, but these things … These demons left a trail of destruction. They ruined Ricky's life and tried to destroy mine. My baby doesn't have much time. I'm desperate."

Mia looked at her and tried to get a read, but no. Strand had warned her. She knew this was possible, no matter how convincing this Gabby sounded.

They just wanted her power for themselves.

"Mia, please," Ricky said. "Everything she said is true. Gabby and I only met a few months ago while I was looking for these demons. She's trying to save her daughter and I'm trying to protect my sister. Like Gabby said, there are two of them. One made me kill the only girl I've ever loved."

"Kill? You killed someone?" Mia's voice cracked.

Ricky knew he had screwed up.

"No, I didn't actually kill anybody. It was them. The demons."

Mia's fear tripled. She needed to get away from these people. Now.

"Stay back or I'll scream and run down the road until someone sees or hears me," Mia said.

As if on cue, a car approached from down the road. Mia rushed and stood in the middle of it. "Don't follow me or I'll call 9-1-1. Leave me alone!"

"Please, Mia," Gabby begged as she felt herself start to lose it. Her eyes started to water as desperation took over. She took a step forward.

"Help!" Mia yelled.

The approaching car started to slow down. Their windows were open, and a man stuck his head out of the driver's side. "Everything all right?"

"We're good," Ricky said.

The man stared as Mia ran back to the car, never taking her eyes off them, and sped off. The man was satisfied as she drove away and continued on.

"What do we do now?" Gabby asked.

"I threw a magnetic tracker under the bumper," Ricky said. "We'll catch up to her."

Ricky drove out of the lot and went in the opposite direction for a few miles. He pulled into a gas station and started messing with his phone.

"Is it working?" Gabby asked.

"Yes. Give me some credit."

"Hard to do that right now, considering you basically told her you killed someone and scared her off."

Ricky shook his head. "Yeah, I got desperate."

"So did I. Let's just move on."

Ricky showed Gabby the map on his phone. Mia was traveling up the same road and direction after the fireworks stand. They watched as she made a few turns, which they assumed was her attempt to lose them just in case, but she made a big rectangle and eventually got back on the same road about five miles later.

"Okay, we don't need to stay within her sight and can keep at least a mile between us," Ricky said.

"Make it two miles," Gabby said. "We can't blow this."

"Okay. Two miles it is."

They drove back in the same direction. Gabby kept her eye on Ricky's phone while he drove, trying to make up some ground.

"She's still going the same way."

A few minutes later, the signal shifted.

"She just turned left," Gabby said. "It looks like a farm road."

"We definitely need to keep our distance," Ricky said. "I'll bet there aren't a ton of cars out there."

Gabby nodded. "Or people."

MIA KEPT LOOKING BACK after taking her detour. She still hadn't seen them but felt her entire body shaking. Her thoughts were everywhere.

What if more people come after me?

Am I that dangerous that others would want to take advantage of my abilities?

Then she started talking out loud.

"They said demons. Strand said whatever attacked me at my apartment might be evil spirits. What if these people are telling the truth?"

She got close to the grouping of trees that hid Hollow

Rock and pulled in. She turned back toward the road but didn't see any more cars. She needed to calm herself and her mind before attempting another round of practice.

Mia realized she'd never contacted Strand to tell him that she was on her way. She was so worried Gabby and Ricky, if those were their real names, might find her again and didn't think to give Strand a heads up.

She picked up the phone and texted Strand. *I'm here. Sorry I didn't tell you sooner. Got distracted. Will tell you about it later. Going to practice. Can you meet me here? I don't want to be alone too long.*

She then called her Aunt Grace, who answered on the first ring. "I just got here. The two people from the school followed me, but I'm pretty sure I lost them. Give me an hour before you start to panic. Setting a reminder to make sure I call or text you."

"I'll be here," Grace said.

By the time she hung up, Strand had already replied. *Will be there in 30.*

Mia got out of the car and headed past the huge trees. She looked back and wondered if they might still be following her. If they were, she didn't want them to see her car.

She got back in and drove it a little deeper into the field of sweet corn so that someone would have to pull in to have any chance of seeing it. She figured anyone new would see the trees and ignore the crops. Wasn't the best way to hide it, but best she could do on short notice.

She entered the cave.

Mia was shaking a little as she got to the table where the pouch with the geode crystal and the ceramic cup still sat. She heard the water moving from the stream. It was a faint but calming sound, but her thoughts about demons and the couple who had followed her made her feel anything but calm. It wasn't going to be easy to concentrate.

~

"She's stopped," Gabby said. "It's only a few miles ahead. It's an even more rural road. We'll have to be extra careful so she won't see us."

Ricky nodded as he sped up and eventually made the turn.

"Straight down this road?"

"Yes, to the left, in about a mile or so. There's nothing out there. She's going to see us."

"We'll have to walk, then," Ricky said as he slowed down.

When they were about half a mile away, Ricky pulled the car to the side and gently eased it into the cornfield until the entire car was surrounded by crops, similar to what Mia had just done a few minutes before. The car wasn't particularly well-hidden, but it was enough in a pinch. They got out of the car and started walking. A lone car came down the road and they ducked into the stalks. The car passed without incident.

They kept quiet the rest of the way. There were no more cars as they reached the tracker spot. They looked around and saw nothing but large trees.

"You see any kind of house or anything?" Ricky asked.

Gabby shook her head. "You think she found the tracker?"

"Not sure. She was pretty rattled."

"You know, those trees are big enough to hide some-thing," Gabby said.

"Look," Ricky said, moving toward some broken corn stalks.

He looked around and then saw Mia's car. It was maybe a foot into the tall grass.

Gabby pointed in a different direction.

"Look over there," she whispered.

She led Ricky past the trees and under the thick surrounding dirt and grass, they saw the shape of something.

"Some kind of bunker or cellar?" Gabby asked.

Ricky just shrugged. This has to be it.

They got closer and saw the two big doors. One was open.

They walked toward the opening and checked it out.

"If she's in there, why would she leave this open?" Ricky asked. "Should we go in?"

"No, she's spooked. She probably left it open so she could hear us coming. She's probably down there with other people or weapons. But we need to know what's going on and why she's here."

"So we hang out here in the corn and trees?"

"Yes, let's stake it out for now. The car has the tracker. We know we can get to her. She could have called the cops by now, but it doesn't look like she did. Once she leaves, we can head down there and check."

Ricky nodded. "I think that's the smartest play. We'll wait it out."

They moved back into the corn stalks near Mia's car and hid. There was a rusted tractor nearby that looked like it had been put out to pasture for many years.

Ricky was checking out the tractor.

"Don't touch that," Gabby said. "All that rust might earn you a tetanus shot. We don't have time for an ER visit."

He pulled back.

"Wait. There's another car coming," Gabby said.

They looked out at the lonely road that led them there. A black Cadillac Escalade was approaching fast. They snuck further into the field and crouched by the aging tractor.

The vehicle slowed down and turned into the makeshift parking area by the trees.

Gabby and Ricky stayed hidden but had a clear view.

A man in a hat and jacket got out, matching the description that the student Gabby spoke to gave about the man Mia spoke to at school. The man turned toward the passenger side and that door opened. A young woman followed. She looked sickly as she proceeded to the back door. She opened it and after a few moments, she pulled out a baby girl.

The baby looked malnourished and pale, like she hadn't seen the sun in weeks. She didn't cry, just turned and looked out, not paying attention to much.

Ricky looked over at Gabby. Her face was white and she was tearing up.

"That's how my Ally looks on the outside," she whispered. "Did they steal this baby's soul, too, or could that child be holding my Ally's soul inside?"

"There's no way to know. We'll find out soon enough."

Ricky's gaze shifted from the baby to the girl. She looked like she was in her late teens at most. Her eyes were dark, like she hadn't slept in days. She had a blank expression, just like the baby.

"Gabby, look at the girl. Is that the one that kidnapped Ally?"

Gabby looked away from the baby and focused on the girl.

"No, that's not her. The girl I saw was younger."

The new arrivals walked toward the doors and the man

in the hat pulled the closed one. They entered, and he shut both doors behind them.

"This Mia is involved in something bigger that we realize," Ricky said. "That man's face looked like he had a purpose."

"We're so close, but what if that's my Ally? Or maybe somebody else's child? I have to know!"

For now, all they could do was wait.

Chapter Twenty-Five

MIA WAS HIDING at the back of the cave, holding a rock as a makeshift weapon, when Mr. Strand, Anna, and Annika entered.

"Mia, is everything okay?"

"It's been a crazy few days," Mia said as she walked back out into the main room. "I thought you might be somebody else, but I was definitely noticing improvement before you got here."

"Maybe the child will bring you inspiration."

Mia smiled as Anna handed her Annika. Mia held her and although she was used to the baby not showing much emotion, the baby squeezed her just for a moment and rested her head on Mia's shoulders.

Annika. Or could it be Ally?

"You look like you were ready for a fight," Strand said. "I heard something happened at the university."

"Did the professor tell you?"

"No, he told his colleague, who then informed me. It was to be expected. Have you seen your visitors since?"

"Yes, after I left school today. They followed me and

bumped into my car so I would pull over. They tried to feed me some elaborate story."

"What tale did they weave?"

"It was a young man and woman. The woman said that her baby was missing its soul. A soul that was taken by demons. I almost believed her, but I caught them lying to me. They did almost exactly what you said they might. They tried to manipulate me for whatever it is they really want."

"As I told you, there are those that want to test your power and use it to their advantage. This place has been quiet for many decades, but the power you are generating has attracted the natural and the supernatural. From now on, I do not wish you to come here on your own. For your own safety."

Mia nodded. "I do feel better now that you're here. I left one door open so I could hear if anyone was coming. I took a different route so they wouldn't follow me and think I lost them but can't be certain."

"Excellent. We will wait here in the shadows to give you space. Please continue when you are ready."

Mia nodded as she handed Annika back to her mother.

She returned to the table, grabbed the cup, and refilled it from the stream. Her control had improved, but she was still struggling to reach the next step. She figured it was the distraction of the two strangers and the talk of demons and souls that she couldn't stop thinking about.

Stop it, Mia, she thought to herself. *This is all that matters.*

She lifted her hands to her temples and pictured her own head as the stone, filled with water, then pictured the water flowing out of her ears and taking her distractions with it. Her mind was clear. For a few seconds, at least.

What had she been doing wrong? Imagining the stone being porous did allow some water to penetrate through the outer stone and around the center. Picturing a central eggshell helped get the water into the center, but it leaked out as soon as it penetrated.

The problem is the eggshell.

She turned back to Strand. "I don't know what to do. The limited success I've had started by imagining the center as an eggshell and the water passing through without cracking it, but the problem is that I can't keep it inside. It flows in one end and then out the other. I can't get past the eggshell concept and am not sure what to use as an alternative."

Strand was silent as he contemplated.

"An eggshell is so delicate," he said. "Something you've known your entire life. Maybe try something similar that is not as fragile. What do you normally picture when you think of eggs, besides cooking?"

She thought for a moment. Aunt Grace taught Mia how to make eggs scrambled, boiled and over easy. Every time she pictured the egg, she knew it would eventually be cracked.

What else do we use eggs for?

Her thoughts filled with Easter Sunday and the plastic eggs used to hide candy and money during the family egg hunts, which they still did for her nephew and nieces and some extended family every year. And then there was always the wild fight to crack eggshells on each other's heads.

"*Cascarones,*" Mia whispered.

"What?" Strand asked.

"It's an Easter thing. A family tradition. Every year we save or buy eggshells, cut a hole at the tip, and stuff them with mostly confetti."

"What do you do with them?"

"Crack them over each other's heads."

"Why would you do that?"

"I'm not sure, but it's like a fun game. The confetti gets in everyone's hair and down their shirts. Well, it's fun until you have that one cousin that fills an egg with flour or uses a real egg. But the thing is, when we make them, after we fill the shell with confetti, we cover the hole with tissue paper and some kind of adhesive. We call them *cascarones*."

"Does that memory somehow help?" Strand asked.

"It might," Mia said as she drifted in thought.

Strand didn't say another word. He could feel that she was trying to work through something.

Mia picked up the stone again. She again imagined the fragile eggshell in its center. But this time, she mentally painted it a mix of yellow and blue streaked colors, then pictured peeling away a piece at the egg's tip. She imagined covering the hole with a soft piece of tissue.

She pulled the water stream from the ceramic cup. Once again, it massaged the outside of the stone, but she didn't create multiple holes and craters. Still, this part was effortless. Almost instinctive.

Instead of letting the water penetrate the imagined craters, she shifted it toward the cracked opening at the tip. She transformed the water into smaller pieces of liquid confetti and eased each piece into the shell.

She let the eggshell center fill, then imagined immediately placing a tissue paper covering over it.

But then the water started to flow back out.

She shook her head.

The water will soak right through the paper, genius.

She needed something else. Something less porous than tissue paper.

Maybe a mesh of some kind.

Mia thought of a flexible, waterproof Band-Aid. When she used one to cover a cut or scrape, it would stay in place even after a few days of showering. Water simply didn't get through.

She tried again. The water shot from the cup, massaged the outside of the stone, rolled up the egg and into the hole, and just as it all was about to spill back out, she covered it with the bandage she pictured in her head. The stream struck the waterproof cover and exploded against it, splashing back into the shell. She made the Band-Aid in her mind disappear, and allowed more water to flow in until the center was full, setting a fresh protective bandage fabric over it each time.

The water held.

Mia broke her concentration and lifted the stone with her hand. Her imagination and improvisation had become reality.

The center of the stone was full of water, and it wasn't going to escape until she decided to do so.

Finally.

"It's done," Strand said with a low-pitched excitement. "You've done it, Mia."

She took in a deep breath and checked the rock. She turned back to Mr. Strand and held it out.

"Yes. I just had to change a few things around in my head and trust it."

"I knew you could do it!"

A thought occurred to her as she admired her work. She had been working so hard on succeeding at the task that she didn't think about the overall purpose. Not until now.

"So, how will this help me get Annika's soul back? What happens next? Can we try it now?"

"Oh, no. Not now," Strand said. "We have three days. You must be at full strength, and I need time to prepare.

You should continue practicing to ensure you can repeat this process every time. They will be pleased."

"They?" Mia asked.

Strand cleared his throat and his eyes shifted to one side.

"The family. Anna's cousins and my sister. They will be pleased to know Annika may yet live."

"How am I supposed to do this? I'm not going to be shooting water into the baby, am I?"

"No, it's not as simple as thrusting water into a stone, but a similar concept. Take the next few days to practice, then you'll need to rest and try not to use any of your abilities on the third day to conserve your energy. Thank you, Mia. I knew it would be you. You are most definitely a special young woman."

Mia nodded. "I hope you're right, Mr. Strand. I'll be waiting."

She walked up to the baby and gave her a kiss on the forehead. "You'll be okay soon, Annika."

Anna turned toward Mia but still looked down.

"Thank you, Mia," she said in a low whisper.

"Let us go now," Strand said. "There is much to do."

They all exited Hollow Rock as Ricky and Gabby watched, holding their breath until Strand and Mia's cars were both almost out of sight. They waited an additional few minutes before walking out of the brush.

"What was that about?" Gabby asked.

"Let's find out," Ricky said as he approached the doors. There was no lock, but he opened them carefully. He looked down.

"It has stairs."

They moved down quietly, unsure of what to expect. They entered and smelled the water, and the blue shimmer on the walls glistened as they moved into the light. They saw the table, the stream, and the dark cave that tunneled even further back.

"What is this place?" Gabby asked as she approached the table.

"No idea. It's beautiful, though."

Ricky walked over to the stream and looked in. The water was calm, barely making any ripples.

"This table is still wet," Gabby said. "They were doing something on it."

Ricky noticed the small pouch on the table and pointed.

"There."

Gabby picked up the pouch and pulled out its contents. A rock and a small ceramic cup. She held the rock up. "This stone has liquid in the center. I think it's water."

She shook it and felt the liquid moving inside. "Not sure what it means."

Ricky crouched down and grabbed his stomach.

Gabby moved down toward him. "What's wrong? You okay?"

The stone went flying out of Gabby's hands and hit the cave wall. It fell, still intact.

"We need to leave," Ricky said.

"Why?"

"The demons we've been looking for all this time," Ricky said. "They're here."

Chapter Twenty-Six

RICKY HADN'T FELT the sensation of power and darkness since the night he destroyed half of his downtown city of Stone Creek and killed the only girl he ever loved. The day that changed his life forever.

A low growl filled the cave and the room turned cold.

Gabby looked back at the cave but didn't see anything. "Is that them?"

"Yes," Ricky said. "The demons. They've been here. Waiting."

The water in the stream moved. It rippled and spilled over. Gabby saw yellow eyes in the water. The same yellow eyes that, along with the Shadow Demon, had stolen her baby's soul. The eyes were there, and they were angry.

Ricky clutched his chest. It had been so long he had forgotten what it felt like. The demon that fed on fear was snacking. The sensation he felt was sudden but total. He couldn't have hidden it if he wanted to. He flung his arms out. Gabby felt something pushing her backward.

"Ricky! Are you doing this?"

"No!" he managed to yell, trying to stifle the pain.

"Not me. The Shadow Demon. It's trying to get inside me. Possess me."

"Fight it!" she yelled as she felt herself being pushed back with each step.

"Stronger. So much stronger than before," Ricky muttered.

All this time searching. All this time waiting. He couldn't lose control. Not again.

Gabby continued her backward movement until she was inches from the water. Just as her back rear foot was about to land in the stream, water shot up and wrapped around her torso.

She screamed as she fell in.

Gabby tried to fight her way out of the shallow stream as multiple demon faces and yellow eyes filled the water. She wanted to yell for help, but water was shooting up her nose. She was on her stomach, just under the wet surface, but she couldn't steady herself enough to get up. She tried to cough it out, but instead her throat filled and she couldn't breathe.

Ricky crawled a few feet and then fell as he felt himself being invaded. He thought of his sister. He thought of Gabby. Then he thought of Ellie. He pictured the day he pulled the trigger. The last moment of her life, taken by his hands.

Never. Never happening again.

Ricky screamed as he fought enough to pull himself up. He reached into the stream and saw the Reflection Demon laughing in the ripples. He pulled Gabby up by the shoulders and eased her out, preventing her from drowning in only inches of water.

Gabby had a coughing fit as both demons laughed over her hacks.

"So, you did follow her," a voice said from behind.

They both turned and the man in the hat and coat stood there with his hat pulled down, wearing a sinister smile.

"My friends told me about you. They are grateful that you both gave them their greatest prizes on their path of destruction. The Demon of Shadow gained his strength from you, Richard Luna, when you destroyed those you loved. The fear generated in your hometown that day was unmatched, and as hard as he tries, he has not been able to repeat it. He's strong enough now. And the Demon of Reflection gained his strength from your life, Gabriella Mendez Alfonso. Such evil around you both, and within you as well. A drug addicted mother, a pervert for a boss, and the murder of a husband. However, the soul of that child. That was what led them here. They realized that soul could give them what they desire most. It could give them a true life here on this plane. One where they could do as they wish without living in shadow."

"Who are you and why are you helping them?" Ricky asked.

"I am Soren Strand. They are me. I am them. They have already given me some of the things I desire, and once they are of this earth, I will stand by their side as they take whatever they choose from the pitiful lives of others."

"They want to conquer this world?" Gabby asked. "Why?"

"Oh, they have no such delusions or need to take this world. They only want to feast and thrive on all that this world provides. You were both a means to an end, and they thought the strength and soul you gave them would be enough to cross into this world, but they had almost given up. That is until they found Mia. You cannot stop them, and they are almost ready."

Strand moved up and stared into the stream.

"You must retain your strength. You cannot waste your energy on these humans."

There was a low buzzing sound mixed in with some grunts. Strand turned back toward Ricky and Gabby.

"Now, what to do with you two?" Strand said.

Ricky rushed him, but the Shadow Demon appeared and struck Ricky, knocking him aside well before he reached Strand.

"Thank you," Strand said. "I think you should subdue them and keep them in the recesses of Hollow Rock. Just be careful. If you must feed, do so sparingly. Save your power and their fear should you need it."

The buzzing got softer as Strand turned toward the pair.

"Richard and Gabriella, please follow them into the cave. You may be spared for now. However, I do hope they save you for our special night before they choose to destroy you."

The stream shot up and Ricky felt the Shadow Demon tugging at him. He wanted to run, but the shock of what had happened had exhausted him.

"We need to get out of here," Gabby said. "They have Ally."

"We need to retreat," Ricky whispered. "Alter our plans."

"What if those demons make you kill me?"

"How do you know they won't make you kill me?"

Gabby didn't know how to respond. She wasn't sure of anything other than they were out of time.

"You will go now," Strand said.

"What if we just leave instead?" Gabby asked.

Strand smiled. "You could not leave if you wanted to. Please, I insist that you try."

Gabby didn't hesitate. She rushed toward the steps.

Ricky didn't bother. He felt the demon's power and his lack of it. He knew he was too weak. They needed a plan.

Gabby reached the first step, but her foot froze in mid-air. She tried to step back but couldn't move.

"What are you doing to me?" Gabby asked.

"Oh, I am doing nothing. It is your old friends that are. This place. The thin walls between our world and theirs give them a boost. You will not interfere. We are too close."

A strong force pulled Gabby's body backwards. When she reached Ricky, they were both thrown back and plastered to the wall, unable to move. It was like they had invisible ropes holding them down.

"Death will not come to you today," Strand said. "We cannot spill blood or perform any acts that will spoil this place. It must be kept pure."

He looked off to the side as the stream defied gravity, pushing upward about eight feet. The reflection coming off the flowing water was only a face and a thin, rotting body of the Reflection Demon.

The rear part of the cave was darker. There were eyes in the shadows.

Strand spoke in guttural sounds and deeper ones returned, echoing through the cave.

"So you speak to demons?" Ricky asked.

Strand ignored him and kept communicating before turning back to Ricky and Gabby.

"That I do. I am the human liaison that will help them achieve what they desire."

Ricky shook his head. "You really think they'll let you live once they get what they want?"

"They are bound by their word. They thank you both for helping them reach this point in their long, difficult journey. We would not be on the precipice of their return without your aid."

"If you're not going to kill us, then what?"

"We have decided we only need to set you aside for now. If I remove you and kill you outside of Hollow Rock, it could lead to questions and interruptions that would be problematic. The safest option is to keep you here, where we can observe you. Once all is done, it will not matter. You will be inconsequential. Maybe your screams will be the first thing the Demon Brothers will enjoy as a celebration of their freedom."

"So we're just going to stay here stuck to this wall?" Gabby asked.

"Oh, no. You are too visible. No distractions."

He turned back to the water and shadow.

"Take them."

Gabby and Ricky floated deeper into the cave as the Shadow Demon descended.

They heard the doors close as Strand left the cave.

Ricky was drained. After all this time of being dormant, his connection to the Shadow Demon had returned. He figured being so close to its presence again re-triggered their old bond. But Ricky sensed the demon was straining. It was stronger, yet weaker at the same time.

Ricky and Gabby floated for what had to be at least a mile in. They were then brought down to a seated position, backs to the wall, facing the stream. A thin tube of water broke in two and wrapped around them. The Shadow Demon extended its claws in their direction and the water hardened. It formed a sticky, gel-like substance that solidified within seconds and they felt the force that had moved them disappear. Then the demons were gone.

The cave got so quiet they could only hear each other's labored breathing. They both tried to break the sticky substance that held them, but it did no good. They were covered from their shoulders to their waists. Their heads and feet were free, but it made no difference.

"What do we do, Ricky?"

"I'm not sure how, but my old connection to the Shadow Demon is back, and I don't think it realized it. I can feel its power. I might be able to use it to get us out of here."

"What are you waiting for, then?"

"I'm drained. That took a lot out of me. Plus, what if the same thing happens like before? What if I can't control it?"

"I don't think we have much of a choice," Gabby said. "If I could get to the knife in my pocket, I could try to cut through, but this gunk, whatever it is, won't let me move. And I have to pee!"

"I'll think no less of you if you do. Just try to aim it that way," Ricky said, motioning to another part of the cave.

"What are we going to do?" Gabby asked. "If we try to run, they'll just take us out."

"You heard him. The demons need to maintain their strength to do whatever it is they have planned here. Mia is going to help them cross over somehow. I just wonder if she knows what she's doing."

"I don't think so," Gabby said. "She thinks she's helping them save that baby and doesn't believe that child's body is just a shell holding my Ally's soul."

Ricky waited. He couldn't sense the Shadow Demon and wasn't sure if the Demon Brothers remained in the cave or were out somewhere destroying someone else's life.

Ricky took in some deep breaths and reached inside for his rekindled dark power. It was weak, but it was there. He thought of the gel bindings keeping them prisoner and felt like he could grasp them with his mind.

Just like riding a bike, Ricky.

A bike on fire that just rode out of hell, but a bike nonetheless. He gripped and squeezed. He heard his bindings crack, but that was as far as he could go.

"How did you do that?" Gabby asked.

"Just being near them. It woke up my old power, and just as he can feed off our fear, I can pull from the power I sense. I can still feel it."

"It's working," Gabby said. "Keep going!"

Ricky stopped. He looked at her. "I can't. I remember the limits. What they felt like, at least."

"I only got a small taste of it," Gabby said.

He looked down and saw the cracks in his binding. They were small and insignificant.

"Is there anything you can do to make it stronger?" Gabby asked.

"I need to goad him. Need him to engage so I can use more of his power and hope he doesn't realize it. Even though that Strand jerk told them to lay off, I think I can get them both riled up."

"Then do it!"

"Gabby, I have no idea what this will do to me. He could hurt us worse. Turn us against each other."

"I'll die for my daughter. You should know that by now. The one thing I'm sure of is if we're stuck here, we can't help anyone. Our choices are limited, so we have to take the risk."

Ricky stared at her for a long moment, then nodded.

"Understood. If I try to kill you, I apologize ahead of time. Please do your best to stop me if that happens."

"I will. I promise."

Ricky closed his eyes and tried to zone in on the Shadow Demon's power. He sensed it in the cave somewhere, but it was only a small pulse.

"I am here," Ricky said. "You destroyed my life. You

took my love, but you didn't break me. Do you know why? Because you're weak. You're a joke. You need your brother and his lame reflection power to be worth anything. What you are is not only an abomination, but a cheap one. You want to break into this world? Why? You'll be as worthless as you are now, having to manipulate humans that are beneath you to get your way. You can't harm us."

Ricky laughed.

"You're nothing."

The retaliation was swift. The power of the Shadow Demon surged, and Ricky felt it up against his face, raging.

His chest felt like it was going to explode as the demon dipped into his soul.

Ricky screamed.

"Come on, is that all you got? It tickles, you bastard!"

Ricky gasped as his breath sucked in and he couldn't release it. It felt like fingers were pulling his mouth apart and a windstorm was blowing towards him. Pain was everywhere.

"Ricky!" Gabby yelled. "Whatever you're going to do, do it now!"

A stream of water struck her in the face and the reflection demon filled her head with images of the demon's rotting flesh.

Your daughter is ours.

The Reflection Demon's voice boomed inside Gabby's head.

She will bring freedom. Her beautiful soul. Delectable.

Gabby's head filled with images of Ally at her sister Teri's house. Ally was in her crib, and Gabby was standing by it, smiling down at her daughter. Ally stuck out a tiny hand and as Gabby tried to reach for it, Ally's fingers turned into claws. Then her eyes turned yellow and her skin peeled into torn pieces of muscle and blood. Her face took the shape of a smaller Reflection Demon.

My daughter now. Our daughter. Part of us forever.

Gabby screamed as Ally's tongue shot out, now a forked, black muscle.

Gabby shut her eyes. "No, no! Stop! Please leave her alone!"

Ricky heard Gabby's screams and could sense what she was seeing. He took the pain that was ripping him inside and threw it back at the Reflection Demon. The water exploded and the reflection turned toward his shadow brother.

Ricky's pain subsided as the Shadow Demon turned and faced the stream.

"Stop," a voice echoed throughout the cave.

The Reflection Demon was speaking to his brother.

"Must conserve. The boy. Has your strength. Tries to weaken us. Leave them."

Ricky felt the Shadow Demon release his grip. The sharp pain was gone, but a throbbing spike of it remained.

The demons disappeared.

Gabby was crying uncontrollably.

"Gabby!" Ricky yelled. "Wake up! Gabby!"

Her head flipped side to side, then she opened her eyes.

"It wasn't real," Ricky said. "It's okay."

She turned to him, her eyes lost.

"It's okay. It's okay now. Ally's fine. I promise."

Gabby blinked as she snapped back to reality.

"It was so real. You pulled him off of me?"

"Yes."

"Why didn't you stop the Shadow Demon?"

"You don't understand. That power he gave me. I could have fought back, but I held back."

"Why? Why not destroy them now?"

"I'm not that strong, but I think I took enough from him to try to escape. If I go into direct combat now, I don't see a way to beat them both. Whatever's happening is happening soon. We need to find out the details."

"So you're saying we stay here?"

"Yes, until we know enough to have any shot of stopping them. At this point, they don't see us as enough of a threat to take out."

Gabby nodded. "Staying here is insane, but I understand you. We wait it out. We observe. And once we know what's happening and what we're up against…"

"We can figure out how to beat them."

"Assuming we can escape in the first place."

"Exactly. We can't stop anything if we don't know what we're stopping."

Gabby nodded. "Okay, I agree."

"So, we'll have to hold it a little longer if we have to pee."

"Too late," Gabby said.

They slept the rest of the night and woke up at some point the next day. They had no way of measuring how much time had passed. They could only hear the flowing stream. Gabby woke up first and was looking at Ricky when his eyes opened.

"Have you been up long?" Ricky asked.

"No, I just wanted you to rest. If we get free of these restraints, we need to be prepared. We should have never come into this place without a plan. It was reckless and stupid. I pushed it and I'm sorry and I won't do it again."

"No, you were right to push. I know we're running out of time. We had to move."

They talked about strategy and whispered, unsure of who or what was listening. Ricky felt the Shadow Demon's presence, but it was not engaging. The demons were resting, too. Resting and waiting.

It had been hours, but they weren't sure how many when they finally heard something in the distance. The doors had opened. Even this far away, the silence picked up the echoes of footsteps.

He felt the Shadow Demon stir, and a stream of water formed a small wave as the brothers rushed toward the entrance.

Now they needed patience and hoped Ricky's gamble to delay their escape wouldn't cost them their lives.

Chapter Twenty-Seven

STRAND CALLED Mia earlier that morning to meet. He made no mention of the cave prisoners.

Mia left for Hollow Rock almost immediately. She notified Grace but didn't bother to contact Tino. She knew time was against them and she didn't want to deal with any more distractions than necessary.

Strand's car was there when she arrived. He didn't say a word to her as she entered the cave but motioned to a hard shell case about four feet long and three feet wide he'd set on the table.

Mia walked up to the table as Anna and Annika observed against a wall.

Strand opened the case and pulled out some kind of a medallion that was slightly larger than an adult hand. It had eight sides and was filled with shiny, brilliant gems. Strand placed it on the edge of the table where the ceramic cup usually sat.

Then Strand pulled out a larger object. It was a plain wooden cross about three feet tall. It had metal caps on each of the four ends of the wooden planks. The caps were silver and lined with small round gems that looked like glass pearls. He placed the cross against the wall on the far side of the stream.

Strand then got on his knees and seemed to start praying or chanting.

Mia started to ask what he was doing, but Anna put her finger to her lips, motioning for quiet. Mia held her tongue.

After a few minutes, Strand stood up and turned toward Mia.

"Mia, we are ready. This will be somewhat different from what you have been practicing."

"Will we be restoring the baby's soul now?"

"No, this is more important, as the restoration cannot be completed without this step. It is a new element. We are preparing a vessel. Something that we could not attempt until we knew if it was even possible. In order to restore Annika's soul, we must use something powerful to extract it. Something dark."

"What does something dark mean?"

"I have established a connection with two spirits. A bargain we struck that ensures their assistance. They pose no threat to you. They may be startling, but it is the only way to return Annika's soul. Do you understand?"

"Are these spirits the same ones that attacked me? The ones speaking to me?"

"Yes, I believe so. They want to ensure our bargain is fulfilled and knew you were key. They acted without my knowledge."

"You say spirits. But that could mean many things. And from what I've sensed, I think it's worse than just spirits. Are they demons?"

Strand pondered for a moment before he spoke.

"Yes, they are."

Demons.

The spirits that tormented her and almost killed her. The ones inside her head. Demons. Like she suspected.

Like what the couple told me.

"Why would you make a deal with demons?"

"Because it was demons that took my Annika's soul. We require demons to get them back."

"How do you know they aren't the same ones that took her in the first place?"

Strand stepped closer to Mia and placed his hand on her shoulder.

"Mia, there is one thing I have yet to disclose to you. I stated I suspected, but could not prove, that Annika's soul was stolen. However, I have known for some time it was. These two demons I have bargained with are the same thieves that took her soul."

Mia stepped away from him.

"What? You're working with the same demons that did all this? Why?"

"These demons took her soul because they craved its power. However, they did not understand how to use it for their gains. Part of my bargain with them is a promise to aid them without harming my granddaughter or any other living creature, so long as they help me return her soul."

"You've known all this time. Why haven't you just tried to destroy them?"

"Have you not realized I will do whatever I must to save Annika? If I destroy them, her soul is also destroyed."

"So you trust demons, actual demons, to keep their word?"

"No, my dear Mia. I do not fully trust them, but the

reality is, only they contain the power necessary to return Annika's soul. What they have stolen resides within their essence, but we must create a container that you can control in order to extract it safely. If the soul were to be taken by brute force, Annika would not survive the transfer."

"Meaning they're the only way to save her? And that's only assuming they keep their word. I'm not prepared for this. I don't think I can help extract her soul until I'm able to fully understand everything you're just now telling me."

"Today," Strand said, "you are only making them ready. In two days, we will use what little of Annika's soul that is still inside her to attract what the demons have taken. Similar to sticking a piece of adhesive tape onto something and pulling it back, bringing the material along with it. Once the soul is contained within these containers, you should be able to extract the entire soul from both demons and Annika to make it complete before restoring it into her body. This will finally make my Annika complete."

Mia's head was spinning. She was trying to understand, repeating in her head all that Strand was telling her. It made just as much sense as it didn't. She was taking shallow breaths and shaking.

She needed to get back to something that made sense.

Stick with the process, Mia.

She moved towards the table. "Where are they?"

"They are here in Hollow Rock. They will appear between the table and the stream. Close enough for you to see and work with them. Just follow through with the process, the process you have worked toward. You will have to perform it twice, once for each demon. This artifact, this Purifying Medallion, will purify and protect the water you pull from the stream. Water you will use to fill the vessels you will create. The demons are like the hollow geode crystal stone you have practiced with. Inside them is a crevice, an empty hole, and we must prepare them to accept and hold the essence of the soul."

"Prepare them?" Mia asked. "Why would I prepare them as a target to transfer a soul into? I thought we were taking Annika's soul back from them."

"It is all about transformation," Strand said. "There are three pieces of Annika's soul. The parts contained within both demons and the little that remains within Annika. What we are attempting must take place at a specific time, when the ability to transfer is strongest. Two days from now will be that day. The demons must be ready for that transformation, or the soul exchange will not succeed."

"I don't fully understand," Mia said.

"That is perfectly fine. You will comprehend soon enough. For today, you only have to perform a slight modification to what you have already accomplished. It is on a larger scale and more frightening than the stone, but you will be able to do this. Of that, I am sure. You must be brave, and you must be prepared. Anna and Annika will remain against that wall, so if you require inspiration or a reminder of why you are doing this, simply look behind you."

Mia sucked in a deep breath and looked back. She moved toward Anna and then picked up little Annika.

Annika once again hugged her, but a little tighter than before.

Mia looked at her pale face. She looked worse every time she saw her. She knew time was their enemy, but if things worked out, Annika could regain her soul in two days.

Mia's shaking stopped. She handed the baby back to Anna and returned to the table. She looked up at Strand.

"I'm ready."

Strand started to grunt and speak in the demon-tongue.

The water in the stream rose and moved towards the table, but instead of heading toward the cup, it dripped to the ground, leaving a thin pool of water.

"Is this the water we're trying to purify?" Mia asked.

"Not exactly. This is not just water from the stream. It contains the essence of these beings within it."

"You mean the demons when you say beings, right?"

"Yes, I do."

"Can you please just stick with demons, then? Don't leave out any more details."

"I shall do my best."

"So you're trying to tell me I'm supposed to treat demon gunk and water the same?"

"Mia, does it matter? I am sure you now realize I have some ability to communicate with the other side. The demons are too weak to do anything with the soul they have taken and are also easily manipulated, which is why I struck this bargain. Even if they cannot be trusted, they can be controlled. So I ask again, with Annika's soul at stake, does it even matter?"

Mia looked back at Annika and then at the wet matter on the cave floor.

"I guess it doesn't matter in the end," Mia said. "As long as we save Annika."

"I agree wholeheartedly. Shall we begin?"

Mia looked at the pool of water on the ground and saw it had a strange shimmer to it. The water in the stream had always looked blue and unblemished, but now it had a tinge of darkness. Something was moving within the water itself.

Strand muttered a few words and Mia felt a strength coming from the pool of water. She looked at it as it expanded and started to form a torso. It was partial and had no head or legs, but it was a chest from the neck down to about the stomach, all formed and shaped with the water, but broken.

"Can you see and feel that?" Strand asked.

"Yes," she whispered. "I can see it and am starting to feel something, but it's everywhere. Beyond this partial body I'm seeing in front of me."

"Yes, grasp it. Just as you formed the eggshell and the porous outside of the stone, this vessel is already porous. You may have to solidify some of it yourself, but notice the center of the creature's chest. The broken hole inside. Do you see that distinction yet? Can you feel it?"

She looked and concentrated but could not feel a connection to the separate parts of what was before her. The water was everywhere, and the partial body, even though it was shaped in water, was hard to ignore.

"Trust your instincts and not your eyes. There is the body. Find the center. It is continuing to form."

Then there was a glow. A dim orange color that filled the chest. Mia saw the shape forming with a more defined center. She felt it growing. Then she imagined the oval shape of the eggshell she had been picturing within the stone, but this cavity was larger. Almost the size of football. She grasped it.

"I see it. I feel it."

"Hold it tightly," Strand said. "Make the center complete."

The shape growled as if it was in pain, although it had

no discernible mouth to growl from. Mia lost her concentration.

"Ignore what you hear. It is confused, but it has given its word not to harm you. Not while I am here."

She pushed harder and tried to drown out the sounds coming from the writhing water thing before her. This demon. She was working with a demon.

It doesn't matter, Mia. Demon or not, this is how to help Annika.

She squeezed her fists and closed her eyes, trying to shut everything else out. Her grip tightened.

"I have it."

The partially formed hole in the chest started to solidify. It was an oval shape turned on its side.

"Excellent, Mia."

The chest completed forming.

"Now, the water?" Mia asked.

"No, not yet."

Strand lifted the medallion and pulled something else out of the bag. He placed a small piece of wood on the table and placed the medallion on it.

"The remaining pool of water on the ground must be drawn through this medallion. Passing through it will turn that water and any elements within it into something purified, worthy enough to house a soul. Simply pass the water through the medallion and nothing more."

Mia reached out to the water on the ground, as well as some dripping around the torso. She was able to unify it and sent the stream of water toward the medallion. She held the stream in front of the medallion's center. Its glowing stones glistened as Mia pushed the stream through them like she was threading the water through a much larger eye of a needle. As the water penetrated the gems, a bright light lit up the cave like the sun piercing through stained glass.

The water changed colors as it passed through. It was as if a light had been captured inside the stream. It pulsed in a mix of blue and orange colors. Mia felt the power. It was different than before. The water she had been working with all this time suddenly had weight to it. She had to concentrate even harder to maintain just keeping it airborne. She heaved the water stream up with her mind, but after a few more seconds, it was no longer a struggle. The water shifted through easily and danced around the wet shape of the demon's partial body.

"Now," Strand said. "This is what you have practiced. What you have prepared for. Take the purified water and place it within the demon's chest."

Mia pictured the water entering the floating torso, but the newness of the situation and the texture was difficult to grasp beyond getting the water there. She had to change the demon's form in her head.

She took the memory of the dark visitors she had in her apartment and pictured the partial body transforming to the dark flesh she saw that night. She thought of every zombie movie she'd ever seen, and in her head, the torso before her turned to flesh, rotting and barely hanging on to the bones beneath it.

Progress.

She shifted the surrounding stream and felt more in control.

As the water hit the demon's body, it writhed in pain. Its partially watery hand turned to flesh and reached towards her. She jumped back.

The stream fell and splashed back to the ground as the demon's torso reverted to its watery form.

"I'm sorry," Mia whispered.

"It was only your first try," Strand said. "Remember who and what you are doing this for."

She looked back and saw baby Annika. The baby just stared blankly, but then reached her little arms out.

That's all Mia needed. She turned back, and this time lifted the stream with confidence.

It shot through the medallion, and she changed the body's flesh color to a burning orange without much effort. She wanted a full distinction of color for what she was about to do.

The body spasmed.

"Stay there and shut up," she said to it. "This baby's life is more important than your pathetic one. You took a soul that didn't belong to you and were too stupid to know what to do with it. I know you only agreed to do this for your own gain. I hope you suffer."

The stream flew straight into the demon's body. It grunted in pain. She felt the pulsing hollowness of the container now fully formed in its chest.

Mia moved the stream around the chest container like she had before with the eggshell in the geode crystal.

The water was under her control, waiting to enter its orange container.

She repeated her Easter egg procedure. She pulled the top off the torso, in her mind the container, and let the stream seep in. It flowed inside without hesitation and remained in its orange shell. Once it was filled to almost the top, she needed to enclose it. She imagined the same bandage, only much longer and thicker, wrapping around the open tip and sealing it. This time, however, once the crack closed, she used her newfound energy to seal it closed. The bandage was no longer necessary.

The orange center was whole and sealed with the purified water within, safely awaiting a soul.

"You've done it," Strand said. "On the second attempt. That is amazing. I thought we would be here for hours."

The demon's form returned to its watery skin as Mia let go, but its orange football shaped container remained. The container and the remains of the demon floated back into the stream. As it hit the water, the stream glowed with a brilliant light.

"That was only the first demon, and the second is just as critical. Are you prepared for the next one, Mia?"

She felt like she could conquer the world as she stared back at Annika, feeling hope for her.

"Yes, bring it."

Strand spoke in his demon tongue and a dark shadow appeared from the inner cave. It moved slowly, and it was impossible to see past it as it moved.

It was the shadow that had been in her home. Mia shuddered. This was the being that scared her the most.

"I know he is terrifying," Strand said, "but remember, this demon, although it used an extreme method, frightened you enough to stimulate your power. It may have been terrifying, but it worked. You are here. You are powerful. Set aside the past. This creature is strong and a key to your success. Please, proceed."

Mia took in a deep breath and sensed her body shaking again.

Annika's all that matters, Mia. You're controlling this thing now.

Mia looked back at the demon that tried to kill her. The last time it had been semi-transparent, but this time she could see the body approaching. It was a much darker sense than what she felt from the first demon. There was no light. No hope within it.

The shadow passed over the stream and stopped, as if it was inspecting its surroundings. The stream glowed briefly and the shadow moved closer to the table. It covered the table with its darkness. It was as if a dark cloud washed over the table and medallion and then it partially solidified.

Mia watched and waited as the shadow settled. She could almost sense it hesitating. Once it calmed, she didn't say a word and turned back to the stream and shot it up. It again went through the purifying medallion, faster than before, and she had it encircling the shadow a few seconds later. She looked into the demon, but something was different.

"I can't see its soul container. It's too dark."

"Just use your mind," Strand said. "The first demon required the water for its reflection. Now there is only shadow and darkness. You can overcome that. Form the entire container yourself. Build it into something you can see and feel."

It's just a different approach, Mia. Just one small roadblock.

She let the water spin and then concentrated on the shadow body. She thought of a dark set of storm clouds approaching at night. They were too dark, so she imagined they were coming during the daytime. Daytime clouds that could blacken the daytime sky while revealing a small glimpse of the sun beyond them.

Light cut through the torso from the inside. She thought of the shell again but pictured it cutting through the small cracks of the darkness. The shadow didn't completely disappear, but it opened enough for her to see and feel its insides.

Rather than repairing the rotting flesh of a partially formed container like the first demon, she imagined forming her own shape from the dark mist. She grasped the mist and pieced it together into the same oval football shape as before. It came together quickly, and once it was complete, she made it glow orange again.

The rest was easy. She repeated the entire process.

Easter egg. Rip off the top gently. Let the swarming stream enter until the soul container was full. Finally, top it off again. She didn't need the Band-Aid at all this time. She simply capped it with energy and watched as it healed along the cracked lines.

It was done. After all the practice and not knowing her capabilities, it was done. The baby had a chance.

There was hope. Real hope.

Chapter Twenty-Eight

GABBY AND RICKY were still strapped to the wall, tired, but biding their time.

While Mia was experimenting with the demons and building their soul containers, Ricky felt everything during her interactions with the Shadow Demon. He felt the pain, its hesitation, and its thoughts, wondering if this human could give them what they needed.

As the center of its core was being readied, the demon writhed as its power spiked.

"It's time," Ricky said. "It's distracted."

He harnessed the power that the shadow was emanating, allowing himself to sync with the demon that altered the course of his life. He hoped to never feel this connection again, worried it could lead him on another path of destruction. But this time, it was necessary. The telekinetic power the demons had once brought him was reborn.

The restraints around Ricky and Gabby broke away like rotted wood.

"You think they sensed that?" Gabby asked.

"No, they're in pain and focused at the same time. Mia

is involved. She's doing something to them, but I don't know what."

They moved silently toward the entrance to the cave, stopping several yards before the main room and remaining out of sight. They were able to hear some of the conversations, and they realized whatever Mia was supposed to do was complete.

"Now that this is done, what's next?" they heard Mia ask.

"We wait," Strand said. "You only need to stay strong. Stay focused."

"What exactly happens in two days?" Mia asked.

"Mia, I cannot thank you enough for what you have done," Strand said.

The water kept rippling, with dark shadows dancing in and out of the stream. The Shadow Demon was reforming its strength as the process had left both demons feeling renewed. It was more focused than before. There had been only darkness when Ricky first sensed the Shadow Demon, but now there was a dark hope.

Mia's adrenaline waned, and she felt faint. She caught herself on the table and groaned.

"What's wrong with me?" she asked.

"This is power you had yet to experience," Strand said. "It can be taxing."

"No, it's not that. I feel like something's wrong. Are you sure the baby's okay?"

Mia moved toward Annika, but she buried her head into her mother.

"Can I please hold her?" Mia said.

Strand nodded and Anna handed her the baby.

"She will be okay, right?" Mia asked.

"Of course she will," Strand said. "All we have accomplished is for her."

"Please tell me what's so important about two days from now? What will I have to do to help her now that these containers are in place?"

"Do you see that cross?" Strand asked as he pointed to it.

"Yes," Mia said. "There's something about it. I can feel it."

"It is said that several pieces of the original cross where the disciple Peter was crucified, allegedly upside-down, were used to build that cross. It is truly special."

"Special how?"

"Prayers, thoughts, and good intentions are said to filter through this cross when it is near. A direct line to the ears of the celestial worlds. To angels, God, or whomever may be listening and able to hear."

"Incredible," Mia said. "How is that going to help?"

"The containers you created and prepared inside the demons. They will be filled with that soul power. And any positive prayers, chants, and intentions will be absorbed and grow in strength from that cross, and then must be relayed through the Purifying Medallion. The combined power generated should be enough to pass whatever is left inside Annika to the demons and then bring her entire soul to completion so it can be transferred back to the baby."

"That's bullshit," Gabby whispered to Ricky. "She needs to know!"

Ricky closed his eyes and tried to send his words to Mia.

It's a lie, Mia, Ricky thought to himself. *These are the same demons that took her soul. They have no intention of giving it back.*

Mia suddenly thought about what Ricky and Gabby had told her.

"You said you had an agreement with these demons. Are you sure they'll give her soul back?"

Strand frowned. "After all you have felt, all you have experienced, you still have doubts? I believe you are allowing that troubled couple to influence you, Mia," Strand said.

"Then tell me they will give it back. Tell me you're positive they will."

Something inside Mia clicked. She focused on Annika and somehow knew the answer.

"Never mind," Mia said as she handed Annika back to her mother. "They never intended to give her soul back. They need our help to take the rest. I feel it. I'm not sure how, but I do. Why wouldn't you tell me this?"

"The truth, then," Strand said. "Yes, these demons have other intentions. I confess I did not wish to distract you and apologize for not being fully forthcoming. In order to retrieve and rebuild Annika's soul, we must take it back directly from the demons that took it, as I told you. No, they cannot be trusted and I never doubted their true intentions, but with your power, their desires are insignificant. When the energy required for them to take the rest of her soul is achieved, our combined forces along with the cross will provide the ability to do whatever we wish. Including returning her soul instead of allowing them to keep and manipulate it. Yes, it will be a fight, but one we had no chance of winning until now."

Mia's head clouded. Maybe Strand was telling her the truth this time, but it bothered her how easily he was able to lie to her.

"Then what can we do to be ready?"

"All you can do is wait. We require the power that the cross will help generate and your special abilities, and it must happen during the one special night it can succeed."

Mia tried to process what Strand was saying.

"The demons are prepared to receive what's left of

Annika's soul," Mia said. "And once it's in their bodies, this final ceremony will put her soul back together and I'll move it back into Annika, making her whole again. All the while fighting off the demons who want to take it for themselves. Am I missing anything?"

Strand saw Mia working something out in her head.

"You are correct. The soul must be united and purified and the Demon Brothers defeated. Only then can the soul be used to save Annika."

"Souls. Souls belong to the living. And it's something spirits and demons all want, or they wouldn't have taken it from Annika in the first place, right?"

"Mia, why so many questions?" Strand asked. "The baby will be fine."

"It just doesn't add up. I sensed the water and the power that just went into those demons. They are strong and want nothing more than to break through the barrier between our worlds, but they didn't even try to fight me or you today. And Annika is right there. If they want her soul so badly and took most of it, what's the problem? You said they don't know how to use her soul, but if that's true, why did I pick up nothing but the desire to use it to cross over? Why bother with all this ceremony?"

"They thought they had enough of Annika's soul to get what they wanted. What they did not count on, however, was the power from the love of Annika's mother was enough to save the small piece that still lives within her. The demons—"

"No!" Mia said.

She shook her head. Something still wasn't right. Her head snapped upward and, like she had with Tino, she grasped Strand's mind. Only this time, she knew what she was doing.

Strand didn't try to resist. Or maybe he couldn't.

232

Instead of trying to squeeze the lifeblood from him, Mia locked onto Strand's sixth sense. She absorbed some of it and replayed his actions in her head.

It didn't take her long to learn what she needed. His body was never threatened, but his mind had been, and he allowed it.

"You're lying. You have been about almost everything."

Strand let out a grunting laugh.

"I am surprised it took you this long to test your abilities on me, but I am relieved. I'm tired of the lies, but this also tells me how much your abilities have matured. Your feelings and emotions are not betraying you. I have been deceitful, but not about everything. The cross, the medallion, and the transfer, those are all accurate. However, they are not giving up a soul or pieces of souls, and I did not agree to help them find another way. There is no other way. What you have done is prepare them to receive the completed soul they require. What you did today was create a grand conduit. It has taken them years to collect the power necessary to reach this point, and now they are on the cusp of crossing over. Thanks to you."

"And what do you gain from this?"

"I will be there to guide them once they cross and will receive the reward of thriving in the new world. You will too, Mia. They are grateful and will reward you as well. All these years of work would have been for nothing without the ability to hold and absorb the soul they require. You gave this to them."

"All this. This grand story. And all you did was use me."

"I am giving you a gift. Reciprocating the gift you so willingly gave. You have already been granted a strength that will last far beyond this day. A strength and confidence you would have never realized on your own."

"I only did it to save Annika's soul!"

"That is unfortunate, but please, do not try to convince me that you do not relish this power. I sensed it. In your class and around those you love. You have enjoyed this surge of power and opportunity. Am I wrong?"

Mia looked around as her eyes started to water. He was right. She had loved the power. It was overwhelming, but it made her feel important. It made her feel strong.

"Yes, I admit I enjoy it. It doesn't change the fact that it was Annika that was driving me. That was always the priority. You lied to me and now you're telling me I'm taking the soul from this child and using it to give two demons the ability to come into our world and destroy lives? No. No, that can't happen. I can't be a part of that! I did this to save her, and you want to kill her?"

"But Mia, my dear. You already are a part of this. A major, treasured part."

"I'll stop it!"

"There is no stopping it now. We still need you, and I hope you understand nothing will prevent you from being here. It is inevitable. It would be preferable to have you here willingly, but I will gladly take you kicking and screaming. You should be happy and celebrate with us."

Mia turned back to Annika and her mother.

"Anna, how can you let them do this? To your baby?"

"The child's body you see is no more her blood than she is mine," Strand said. "She was a dying, abandoned child the Brothers found along the way. Now she is a vessel to help hold what's left of another's child's soul. We gave her unwanted body a longer life. A purpose."

Mia's lower lip trembled. "One child's soul and another child's body. Was either child even named Annika? And what about the soul inside her? Does that belong to the daughter of that lady, Gabby?"

"Perhaps. I never cared enough to ask who either child's parents were."

Mia started to cry and reached for Annika, but Anna held her closer and refused to hand her back.

Mia took another step, but part of the Shadow Demon appeared between her and Annika.

"Stay where you are," Strand said to Mia. "You can help willingly. Or be coerced."

"My aunt knows I'm here and is going to call the police if she doesn't hear from me soon."

Strand moved toward her and touched her forehead, reading her essence. Mia was too taken aback to fight it.

"I would expect a bluff, however, it seems that you are telling the truth. Pity. We shall take you above and issue a text on your behalf. It seems you have to return to the school for an all-night study session for an upcoming test. Your aunt and boyfriend will understand. You are ever the studious one."

Mia knew that excuse could work. She'd had to pull a few all-nighters before.

"Why would you admit to all this now?" Mia asked. "It makes no sense. There's no way I'm going to help you."

"There is no hiding our true intentions with the final ceremony. Better to tell you now so that you help us willingly. We need you, but know that you will not be harmed for the same reason we did not kill the two that invaded this place last night."

"Who? That couple that came looking for me?"

"I am sure they are the same. This place must remain pure until this is done. No killing of anyone. The demons must also remain free from any violence within this cave or it may risk their fragile status. They must protect their soul containers that you so generously provided them. Let there be no doubt, Mia Morales. You will help us."

"Never!"

"We shall see. For now, we must leave. It is time to notify your loved ones you will not be available."

"And what happens to me after this is all over?"

"That is entirely up to the demons. They may choose to feast on you or spare you for what you've done. Provided you do not threaten their passage."

Strand waved at Anna and Annika. "Join us willingly, Mia. You will be comfortable in my home as we await. No harm will come to you today."

The group moved up the stairs and out of the cave.

As soon as the doors closed, Ricky rushed from his hiding place. "Gabby, we have to move now!"

Gabby hesitated. "He said the demons had to remain calm. Do you think they'll listen?"

"I guess there's only one way to find out."

Chapter Twenty-Nine

RICKY BROKE into a run and flew into the main room.

Gabby was a few steps behind him when a stream of water slammed them both against the table.

As they turned, the Shadow Demon's form was above them. It was over eight feet tall and almost as wide, ready to envelop them.

Ricky threw out a power surge and the Shadow Demon flinched, but then came back at them. The shadow hit them as solid as a cement wall and they lost their breath as they were knocked back.

"You are risking your souls!" Gabby yelled.

The shadow held fast.

"Are we worth all the time you've waited?" Ricky screamed. "If you harm us, you could lose your only chance."

The shadow stood its ground as the stream retreated, then inched forward.

Ricky felt the demon's rage compounding.

"Come on, dickhead," Ricky said. "I'd happily let you

kill me if it meant preventing you from crossing over. Let's go. Take me out. Come on!"

The shadow moved closer. Gabby wanted to goad it but could only think of her Ally.

"Ricky, stop. Please stop. You know what we're risking."

"Gabby. If they break into our world, they destroy everything. Ally included."

He turned back to the demon. "I'm getting out of here, and the only way you can stop me is to kill me. I dare you, you bastard. You took my Ellie! You took my life! I'll take you down with me without thinking twice."

Ricky moved toward the demon and images filled his head. It was Ellie staring back at him that day in the downtown streets. He used every ounce of his strength in his being to resist, but still he raised the gun and fired. It fired every time. Almost every night he dreamt of it, and he had to distract himself multiple times a day not to think about it. It was there. It was always there. He did everything he could to try to stop it, but he couldn't.

A hard splash to the face knocked Ricky back to reality. The Reflection Demon moved between Ricky and the shadow.

"Stop this," the Reflection Demon hissed. "Trying to weaken you. Long we have waited. Now on the cusp. Feast on the world. Human is insignificant. Human is nothing."

The shadow backed off, and Ricky didn't hesitate.

"Run!" he told Gabby as he rushed toward the stairs.

Gabby hit the back of his heels twice as they flew up the steps and flung the doors open.

The first thing they saw was Strand closing the rear of his vehicle. They heard Mia whimpering within.

"Let her go!" Gabby yelled.

Strand turned toward them. "Ah, our intruders. I

should have expected you would both be clever enough to escape. Do not worry. Mia will be fine."

Gabby and Ricky rushed him. Anna dropped Annika on the ground and jumped on Ricky's back. The baby barely reacted.

Strand moved faster than expected. He always walked with a slow purpose, but he was moving like an athletic teen now. He shifted as Ricky first reached him while trying to shake Anna off his back, but Gabby was there two steps later. She kicked sideways at Strand's feet, making him lose his balance, but he adjusted and didn't fall. Instead, Strand swept his arm sideways and hit Gabby on her ribs. She fell on her side as the strike knocked her breath out.

"Help!" she heard Mia yell.

Ricky threw Anna off him and tackled Strand to the ground. They struggled as Anna jumped on him again. Gabby was ready to help, but she heard Mia pleading.

Gabby ran to the vehicle's driver side window. She picked up a rock from the ground and threw it, but it was too small to make an impact. She pounded the windshield again, but it didn't crack.

She heard Ricky still struggling. She had to move fast.

Gabby picked up a larger rock, then took several steps back. She sprinted and flew up, bringing the stone down and through the window.

Gabby's hand crashed through it. A few pieces of glass sliced into her arm, but nothing deep. She didn't feel it with the adrenaline rush.

Gabby pulled the door open and hit the tailgate release. It popped open.

She ran back and Mia was sitting there, shaking.

Gabby held her hand out and offered it to Mia. Mia

took it and jumped out of the vehicle. As she stood there, Gabby moved past her and pulled up the rear mat.

"What are you doing?" Mia asked.

Gabby lifted the mat and yanked out the standard crowbar by the spare tire. Mia stepped back as Gabby ran past her. Strand and Ricky were struggling on the ground while Anna was pulling on Ricky's hair. The baby was on the ground and looked safe, but paler. Gabby thought of her Ally and ran toward the fighting crowd. She leapt and landed a kick on Anna's back. As Anna fell, Gabby swung the crowbar hard at Strand.

She struck his arm and he stopped fighting. Ricky got up and punched him a few times.

Anna pulled him back.

Strand reached behind his back and pulled out a dagger with a blue gem on its handle from his waist.

"This dagger is worth over two million dollars," Strand said with a menacing smile. "A Roman artifact. It is one of my most treasured items, but I will not hesitate to use it on you. Leave now. No blood will spill. You cannot stop what is destined. It is now an inevitability. The demons will not let you back in, and I will stand guard here until it is time. Go!"

Ricky looked at Gabby. "We can try to just end this now. If we take out Strand, I think it would be over."

Strand scampered toward Annika and picked her up, holding the dagger near her face.

"I will destroy this child if there is no hope of completing the ceremony. Your daughter will lose her soul and die now instead of two days from now. I give you a choice. Go. Plan. Spin your best vengeance. You shall not stop this, and if you are somehow able to convince authorities to come here, they will not be able to reach us."

"How will you do that?" Ricky asked.

"Be careful, Ricky," Gabby said. "He has her."

"He won't kill her. Not yet."

"You don't know that! We need to regroup. Don't gamble with my Ally's soul!"

Ricky hesitated. He knew she was right.

Strand started to mumble something and he pulled the dagger up to Annika's ear, slicing it just enough to draw blood.

"No!" Gabby screamed.

Strand rubbed the tip of the dagger on the blood, still chanting, and jammed the dagger into the ground.

There was a bright flash, blinding them all.

Ricky was face down and Gabby was writhing in pain on her back. Mia was on her side in the fetal position, coming to terms with what had just happened.

Gabby crawled toward Ricky and checked him. He was breathing.

She shook him a few times until he finally groaned.

"What happened?" Ricky asked.

"I don't know," Gabby said. "There was a flash and now we're on the other side of the road. At least I think we are."

Ricky looked across toward the trees, but saw only crops and an area of flat grass.

"Where did everything go?" he asked.

Mia stood up. "They hid it somehow. It's not there."

The three of them ran across the road to the same spot where they had been only moments before. There were only the crops surrounding the flat area where the trees and cave entrance should be.

"How did he do that?" Gabby asked.

"The planes," Mia said. "This is a spot that is ready to

be breached, and Strand told me the planes were thin. He lied to me about many things, but that part seems to be true. The new power they gained with what I did tonight. They must have been able to mask this. Hide it from the world."

"There has to be a way to get through," Ricky said.

He groaned. He lifted his shirt and saw he was bleeding. The dagger had cut him. The wound wasn't fatal, but it hurt.

"We have two days to figure it out," Gabby said.

"They've won," Mia said. "We can't defeat them if we can't get to them. I did this. I was stupid enough to believe everything. That poor baby's soul."

"That is my baby's soul," Gabby whispered as the tears flowed down her face. "My Ally's soul, just like I told you."

Mia heaved a sob. "I'm sorry. I should have believed you. I'm so sorry!"

Gabby offered no words of consolation. Her daughter's soul was going to be used to help demons, and her body would die back in Texas if that happened.

Ricky walked toward Mia. "Mia, you had no reason to trust us. We were desperate because we felt time was short. We should have found a better way."

"I should have listened," Mia said. "Everything was too good to be true. I enjoyed the power. I enjoyed it too much. My vanity. My stupidity. Tino was right. I should have just quit school and let him take care of me. I'm worthless."

Gabby fell to her knees.

Mia stood there, unsure of what to do. She was lost and riddled with guilt.

Ricky paced in a circle, trying to harness the power of the Shadow Demon, but it was gone. He got angrier with each step and wanted to mentally smash something, but he couldn't even grasp a rock.

He fell on his back in the middle of the grass.
Gabby looked up and finally spoke.
"Mia's right. It is over," she said. "They've won."

Chapter Thirty

THEY SAT down in silence for several minutes until Mia stood up.

"If this is the end, then it's the end, but we aren't going to get anything accomplished sitting here doing nothing. If we're going down, let's at least go down fighting."

Neither Ricky nor Gabby said anything for a moment.

"Mia," Ricky said. "We only heard the end of whatever was going on in there, and only parts of the conversation. Why didn't they just kill you? He said they needed you, but why? What did you do in there today?"

"They didn't kill me because they still need me. If you hadn't saved me, they'd have me locked up."

"But up until today, you were doing all of this willingly, weren't you?" Ricky said. "Why would they have you restrained and thrown in the back of Strand's truck? What changed?"

"They tricked me," Mia said. "Strand lied and I believed it all. I was blinded by saving Annika ... I mean, Gabby's daughter's soul."

"Ally," Gabby muttered.

"I only wanted to save Ally's soul. Instead, I prepared two demons to take the rest of her soul and kill us all."

"Tell us," Ricky said. "The entire story from the beginning. We have to know every detail."

Then she told them everything, ending with, "But I'm not going to help them."

"But if you don't," Gabby said. "They won't need Ally's soul anymore."

"Then what do we do?" Mia asked.

Gabby shook her head. "I don't know."

"After all this time, I finally tracked them down, but they beat us," Ricky said. "We can't get to them. We can't even see them. There's only one thing we have to work with."

"That they still need me?" Mia asked.

"Yes. They're going to try and grab you at some point," Ricky said. "But right now, I'm so beat I don't know what to do with all this information. Anyone else?"

They went silent for a few minutes.

"You've both been together for some time now," Mia said. "What have you done when you've been stuck?"

"We regroup," Ricky said, staring into nothing.

"Then we regroup — now," Mia said. "For Ally. For your friend and sister, Ricky."

Ricky looked back at her and got up. "Then let's get back to our hotel, get cleaned up, and see if we can come up with something. We knew we didn't have much time, but now we know the clock is ticking. We have maybe 48 hours."

They got in their cars and left. Mia called Aunt Grace on the way to the hotel and caught her up. Once they all arrived, they settled into the room. Ricky took out his laptop and set it on the table.

"How do we start?" Mia asked.

"Nothing really formal," Gabby said. "We talk about what we know and don't know and go from there. Ricky sometimes uses contacts he has in cyber land."

"Okay," Mia said. "Then what do we know?"

Ricky created a blank document, then looked up at Gabby. "We know they need Mia."

"And we know whatever they're planning is in two days," Gabby said.

Ricky's head perked up. "What is today's date?"

"October 30th," Gabby said after checking her phone. "Halloween is tomorrow. I could understand that, but what's on November 1st?"

"November 1st is All Saint's Day," Mia said.

Ricky stood up. "And November 2nd is All Souls Day, but it's also *Dia de los Muertos*. Day of the Dead."

"How does that relate to anything?" Mia asked.

"Hold on," Ricky said, as he started clicking furiously on his touchpad.

"I've seen that look before," Gabby said. "You have something?"

Ricky raised a finger, signaling her to hold on.

"I'm sending a message to DeadBlogger," Ricky finally said.

"What are you thinking, Ricky?" Gabby asked.

"Ellie."

"Who's Ellie?" Mia asked.

"The girl the demons killed through me," Ricky said. "Ellie. Back when all this first started, Ellie told me more about *Dia de los Muertos* than I ever knew."

"Such as?" Gabby asked.

"My grandmother had an altar to my long-dead grandfather in her room. An *ofrenda*. I knew a little about the traditions, but Ellie taught me how some people have these altars in their houses, but during the two days of *Dia*,

November 1st and 2nd, people also visit cemeteries that they clean up and often decorate to build their own *ofrendas* there as well."

"Yes, my Aunt Grace took me and her family to the cemetery after my parents died," Mia said. "I'd take my dad's favorite drink and my mom her favorite flowers."

"That was never a thing in my family," Gabby said. "But we went all out on Halloween. What's the purpose of the altars?"

"To remember them and invite the dead to cross over and visit you that one night. More of a celebration."

"How does that help us?" Gabby asked.

Ricky typed furiously on his computer.

"There it is," Ricky said. "I couldn't remember the details. In Mexico, November 1st is also referred to as *Dia de los Angelitos*. Day of the little angels. This is to celebrate and remember children who have passed."

"I think I follow," Mia said. "It would be the perfect time to try and get a baby's soul to cross planes."

"But how?" Gabby asked. "What does that mean for Ally and what the demons are trying to do?"

"I'm not exactly sure," Ricky said. "But I asked Dead-Blogger if he knew of any ties to the Day of the Dead dealing with demons or resurrection."

"Strand," Mia said. "Strand said, more than once, how prayer would save Annik — I mean, Ally. He brought a cross today. A special one that is supposedly made of wood pieces from the disciple Peter's original crucifixion cross."

"As in one of the twelve?" Gabby asked.

"Yes. Those disciples. Strand said it could use prayers and positive thoughts as power. I always thought he was just praying for her soul, but what if—"

"My grandmother always said there was power in prayer," Ricky interrupted. "What if he means to use that?

I mean, think about it. If there are so many people offering prayers and gifts to their loved ones, maybe there's something there that can be harnessed."

"Do you think a bunch of random prayers for children we don't know could actually help?" Mia asked.

"Did you believe demons existed before recent events?" Ricky asked.

"I mean, I guess I believed they could exist, but not like in regular life."

"Now you know they not only exist, but they are here now. If we buy that they exist, then maybe we should go all-in. Meaning, if there are demons, there are exorcisms."

"You think we need a priest?" Mia asked.

"No, my point is that exorcisms are all about prayer. During my experience, both my mom and I were partially possessed, but like with Gabby, it was the demon's ability to influence that was strongest. Prayer is a strength against that. Against evil."

Ricky's computer dinged.

"It's DeadBlogger. He says he found a few references to Mexico City. One from the mid-1800s and another from 1919. In both cases, there was a mass gathering at a cemetery on *Dia de los Muertos*. The one in the 1800s talks about a series of child murders. The people asked the dead to help find the killer and prayed together. They claimed a church deacon burst into flames during the prayers. After searching his belongings, they found out he was the child murderer. He used his position to gain trust and then kill at least seventeen kids."

"Is that verified?" Mia asked.

"He sent some writings about it. Seems legit."

Gabby leaned into the screen. "What about the one in 1919?"

Ricky clicked the document. "This talks about how the

Spanish flu pandemic ravaged through Mexico in 1918 and 1919. Again, people gathered at a cemetery and prayed to God and the dead to help them. Witnesses swear everyone within a mile of one of the largest cemetery gathering ever recorded experienced a mass healing. Even people that were sick with other ailments. There doesn't seem to be anything proven, but there are some documents where several people claimed it really happened."

"Not like we can get a mass gathering together to stop these demons in the next two days," Gabby said.

"No, but if these are to be believed, it's a power that could be strong enough to help."

"But how?" Mia asked. "Two instances in two centuries. I don't like those odds."

"I don't know, but I may know someone who might."

Gabby put her hand on his shoulder. "Who are you talking about?"

"Dr. Jackie," Ricky said.

"Who is that?" Mia asked.

"Dr. Jacqueline Baker. She was my grandmother's professional partner. They were both anthropologists and saw all kinds of strange things in their time."

"When was the last time you spoke to her?" Gabby asked.

"Before my family went into hiding with new names," Ricky said as he picked up his phone and dialed.

A woman's voice answered on the second ring.

"Hello?"

"Dr. Jackie, it's Ricky."

"Oh, my God! Ricky? I'm so glad to hear your voice. Wait, are you supposed to be contacting anyone?"

"No, I shouldn't be."

"That means it's something serious. Please, tell me."

"I found them, Dr. Jackie. With the help of some friends, I found them."

"Understood," Dr. Jackie said. "Please, catch me up."

Ricky told her as much as he could.

"How can I help?" she asked.

"They plan to do this during Day of the Dead. I read about two instances where a mass gathering and prayers were strong enough to kill a killer and heal hundreds of sick people. Can you think of anything in the history of your work with my grandmother that could help us use this information?"

Dr. Jackie didn't say anything for a few moments, then, "I'll need to go through some of my journals. I should be able to get back to you later today."

"Thank you, Dr. Jackie. I can't emphasize enough that time's against us. Please just call or text me back at this number when you're ready," Ricky said.

They tried to plan some more, but went nowhere until Gabby finally said, "I think we're too beat after being up all night as hostages. I feel disgusting."

"Then let's get cleaned up. Maybe it'll help while we wait for Dr. Jackie."

Ricky and Gabby showered. When they were done, the three of them brainstormed more ideas, but were still so tired they could barely think straight. It was almost 9 p.m. when Dr. Jackie texted. She said she was close, but needed access to some materials she wouldn't be able to get to until the next morning.

"Thank you, Dr. Jackie," Ricky replied. "Just let us know when you're ready."

The three tried tossing around more ideas, but the strain of fighting the demons and Mia coming to terms with Strand's betrayal had taken its toll. After a few hours of running in circles, they decided to rest while they could.

Mia texted Aunt Grace and stayed the night in the hotel in case inspiration struck.

No one stirred until Ricky's phone dinged a little before ten the next morning. It was a text from Professor Jackie.

I have something. Can you video chat in maybe 15 minutes?

Ricky quickly replied, woke up the others, and waited. It felt like an hour, but seventeen minutes later, his video chat sound was ringing.

"Oh, Ricky," Dr. Jackie said. "It's so good to see your face. Who are these lovely ladies with you?"

Ricky introduced his companions. "We've all been affected by these demons, Dr. Jackie, but if they're let out, everyone is in danger."

"Yes, I understand. You no longer look like that high school boy I last saw during that horrible time. You're a man now. Locked in and determined. Much like your grandmother. I hope your mother and sister Myra are okay?"

"Yes, they're fine. I speak to them every few days. Everything I've been doing, it's all been for Myra. To protect her. And now I'm also doing this to save Gabby's daughter."

"Then let's not waste time."

She had a journal in her hands and started thumbing through it.

"Yes, here. More than forty years ago, your grandmother and I were doing research in Australia and visiting one of their many Aboriginal tribes. During our time, we met several healers that are known as Ngangkari. They specialize in traditional spiritual, mental, and physical healing. Most are like holistic healers, but there was this one unusual female Ngangkari we got to know."

She thumbed through her notes.

"Here it is. Your grandmother Bea and I saw this

Ngangkari enter a family's dwelling. All five members of the family and one of their neighbors were experiencing some unknown illness. The Ngangkari woman was brought in from another area because she was known to be the strongest spiritual healers of her time. In under an hour, the family, who were all bedridden, sat up and their fevers and pain were gone. We later found out the neighboring family was seemingly healed at the same time."

"How is that possible?" Gabby asked.

"We spoke to the healer through a translator and asked how she was able to heal so many at once. She pointed to two wooden pieces in the dwelling with circles on them. The circles were symbols that represented people gathering. She placed a third one in the neighbor's home as well. She claims she was able to channel her ability to heal their spirits into the wooden piece and carry it through the one in the neighboring family's place."

Dr. Jackie glanced at her notes and then closed the journal.

"You're saying we need something to channel that energy?" Ricky asked.

"Like a kind of conductor of some kind," Mia added.

"I believe so. In this specific case, it's how the Ngangkari did it," Dr. Jackie said. "Of course, this is no guarantee, and you're talking about a much stronger burst of energy based on the strength of these creatures."

"Thank you, Dr. Jackie," Ricky said. "I think you've helped more than you realize."

"Please let me know if you need anything else," Dr. Jackie said. "Good luck."

Ricky hung up and looked back at his companions.

"What is it, Ricky?" Gabby asked. "Do you have an idea?"

Ricky reached into his backpack and pulled out the one memory that had refused to leave him since he lost Ellie.

Ricky held out his sugar skull.

"The skull?" Gabby said. "How does that help us?"

"This skull held my grandmother's spirit for weeks. I still can't get rid of it."

"I think I get where you're going with this," Mia said. "Right now is the perfect time."

Gabby shook her head. "Perfect time for what?"

"We'll need as many as we can get our hands on," Ricky said.

"Will one of you tell me what you mean?" Gabby said.

"Conductors," Ricky said. "Right now, before Halloween and Day of the Dead, is when sugar skulls are the most available. We need as many as we can buy."

"Is that all we'll need?" Gabby asked.

"No. We need power. We need to put together a way to stop them and this ceremony they're planning, and we have to assume that somehow Mia will be there."

"I don't plan to be."

"I didn't plan to destroy people I cared about. Gabby didn't plan to have her daughter's soul taken. The only way we can do this is to prepare for everything we can. You mentioned St. Peter's cross and medallion. That's serious. We're going to need as much supernatural juice as we can gather."

"I need to go home," Mia said. "My Aunt Grace gave me my grandmother's book of healing recipes and spells, but it has a darker section. One that I was hoping we didn't have to use."

"I'm willing to do whatever is necessary," Ricky said.

"Ally is all that matters to me," Gabby said.

"It's your decision, Mia," Ricky said. "One of us can try to use it if we have to."

"No," Mia said as she turned to Gabby. "I may have destroyed any chance for you to save your baby. I'm so sorry."

"It's not your fault, Mia," Gabby said. "They would have found someone else if it wasn't you. They lie. They do it convincingly. It's the root of their evil."

"No matter what, I played a big part in this," Mia said. "I have to make it right. My grandmother said sometimes you have to fight darkness with darkness. No one else can do it. It has to be me. Like Ricky said, we need to be prepared."

"That's only one part of this. We still have more research to do," Ricky said. "We were caught with our pants down at Hollow Rock because Gabby and I were impatient. We rushed in without any kind of plan. That won't happen again. We'll start by going to grab the sugar skulls we need."

"Ricky and I will find the skulls while you go do what you have to do," Gabby said. "We'll keep researching when we're done."

Mia nodded. "What I have to do is going to take time. I'll be back late tonight or first thing tomorrow."

"Then there's no more time to waste," Gabby said. "We all have our jobs to do."

Chapter Thirty-One

MIA GOT in her car and got a text from Tino that his job only lasted a few hours and he was done for the day.

Mia didn't reply but decided to add a stop to see her boyfriend. She didn't tell Ricky, Gabby, or Aunt Grace about it. Mia didn't want to see him, but knew she had to.

Just in case.

Tino was surprised when he opened the door. He was still in his work clothes and sweaty.

"Hello, stranger," he said coolly.

This wasn't something she was going to put up with. Not now. Not if she might never see him again.

"Tino, sit down."

He looked at her. "Yes, ma'am. You sound serious."

"I am. Something's going on. I'm not going to tell you the details, but it's dangerous. It's something I have to do."

"No," he interrupted. "You don't have to do anything dangerous. You're staying with me and it's time you quit school. I want us to get married and we'll live here where I can take care of you. No more of this danger bullshit."

"Tino!" she yelled. "Sit down. Shut your mouth. And listen."

Tino fell back into his seat. She had never spoken to him like that before. He seemed more in shock than angry.

"Like I said, I'm into something dangerous. And I'm going to see it through. You will not be there because you'll only be in the way. I have the power to save a baby's life and you will never dictate to me what I can or cannot do. I am not a dog for you to command, and as much as I love you, I will not stand for any more of your bullshit! Do you understand?"

Tino started to stand up. "Who the hell do you think you're talking to?"

Mia pushed him back into the seat.

"I am not done! I'm doing this, and if I survive, I will not be quitting school, and if I end up making more money than you do, you're going to have to ask yourself if you can live with that. Because, asshole, that money will be ours. Not mine. Not yours. Ours. If you're too much of a coward to deal with that, then just let me know right now so we can end this and move on. I don't give a rat's ass what your father says, because you know what? That attitude hasn't gotten him far, has it? He's alone, and it's his own fault. If that's what you want, then go find someone willing to be your lapdog. This ends now. I don't care if I only live another day or another fifty years, but I will not live like that. I'll ask again. Do you understand?"

She was breathing so hard it was difficult for her to get herself under control.

He stared at her and didn't say anything for a long time. He seemed to be trying to decide if this was really his Mia or if she was drunk. There was no way he was going to ask.

"You're serious, aren't you?"

"You're damned right I'm serious! I have no problem walking away. I know what I'm capable of. I'm capable of so much more. I would never hold you back, and there is no way in hell I'm letting you or anyone else hold me back anymore. Never again. I came here to tell you what I'm going to do, not ask your permission."

Tino sat there, his lip was quivering. He looked at her and looked down at her feet as he tried to understand the person standing in front of him.

"I love you," he whispered.

"I know you love me, idiot! That's not the point. But it's not enough. Not anymore."

He looked at her. He was shaking.

"We do this together or we don't do it at all," Mia said. "Do. You. Understand?"

"I'm sorry—"

A door in the back of the house creaked open, followed by the familiar smell of a cigarette and bad cologne.

"You going to let her talk to you like that?"

Tino's father stood at his open doorway in a white tee shirt and jeans.

"Stay out of this!" Mia yelled.

His father rushed up to her and repeated his son's words. "Who the hell do you think you're talking to?"

A look of fear contorted Tino's face.

Mia laughed.

"Little man, just because you screwed up your own life, you want your son to screw his up, too? You want him to be like you? A pathetic loser?"

Mia didn't blink as Tino's father slapped her across the face. He turned to his son and said, "You should have done that a long time ago."

Tino stood up, stared at Mia and his father, but froze.

"Come on," his dad said. "Try it. This bitch needs to be put in her place."

Mia's cheek was red, but she didn't feel any pain. The anger was too overwhelming.

Tino lifted his hand, but put it back down.

"Man, I can't believe you're my kid," Tino's dad said. "Let me show you how it's done. This *puta* ain't never gonna talk to you like that again."

"You think that hurt?" Mia said as she took a step closer. "My mom slapped me harder than that when she was alive."

"Yeah, well I'm glad that bitch is dead. You're proof she was a shitty mother anyway."

Tino's dad's arm cocked back for another slap, but before his hand reached her face, he flew backward. He couldn't breathe and the veins in his head and neck were popped out. With a wave of Mia's hand, Tino's father slammed against the wall and his eyes started bleeding as picture frames on the wall fell and crashed on the floor.

"Mia, are you doing that?" Tino yelled. "Stop!"

Mia turned to Tino. "So, him you'll protect?"

"It was you," Tino said, his eyes bulging. "The other day at the restaurant. You did that to me. What are you?"

Mia waved both of her hands and Tino hit the wall, landing next to his father.

Mia felt both men's veins pulsing so hard they were about to explode. She only needed a whisper of additional effort to kill them.

She dropped one hand and Tino's father fell to the floor, gasping for breath.

"That's your future, Tino. Old and alone. We're done."

Mia let Tino go and he fell, too.

As she turned to leave, Tino jumped up and put his

hand on her shoulder. She flipped around and made his hand go numb.

"Neither you nor your father will ever touch me again."

Mia walked out the door.

Chapter Thirty-Two

WHILE MIA WAS DEALING with Tino and heading back to her apartment, Ricky and Gabby drove to the local stores and cleaned out their sugar skull inventory before returning to the hotel to continue their research.

Before getting out of the car, Gabby turned to Ricky.

"I'm going to call Ally before we get any deeper into this."

"Yeah, I should call my sister," Ricky said. "While I can. You take the room. I'll stay in the car and call her from here. Just text me when you're done so I don't interrupt."

Ricky called Myra and was happy to see her smiling face as his mother, Lori, walked into her room and appeared on the screen. He didn't want to scare them, but he made sure he told them he was close to finding the demons.

Ricky sent his love to his mother, then asked her if he could have a moment alone with Myra. As much as he and Lori had made peace with each other after so many years

260

of conflict, Myra was the most important person in his life now.

Ricky had managed to keep her safe, and she had been resilient after the events that changed everything. She was his reason for everything.

"I love you, Sissy," he said as he felt his voice crack.

"Are you okay, Ricky?"

"Why?"

"Because you only call me that when you're worried. Or scared."

"I am. Just know that I love you."

"Remember, Ricky. Nothing was your fault. I know you're trying to protect us, but stop beating yourself up."

"I'll try."

"You're still a bad liar. Be safe, brother. I love you, too."

Ricky thumbed through his phone to keep his mind off Myra. He continued to research the traditions of the *Dia de Los Muertos* and *Dia de los Angelitos*.

Gabby's call to Ally was quick.

Her sister Teri picked up the video call in two rings.

"Gabby? How are you? Hadn't heard from you all day,"

"Teri, we're close and we're almost out of time. I can't tell you many details that will make sense, but we have one more day left. If we fail, Ally's not going…"

Her voice cracked. Her sister's eyes welled up. That sister bond told her what Gabby meant without her having to finish.

"I understand. She's right here and no matter what, I'm going to take her to the doctor if she gets worse."

"You already know what's going to happen. If her time is … limited, I don't want her full of needles. They've already said more than a few times there was nothing they could do. Please, can I see her?"

Teri moved away from the screen and returned a few moments later. She held up what used to be Gabby's smiling, well-fed daughter.

Now she was a scrawny shell. Her face was skeletal, and she looked malnourished. Her empty eyes were looking to the side.

"Ally," Gabby said.

Ally turned but couldn't focus on the image on the phone. It was like she was blind but could still hear her.

Gabby stared at her daughter without saying a word.

"Thank you, Teri. Please, hug her for me. I have to go."

Teri nodded and she hung up. Gabby wanted to curl up on the floor and cry, but she knew the best thing she could do for her daughter was to stop Strand and the demons and get her soul back.

Gabby texted Ricky to let him know she was done. He walked from the car into the room.

"Good call?" he asked.

She looked at him and they took in the shared moment of knowing that might be the last time they saw or heard the voices of the people they loved most.

They returned to their research and conversation about what was to come.

Neither Ricky nor Gabby were going to stop trying, no matter how bleak things looked.

Ally. If they could save her, they would save them all.

Chapter Thirty-Three

MIA DROVE to her apartment feeling empowered. The initial fear she'd felt when she almost killed Tino at dinner a few days before was replaced with pride from standing her ground and finally putting Tino and his father in their place.

As her adrenaline settled, she thought of Aunt Grace. She called her and told her what happened with Tino and how she, Gabby, and Ricky were trying to figure out how to proceed. Mia initially hesitated telling her about the book, but she knew Grace was the only person who would understand and didn't leave out any details.

Grace paused for a moment before speaking.

"I understand why you're doing this, even if I don't like it. You know the risks."

"Yes, Aunt Grace. I do. Grandmother even added a warning in the book. I won't take it lightly and will use it only if I have to."

"Are you going to have to take the book with you?"

Mia paused.

"I hadn't thought about that. It's not like I can be walking around with this book in my hands."

"I'm sure you'll figure out something. Mia, please be careful. If you need me to help, you call me. No matter what it is. Do you understand?"

"I do. I'll check in with you as soon as I can. I promise."

They hung up as Mia got to her apartment. She grabbed the book, the ingredients, and materials she needed and got to work.

Three spells. Power, darkness, and fear.

She put the power concoction together and, in the end, it was a liquid. Something she could drink. She took a tiny sip from the cup she poured it in, then gagged and almost spilled it all. The sip was enough to make her body shake. She felt the surge of power, more refined and focused than she'd felt at Tino's.

She transferred the Power liquid into a small water bottle and continued with the next two, the spells she worried about most. Power walked the line of white and black magic, but darkness and fear walked no such line.

They were both dark magic. Black magic. She re-read the passage with her grandmother's words at the beginning of the section.

THESE PAGES ARE to be used only as a last resort when a life is at stake and the risk of the darkness spreading is high … I did not make this decision lightly, and neither should you. Just be sure you are doing this for the right reasons.

MIA CLOSED HER EYES.

"I promise, Grandma. Only as a last resort. Only for a good reason. I know you'll be with me no matter what."

Mia mixed and crushed and failed, but she'd bought enough materials to experiment. She worked late into the night until the Darkness potion was almost ready. It took another five hours and fifteen attempts to complete the fear mix. She separated the potions into glass jars and only needed drops of vinegar heated by black candles to complete it all, but that would have to happen tomorrow.

Mia texted Ricky and Gabby at 4 a.m. with her progress. They were both still up researching and brainstorming, talking to Dr. Jackie and messaging DeadBlogger. All three of them had lost track of time and decided they should try to sneak in a few hours of rest. They had a long day ahead of them and they would have to be prepared.

Mia jumped out of bed at seven.

She had a problem.

Just like she couldn't carry the book with her, how was she going to haul around glass jars full of dark magic? She needed something practical.

Mia ran to her kitchen cabinet and pulled out small plastic containers.

No, she thought. *I need something I can throw. Something that can break. Something I can carry.*

Mia turned on the black candles and held a pot of vinegar over them until they boiled. She poured a small amount into each glass jar, then mixed everything.

A green mist rose from each mix and Mia sealed them. She had no way to test if she had done everything right or if any of the concoctions would actually work, but somewhere inside, she knew.

Mia showered and dressed, then texted Ricky and Gabby that she'd run into a problem but was working on the fix. She took off to a nearby arts and crafts store, got what she needed, and came back to her apartment to finish her work.

She knew Ricky and Gabby didn't fully understand her abilities, but she was about to give them a live demonstration.

If they had any doubt if Mia was with them, she planned to put those thoughts to rest. She was an equal partner now.

Her goal hadn't changed. She was going to save the soul of a child and do everything in her power to succeed, even if it took the darkest and deepest depths of her own soul to do it.

Chapter Thirty-Four

THE DAY of the Dead had arrived.

It was almost 11 a.m. when Mia texted that she was ready. Ricky and Gabby had already been up a few hours and were still trying to research, but they didn't find anything new and hoped they were as ready as they were going to be. Mia gathered everything into a handbag and left to meet them at the hotel.

Mia didn't say much as she pulled several items from her handbag and placed them on the hotel room table.

"What is this?" Gabby asked.

"I want you both to see something."

Mia set the two glass jars on one side of the table and unscrewed the lids. She then grabbed a bag from the arts and crafts store. She pulled out several glass beads. Half were black, and the rest were green.

"These beads are hollow, like the stone I practiced with and the containers that I created for the demons to hold Ally's soul. These jars hold two of the spells I may need, but it won't be easy hauling them around. I've only moved liquids, and the contents of these jars have solids mixed in, so I'm going to try and move the contents into a few of these beads that I can carry and use as weapons if I have to."

"This is how you transfer souls?" Ricky asked.

"It has to be. It's what I've been working on all this time. The prep I did for the demon's containers was different, but familiar enough that I was able to adjust. I expect the transfer itself will also be similar. Even though there are solid pieces of ingredients mixed in, I can already tell that I know I can do this."

"How?" Gabby asked.

"It's the same as my abilities. I don't know how. I just know."

Mia placed five green beads on the opposite side of the table. She closed her eyes, took in a sharp breath, then raised her hands. She opened her eyes as she exhaled, concentrating on the Jar of Fear. She flicked her right wrist and the contents moved upward in a steady mix of liquid, roots, and herbs and hovered over the group of beads. Mia stretched her fingers and the floating mixture broke into smaller chunks, compressed, then dashed into each of the five different beads, with the solids doing exactly what the liquids had done for her at Hollow Rock. She didn't have to imagine the eggshells. She just pictured glass and sand and got all five beads filled on the first attempt.

She repeated the process with the Jar of Darkness and the five remaining black beads.

Ricky and Gabby stood motionless.

"That's incredible," Ricky said.

"We understood you could do this," Gabby said. "But to see it in action is insane. I see why Strand chose you."

"I just hope that helps somehow," Mia said. "I just wanted to give you an idea of what they want me to do. I assume the medallion and cross will be involved as well."

Ricky picked up a bead and moved it between his fingers.

"We've been looking at this all wrong," Ricky said.

Gabby turned to him. "What do you mean?"

"We keep trying to figure out how we're going to stop them. Mia, just like you knew this was going to work, I know somehow you will physically be there performing this ceremony when the time comes. I think Strand was right. It's inevitable. But we can't stop Strand, help you, or save Ally if we can't get back inside Hollow Rock. I think we have enough information for a solid plan, but the thing is, if they don't think we can get to them since we can't even see the location anymore, they're probably not planning any type of counterattack or defense. Why would they?"

"I get you," Mia said. "We need to worry about being able to get through whatever magic they're using to conceal themselves."

"Exactly," Ricky said. "We're worrying about what to do when we get back to the cave, but it's pointless until we can."

"Do you have any ideas?" Gabby asked.

"Yes. My original plan was to take the skulls we had and somehow spread the energy from my original skull through them to disrupt the ceremony and stop the transfer. But that's not the problem. We can't do any of that if we can't even get inside Hollow Rock. But I think I can use the same concept to get us inside."

"What do we need to do?" Mia asked.

"Skulls. We're going to need more. Way more."

"We cleaned out every place we could," Gabby said.

"Only here in town. We need to drive to nearby towns. And we have another problem."

"What is it?" Gabby asked.

"Once we have the skulls, we'll need as many people as we can gather if we have any hope of pulling this off."

"Will they be in danger?" Mia asked. "Are they coming with us?"

"No, they won't be in danger and they won't be near Hollow Rock. We need to get them to a local cemetery. To as many local cemeteries as possible. We need to get these skulls to the graves of every child we can find. Before families start arriving."

"Then go," Mia said. "You and Gabby go get the skulls. I'll get my family to help."

"How many people will that be?" Ricky asked.

"At least four to start with. My aunt and cousins."

"That won't be nearly enough," Ricky said.

Mia looked at her watch. "By when do you need everybody?"

"The cemetery gatherings start a little after dusk. We'll need to start preparing as soon as we can."

"I can get us more, but it will have to wait until about three or so. Can you get enough by then?"

"I don't know, but we'll take whatever we have and meet by 3. Are you sure about this, Mia?"

"I'm trusting you, so now I need you to trust me. Give me all the skulls you have and let me know when you have more. You can get them to me when we meet later."

Ricky nodded. He and Gabby found more locations in the nearby towns, then moved all the skulls they had collected previously into Mia's car before they parted ways.

Gabby drove while Ricky navigated, making calls to see if the smaller nearby cities like Monticello or Midway would have anything, but the only places that had a larger amount of inventory were further north in Georgia. Cairo would be their first stop.

"Any idea how Mia's planning to get that much help?" Gabby asked.

"No idea. Maybe friends? One thing I do trust is she'll do whatever it takes to undo what she's done and save Ally."

～

MIA CALLED her Aunt Grace from the car and filled her in. Grace agreed to pick the kids up a little early from school to help. They would be waiting for her call.

Mia was worried about where she was going next.

The last thing she wanted to do was go to the university, but she parked, rushed up the stairs, and sat outside Professor Cort's classroom, which was already halfway over. When there were only a few minutes left in class, she knocked on the door and got the professor's attention. He waved her in.

"Mia, are you okay?" the professor asked.

Mia realized she probably looked like a crazy homeless woman. Her hair was everywhere.

"Professor, can I speak to the class, please?"

He nodded reluctantly, and she stood front and center.

"Hey, everybody. I know you all know there's something … different about me."

A knowing murmur spread across the room.

"The thing is, you're all correct. I have an ability I don't understand. I can manipulate liquids and their flow, and even some physical objects. I don't know how or why I have this ability, but as most of you have seen, it exists. It's a great thing to have in a class like this, but over the last few weeks, I've learned it can also be dangerous."

The room's mood turned nervous.

"I'm here because I need you all. I know this sounds

insane, but recently I was asked to use my skills to save a child's soul. A baby. I've been practicing on how to do this and that's what caused most of the chaos that happened the other day. Tonight is the only night we have any chance of saving this baby's soul, but I can't do it alone. I need help. Your help. I've helped many of you in this class, and although I didn't do it expecting anything in return, I have to ask…"

She hesitated.

"There's no other way to say this, so here it goes. Today is the Day of the Dead. I want you to come to a few cemeteries and help me place a bunch of ceramic sugar skulls at the graves of children."

The nervous mood turned into fright, shock, and some laughter.

"Are you kidding, Mia?" Laura said. "Talking about dead babies isn't funny."

"I'm not being funny. Have you ever known me to lie?"

Some of the class started to get up from their desks.

"I'll help, Mia," Professor Cort said. "Class, for what it's worth, I believe her."

Some still moved toward the door.

"NO!" Mia yelled.

The students stopped moving and turned to Mia in shock. She had always been soft-spoken and had never raised her voice to anyone at the university.

"I'm not joking. This has to be done. And I'm sorry, but I asked nicely and no longer have time to argue. There's more to this story. There are demons involved. Real hellfire demons like from a horror movie. If we don't save this child's soul, they will escape into our reality and kill us all. You, me, your families. Everyone you care about. All I'm asking is for you to help me distribute these skulls.

That's all. Then you can go home and pray that we're successful. Worst case, you can say you helped a crazy girl and will have a great story to tell for years to come."

"I … I can't move," the student nearest the door said, her voice shaking.

"No, you can't. Let me rephrase what I said, so it's clear to everyone in this room. I'm no longer asking. You are all going to help me."

She raised her hand and a collective breath inhaled throughout the room. Mia locked on and pushed as every student's veins pulsed and throbbed loud enough for each one to hear their own heartbeat. For the next five seconds, no one could breathe or move. Mia let go and everyone reached for their throats, gasping.

"Like I said, I learned my power can be dangerous. It can be used to pass a class, to save a life, or to end one. Right now, worry about the dangerous part. I *am* dangerous. I don't want to harm anyone, but this is important enough that I'd rather take you all by force than risk everyone in this room dying. This entire town and maybe even the world are at risk of being destroyed. Am I clear?"

A few cries let out, but everyone stood up and nodded.

"Follow me."

Mia led them to the parking lot and handed each of them a few skulls.

"We're going to a few different cemeteries in a caravan. Take as few cars as possible and be sure every seat is filled. We should be getting more skulls later. Place one skull at a child's grave, meaning anyone that died under the age of 18 in the last fifty years. Understood? And in case you're wondering, I can still unleash my power if you're ten cars behind me. We'll be done in a few hours, and then I expect you'll never see me again."

273

No one argued. The Sugar Skull caravan left to perform
Mia's bidding.

Chapter Thirty-Five

On the way to the first cemetery, Mia called Aunt Grace and told her where to meet her. Then she called Gabby and Ricky.

"I have a crew. I think we can finish with this batch within the next couple of hours," she said.

"How?" Gabby asked.

"You don't want to know. I did something I already regret, but the stakes are too high. Were you able to find more skulls?"

"Yes," Ricky said. "We had to drive into Georgia, but we have almost double the number of skulls now. We're about 15 minutes away. Gabby and I need to get to the Hollow Rock site, but there's no point until those skulls are in place. Where can we meet?"

"Our first stop is the Old City Cemetery. By the time you arrive, we should be distributing the skulls we have now. Well, my crew should."

"Crew?" Gabby asked.

"You'll understand when you get here."

When Ricky and Gabby arrived, they parked by Mia's

car. They looked out toward the cemetery and saw several students they recognized placing skulls throughout the cemetery.

"Never doubted her," Gabby said.

They moved the rest of the skulls in Mia's car to use for the next cemetery stops.

"Just get to as many cemeteries as you can before dusk," Ricky said. "We're heading to the site and will monitor. Gabby and I are hoping Strand has to leave if he really needs you. And when he does, we figure he'll have to take his cloaking spell or whatever they're using down and we'll see him. Am I counting on that? No, or we wouldn't have all these people out here, but it would make things so much easier. We're going to do whatever we can to keep him from taking you. Just keep in constant contact."

"Okay, thanks. My aunt and cousins should be on their way, too."

"You can tell us later how you got so many to help," Gabby said.

"I will."

"Finish up and then go to your aunt's place."

"No," Mia said. "I think all three of us need to be there."

"The closer you are, the more likely he'll find a way to capture you," Gabby said. "Without you, there is no crossover and Ally will be safe."

"I know I said and still believe it's inevitable," Ricky said. "But that doesn't mean we shouldn't try."

Mia didn't like the option but nodded. Ricky and Gabby left as Mia joined her classmates.

When they were done with the first cemetery, Mia tried to call Grace, but she didn't answer. Mia texted her and Bianca to let them know the next location. Grace texted back: *Sorry, Omar fell and hurt his knee. Cleaning him up, but we're all going. I'll let you know when we do.*

Thank you, Aunt Grace. And don't worry about it. I think we have enough people. If you can't make it, we're covered. I can just head over when we're done.

We'll be there.

Mia led the caravan to three more cemeteries. She, Ricky, and Gabby were texting the entire time. Ricky and Gabby were preparing on their end. Mia wasn't sure what they were doing exactly, but she needed to finish her job.

The crew finished at the fifth cemetery 90 minutes before dusk. Aunt Grace never made it, but Mia knew she was a mom first.

Professor Cort was the first person to walk up to Mia.

"Professor, I want to apologize to you," Mia said. "What I did was inexcusable."

"I've seen what you can do, Mia," Cort replied. "I will never agree with the way you went about it, but if everything you're saying is true, I do understand. Maybe you should reassure everyone before we leave."

Mia called everyone over to gather by her car. Even after over two hours of working together, some of her classmates were still rattled. She could sense the collective fear as they stood near her.

"I just want to thank you all. I know most of you didn't come here willingly and I am truly sorry for frightening everyone. You may think I've lost my mind, but I promise I'm trying to save everyone's lives. I believe what you did tonight just might give you an opportunity to grow older and have children and grandchildren to tell this story to someday. I don't regret what I did, but I don't expect any of you to forgive me or fully understand. Still, this couldn't have happened without you. If that little girl survives, if we all survive, a large part of that will be due to your help. Thank you."

The crowd dispersed nervously. Some of them stared at Mia as they entered their vehicles, half-expecting her to attack them again.

Laura remained. "I'm sorry, Mia. You've done so much for me. But you have to know this is a lot to take in. No matter what, I do believe you're doing this for a noble reason. Or that you believe you are. And if everything is true, I wish you the best of luck. I couldn't have asked for a better lab partner."

"Thank you, Laura. I don't think I'll ever be able to return to the university, but I'm glad to have had you for a partner, too."

Mia got into her car and texted Gabby and Ricky that she was on her way to her aunt's house.

Then Strand called.

Mia stared at her phone on its dashboard holder. She didn't answer, and the ringing stopped. Then a picture message came through.

Aunt Grace. It was a picture of Aunt Grace inside Hollow Rock.

Another text followed: *I think you should answer the next call.*

The phone rang again and Mia answered immediately.

"What did you do to her? She has nothing to do with this!"

"You are quite mistaken, Mia," Strand said. "You must come here now. I believe without your beautiful Aunt Grace, you would not come willingly. So right now, she is the most important person in the universe to me, because she alone will get you here."

"Where are my cousins?"

"After bringing your dear aunt here, I had her send

them a message that she had to meet you alone and your older cousin, Bianca, I think it is, would watch her younger siblings. I guaranteed your aunt the safety of her children, but that agreement is also dependent on you, Mia. I will retrieve them if necessary."

"No, no. Leave them out of this. I'm going."

"And you will remain on the phone with me for the duration of your trip. I think it would be best not to speak to your friends before you arrive."

He hung up and called back immediately for a video chat.

In the seconds before answering, Mia sent a voice-to-text message as fast as she could.

"Stand. No tm to graze," is what went through.

Then she answered Strand's call, not wanting to risk her aunt or cousins from being harmed.

"WHAT DOES THAT MEAN?" Gabby asked.

She was trying to decipher Mia's text and tried calling her back three times already.

No answer.

"Something's wrong," Ricky said. "Stand has to be Strand. But 'no tm to graze?'"

"Cows graze," Gabby said. "No tm - no time. Maybe she meant 'grass' and is meeting us out here in the tall grass. The reception out here isn't the best."

"I'll finish getting ready," Ricky said. "Keep trying."

A car approached ten minutes later. It was driving fast.

Inside the car, Mia was staring at Strand and Aunt Grace on her phone screen while trying to use her peripheral vision to spot Ricky and Gabby. She wasn't exactly sure where they were hiding but saw a reflection of something coming up on her right and put her elbows on the wheel and placed her palms together.

"What are you doing?" Strand asked.

"Praying for you not to hurt my aunt," Mia said as she realized it was Ricky's car reflecting the last remnants of sunlight.

As she passed the car, she turned slightly to her right.

"Did you see that?" Ricky asked.

"She looked like she was praying?"

"Yes."

As Mia neared the location where Hollow Rock should be, the surrounding air shimmered with color as the trees that hid the Hollow Rock entrance appeared.

Grace and Ricky saw the brake lights flip on as Mia turned into the clearing. As soon as she did, the trees and crops disappeared again.

"Praying," Ricky said. "Strand got to her."

"Her aunt," Gabby said. "You also pray when you say grace. He must have been watching her, so she couldn't answer and had to find another way to signal us."

"Strand has her Aunt Grace," Ricky said. "Graze for Grace."

"What do we do?"

"We continue with our plan," Ricky said. "I don't think Strand considers us a threat at all. We just have to add saving Mia and Grace to the plan."

Gabby looked up at the sky. "It'll be dusk soon."

"Then no more waiting," Ricky said. "It's time to begin."

Chapter Thirty-Six

RICKY AND GABBY got back into the car and moved directly across the road from the cloaked Hollow Rock site.

Ricky and Gabby pulled out a small metal outdoor folding table, a glass Superman cup, candles, perforated paper decorations, salt, flowers, and bread. Gabby pulled photos from a manila folder of Ally, Ellie, Ricky's grandmother, Gabby's mother, and Mia's parents and grandmother. They put everything together and set up an *ofrenda*, taping and weighting everything down to keep them from being blown off the table.

Once they were done, Ricky went to the car and reached into his bag. He pulled out a red sugar skull that was almost twice the size of all the others they had bought and set it front and center of their altar.

"I think we're done," Gabby said.

"Not quite."

Ricky pulled out a tube and several small mirrors.

"Wait," Gabby said. "Is that your hair gel?"

"Yes, my water-based gel. Help me set these mirrors. They need to face as many directions as possible."

They set them up around the table at various angles, then Ricky took his hair gel and spread it around all the objects, taking more time on the skull.

"What is the gel for?"

"We know water's a conductor, but I need the gel form to help absorb what's coming."

After leaving the cemetery earlier, Ricky and Gabby stopped every few miles from the site to the cave location and left a trail of skulls. They repeated this on the paths of the other cemeteries Mia planned to visit, with all the trails converging on the farm road leading to Hollow Rock. A network of skulls.

Ricky looked at his watch. "Most people should be arriving at the cemeteries soon if they're not already there. Two of the cemeteries had scheduled activities and one parade ending at one of the larger ones. We have to hope there will be enough people out there visiting their children. And that they show up before Mia tries to bring the souls over."

Back at the Old City Cemetery, where some of Mia's more curious classmates stayed to see if her story had any merit or if she had fully lost it, families began to arrive at the gravesites of their children. Some set up *ofrendas* with favorite toys and spoke out loud to their lost loved ones. A sense of quiet, joy, and peace came over the entire cemetery. More and more people arrived, and within the first fifteen minutes after dusk, hundreds of people were remembering the young ones that were no longer with them.

Ricky and Gabby waited patiently, checking their watches.

"It's been twenty minutes, Ricky. Nothing's happening."

"I know. Just give it a minute."

"Mia and Ally may not have a minute."

Most of the families assumed the sugar skulls that were placed on their children's gravesites were gifts from the cemetery. Some admired and touched them or placed them somewhere more pleasing to their altars, but no one removed them.

As families spoke to the lost children and the praying increased, every set of skull eyes started glowing at the same time. Some people gasped in fear, while others took it as a sign their loved ones were present and fell to their knees.

What Mia's classmates saw as outside observers from the cemeteries was quite different.

The lights from the numerous skulls created a gentle glow around the cemetery. Not bright like a spotlight, but with a soft edge like the approaching sunrise at dawn.

Then the collective light shot out in a direction toward the east.

The students turned as the beam flew past them like a laser. This same event was happening at all the cemeteries they had visited earlier.

What they couldn't see were the skulls Ricky and Gabby had placed on the path from each cemetery to Hollow Rock.

Ricky had placed each *calavera* himself, leaving a small amount of gel on each. As the beam hit each skull, the eye sockets lit up in brilliant white and blue light and the beam continued on to the next skull.

"Look!" Ricky said, pointing to the dark road behind them.

The bright beam of light flew at them and hit the larger red skull, causing a burst of energy that blinded them momentarily. Then a second beam came from the opposite direction and finally, a third beam came from behind. When the last beam struck, Ricky and Gabby were knocked down by the sheer force of what hit them, and when they looked up, the red skull was emitting a beam through its eyes and triangular nose socket that was flowing directly toward the Hollow Rock location. The beam spread into a bubble of light, forming a snow globe-like shell around where Hollow Rock should be, and the surroundings shimmered into a blur.

The light dissipated as Ricky grabbed his backpack and Gabby lifted a duffel bag. They ran past the trees and found the barn door entrance to Hollow Rock.

"We just needed the combined energy and power those prayers and souls provided," Ricky said. "I knew it would work."

Gabby smiled. "No, you didn't, but I'm glad it did."

"This is just the first step," Ricky said. "It only gets harder from here."

"Just be careful. Ally is the most important thing here, but we have Mia and now her Aunt Grace to worry about."

"I know. Just stick to the plan."

He took out some tools and instead of yanking the doors open, he patiently took apart the door hinges. Once he removed them, he put some soft foam between the doors and the base to keep it from making any noise.

Ricky and Gabby gently lifted each door and set them on the soft grass. They grabbed their bags and stared at each other.

"This is it," Ricky said. "Ready?"

"No, but I'm going anyway."

The pair walked with soft steps down the stairs, but their caution was unnecessary. No one would have heard them with the groans and screams coming from below.

The voices came into focus as they moved further down.

"Leave her out of this!" Mia sounded desperate.

"Do as I ask and we will let her go," Strand said. "It is almost time."

There was an underlying roar of darkness. The Shadow Demon and Reflection Demon sounded as menacing as ever, but also laced with a hint of excitement.

"If we let your aunt go, she will notify others and I will be forced to kill her and her children. Do as we ask, and I give you my word she will not be harmed."

Mia was crying. "Okay, fine! I'll do whatever you want."

"Mia, no!" Aunt Grace yelled. "They're going to kill us all no matter what you do!"

Ricky and Gabby neared the table room. Strand was standing by the stone table and Anna had her hands on Mia's shoulders. Aunt Grace was on the ground, tied up, wet, and dirty.

The water stream was glowing bluer and brighter than before, emitting an aura of light with dark patches rising and retreating throughout.

Mia moved toward the table.

"What do you want me to do?"

Strand placed a book with a rotting leather-bound cover on the table. The wooden cross that supposedly contained pieces from St. Peter's crucifixion cross also stood by the stone table.

Anna walked over and placed Annika's body on a blanket by the book. Strand then moved toward the stream and placed the gold medallion on a base within the water so that the medallion was above the stream.

Strand walked back to the table and opened the book

to a marked page and started reading an incantation in Latin.

The glowing light along the stream tightened and surrounded the medallion, causing its gemstones to glow. The light from all five stones then shot out beams that converged to a point on the ground a few feet from the stream, creating an egg-shaped form of light and sparks.

Strand glanced over, then started the incantation again until a second container formed next to the first. He repeated once more.

When the lights dimmed, three oval pods were on the ground with only a foot of space between them. The center oval was only half-formed, like an egg sliced in half with the open end facing up. The other two pods were completed shells. Each pod was filled with light and electric charges shot between each adjacent pod, forming some type of otherworldly link.

Strand looked at his watch, then back at Mia.

"Mia, these pods are your new hollow geode crystal stones. Just as the demons were when you prepared their containers. Now you require a host."

Strand gently lifted Annika, who was frail but still holding Ally's soul. Annika didn't protest as Strand placed her inside the open center pod container.

Gabby stepped forward, but Ricky held out a hand. "We have to wait until the time is right."

"When will that be?"

"I don't know yet, but rushing in already backfired on us. They don't know we're here."

Gabby already had a dagger in her hands. They knew guns wouldn't hurt the demons, and daggers probably wouldn't either, but there were still humans to fight.

"The host is in place," Strand said. "Now for the source."

Strand recited more from the book, raising his hands and voice as the groans and darkness increased from the stream and converged, then broke into two dark shapes near the medallion.

The forms writhed and the Shadow Demon appeared, revealing its menacing teeth. The other form flattened and its reflection off the water and walls revealed the Reflection Demon and its yellow, slitted eyes.

Strand turned to Mia. "You know what you must do."

"No. I won't do it."

Anna moved toward Aunt Grace and held a knife to her throat.

"Your aunt will die first. You will watch as Anna slits her throat and as I personally drag her children in and gouge out their eyes on this table."

"No, Mia!" Grace yelled.

Mia was crying as she raised her hands. "I have to, Aunt Grace."

She looked at the body holding Ally's soul. "I'm so sorry, Annika. I'm sorry they're using your body to hold another child's soul. And I'm sorry, Ally. To you and your mother."

Chapter Thirty-Seven

MIA CLOSED her eyes and tried to shut out every distraction, but with her aunt tied up only a few feet from where she stood and the fate of everyone she loved on the line, it was difficult.

Concentrate on the task at hand, Mia, she said to herself.

She focused on the Reflection Demon. The connection was stronger, like she had to hold something four times the size of what she'd sensed when creating the container within it, but she was practiced and honed now. It felt comfortable. She was the strongest she'd ever been.

The first difference was that the darkness was split into multiple reflective surfaces, but she concentrated on a central point and flexed her power there. The pieces came together in the surge she created in the demon's center. The Reflection Demon's essence was now in one concentrated spot. It was surrounded in darkness, but there was a light underneath, one she couldn't see but felt. It was Ally's soul. The part that the Reflection Demon had already taken.

Mia opened her eyes and glanced at the blue, egg-shaped pod on the right. She tried to move some of the Reflection Demon's dark energy toward the pod, but something was off.

The darkness. Even with Ally's soul inside it, the demon's darkness wasn't compatible with the light around the pod. The light was coming from Annika, who was holding the last remnants of Ally's pure soul without any corruption. And then she felt the cross. Peter's crucifixion cross wasn't glowing or sparking. It was providing a power boost, supercharging the room by just existing.

Mia was in tune with the darkness, soul fragments, and the spiritual relic of power surrounding her. She knew what to do.

Mia took the Reflection Demon's darkness and pushed it toward the gems of the medallion. The precious blue stones served as a conductor and filter at the same time. As the dark energy flowed through each of the medallion's gems, it broke down into five thinner streams.

Just like when the containers were formed, the dark essence now mixed with blue and orange hues of light, turning into a darker shade of purple, and shot through the stones and converged into a center point a few inches from the medallion. Then the five converged streams transformed into a single stream aimed directly at the right side pod container.

Then Mia pushed.

The energy felt laser sharp, like she was threading a needle of liquid light. The container was solid yet gentle, but just as she had practiced before, she surrounded the container and imagined it filled with tiny, porous holes and let the liquid ooze through, sealing the pores as they passed.

This wouldn't be as quick as what she'd practiced with.

The Reflection Demon was much more dense and larger than what she had worked with to this point.

At that moment, Annika's head jerked back, and she turned toward the filling pod. It was the most emotion she'd let out since Mia first met her.

Mia pulled back and Gabby took a step forward.

"Wait," Ricky whispered. "She needs to do this twice. Observe everything she does, even if it means letting the first one through. We have to be sure what we're up against if we have any hope."

Gabby's hands balled into fists, but she held her ground.

"Remarkable," Strand said. "Please continue."

"But Ally's soul," Mia whispered.

"Continue or you seal your family's fate."

Mia's tears fell as she refocused. The streaming continued in long pulses as she drained the Reflection Demon and filled the container. It only took a few minutes before the stream ended. When it did, there was a large crackling sound as lightning and energy filled the container and it solidified, turning a bright green.

"Now, it is Shadow's turn."

Mia took a breath and was overcome with exhaustion.

"Hurry!" Strand said.

"I'm drained! Give me a chance to recharge!"

Strand reached into his bag and Mia winced, expecting a weapon, but it was a bottled water.

"Drink. You cannot stop."

Mia took a few sips and set the bottle down. Then she raised her hands and again reached out. The Shadow Demon was a different sensation. He was larger and much darker. It took additional effort to reach his entire being, and he snarled as she tried to latch on. He wasn't used to being controlled.

"Now?" Gabby asked.

Ricky nodded, and they each pulled flares from their bags.

He started to whisper. Gabby thought it was an incantation but realized he was praying.

"For Grandma. For Ally. For Ellie."

Ricky reached back into his backpack and pulled out another sugar skull. The sugar skull. The one that started it all and couldn't be destroyed. The one that once held the spirit of his grandmother Bea and was possibly the only reason he was still alive.

He raised it, and the light and energy still vibrant and flourishing from the cemetery prayers for dead children transferred through the large skull outside and down into his old sugar skull.

Ricky and Gabby each tossed two flares toward the stone table as the light hit the sugar skull.

Everyone but Annika turned as Ricky and Gabby rushed out with their weapons. Ricky held a metal baseball bat and Gabby had her dagger.

Ricky took a swing at Strand, who was caught off guard, falling in a heap. Gabby rushed at Anna, but she didn't try to fight. Gabby cut the zip ties restraining Grace and turned to Mia.

"Can you save Ally?"

Ricky ran to the pod containers and tried to reach in to grab Annika's body, but sparks shot at his hands, knocking him back. Gabby didn't hesitate and also tried, but with the same result.

"It's too powerful," Mia said. "And it's growing stronger."

Gabby and Ricky nodded towards each other and tried to reach in at the same time. They grimaced and yelled in pain, but with the energy being spread around, their hands reached Annika.

Both flew back as the Shadow Demon, who had not yet been transferred, yanked them away.

Strand jumped up and pulled a long knife against Grace's throat.

"No!" Strand screamed. "Shadow, move away from them. You need your strength. Mia, you will ignore them all, or your aunt dies here and now. You know you cannot stop this. Finish it."

The Shadow Demon retreated as Strand moved his hand slightly, drawing blood from Grace's throat.

"No!" Mia yelled. "Stop!"

"Ignore him, Mia! If they succeed, we all die anyway!" Aunt Grace yelled.

Mia lowered her hands. "I won't do it."

The container housing the Reflection Demon started shaking, its green light spreading out towards Mia. Her hands shot up.

Ricky and Gabby tried to stand, but Mia had already resumed. She had a full grasp on Shadow, and she started threading him through the medallion stones.

"No!!" Gabby screamed. "Stop it, Mia!"

"I can't!" Mia said. "The Reflection Demon—I think it's controlling me!"

The power the demon had already gained from being purified, even only partially, was surging. Mia knew they had no chance.

Ricky stared at Anna, who was observing with a smile.

"Maybe she can break this," Ricky said.

He rushed up and grabbed Anna by the back of her neck and pushed her forward. He placed her body between the wet streams, and Anna screamed as the light penetrated through her chest. But it did nothing to stop the stream. It simply burned through her and reached the last pod.

The Shadow Demon was incomplete, with a part of him inside the pod and the rest still waiting.

Anna's face started to flash in different colors, revealing her skull underneath. Ricky leapt back.

Then Anna's face changed. There were two faces now, alternating with each burst of energy. One of the faces cleared up. It was the face that started it all. The little girl looking for her kitty that first night at his house when everything changed.

"Who is that?" Gabby asked, getting to her feet.

"Ghost Girl," Ricky said. "The one with the cat I told you about. She's been helping inside Anna all along."

Ghost Girl started to writhe, but Gabby joined in and held her. The girl bent over in pain, screaming loudly, and then Anna's body crumbled into nothing as another voice screamed.

"Ricky! It hurts!!"

The face flashed again and Ricky stepped back, falling to the ground, his mouth open in disbelief.

There was a second person inside of Anna. The neighborhood girl he'd loved since they were in elementary school together.

Ellie stared back at him. Ellie, who the demons made him kill.

"How?" Ricky whispered. "Ellie? It can't be."

"Ricky, that night. They took a part of my soul and joined me with the Ghost Girl. My soul gave her the strength to leave the neighborhood she haunted. Our neighborhood. We were tied to the demons until they found Strand. Together, they put us in bodies of young girls that were on the verge of death, moving us to new bodies when the ones we occupied were too weak to function. But in each body, Ghost Girl had control. I've been trapped inside all this time."

Ricky moved Anna's body out of the stream's way as Ellie and Ghost Girl continued to flicker in and out.

"Hi, Kitty."

"Ricky, help me!"

"I like my new Kitty better, but I miss you."

Ricky screamed.

Then the cave was filled with a crack of light and thunder.

They looked at Annika inside the pod. Her face was thinning and dark patches formed under her eyes as what little life she had was being drained from her as Ally's soul within her was being extracted.

"Ricky," Gabby yelled. "We have to stop this!"

"You can't," Mia said. "It's over. They're too strong."

Anna, now with Ellie's face, turned toward them.

"Ricky," Ellie said. "Use us. Our souls. We might be able to stop it."

Ricky's face filled with tears. He couldn't process that he was staring at Ellie.

"No," Ricky said. "I can save you."

"Ricky, I'm already gone. There's nothing to save."

Gabby was trying to grab Annika, fighting back the electric shocks she received with every attempt.

"STOP THIS, MIA!! SHE'S DYING!"

"Listen to me, Ricky," Ellie said. "Do it."

"Dammit, Ricky!" Gabby yelled as she rushed and pushed Anna's body toward the containers. Sparks exploded as Ghost Girl and Ellie struck the pod and ripped in two. Ellie's essence joined the Reflection Demon's pod, while Ghost Girl's entered the Shadow's partially filled one.

Ellie screamed as Ghost Girl laughed.

"Ellie!" Ricky yelled.

Ellie tried to fight the Reflection Demon, but it didn't engage her. She stopped after a few seconds and shot back out of the pod.

"Mia's right," Ellie said. "The Reflection Demon alone is too strong. I can't stop him. And Shadow is even stronger. We can't win."

Strand, who had remained by Aunt Grace, was laughing. "She is correct. None of you are a threat. You have lost."

Ricky looked back at Strand and then at Annika's body. Finally, he turned to Ellie.

"This was all my fault," Ricky said. "All of it, but I think I know what I have to do."

Ricky turned toward Mia, who was still being controlled by the Reflection Demon.

"Mia, don't fight it anymore. Transfer the Shadow Demon into the pod. You're all right. We can't win."

"Ricky?" Gabby yelled. "What are you doing?"

"What I have to. Please, Mia."

"Yes," Strand said. "Listen to him. Complete your task!"

Ricky looked at Mia and silently mouthed, "Trust me."

Mia nodded and gave in. The Shadow Demon screamed loud enough to fill the entire cavern as the rest of its essence strained through the medallion's gems and transferred into the pod.

"Yes!" Strand said. "It is time!"

He walked away from Grace and stood near the pods. With Annika's body in the center and the Reflection Demon and Shadow Demon on either side, the electric surges between them increased and cracked louder than before as the remnants of each piece of Ally's soul began to fuse together.

Ricky ran toward Mia as Gabby stood and stared at the pods in horror. She fell on her knees, screaming.

"We've lost her!" Gabby said.

Ricky reached Mia and pulled her face to him so only she could hear his words.

"Where are your glass beads?"

Mia had forgotten about her black magic spells.

She reached into her left pocket and pulled out different colored beads.

Strand was ignoring them, knowing Mia's job was done. They only had to wait for Ally's soul to drain and feed the demons enough to bring the soul together and give them the power to cross over.

"Black for darkness and green for fear, right?" Ricky asked.

"Yes. And drink this."

Mia pulled out her water bottle, which held what was left of the third spell she'd created.

"This is the spell for power. I took a sip of it earlier and it's strong. Take the rest. You'll need it."

Ricky reached for it and swallowed the entire contents, then took the black beads of darkness from her. "When the time is right, I need you to use the green beads of fear on the demons."

"But they're already in the pods, Ricky," Mia said. "We can't get to them."

"Mia, whatever I ask, no matter what it is, I need you to trust me. Can I have your word?"

Mia looked up at him and back at Annika, who was barely moving.

"Mia, this may be the only way. Ally's soul, your Aunt Grace, your cousins. Think of them. Think of what they mean to you. Promise."

"What are you going to do, Ricky?"

He stared at her and didn't blink.

"What I have to. Promise?"

Mia nodded. "I promise."

Ricky moved next to Gabby and knelt by her. Strand didn't flinch, convinced they posed no threat.

"I need you to stay with me, Gabby. I still need you."

He handed her the black beads. "Darkness. Remember that. I'll tell you when."

Gabby screamed, "What are you talking about? It's too late!"

"Gabby. Come back to me. For Ally. There's still a chance."

He picked up the dagger she'd dropped and put it back in her hand.

Gabby stared at him and heaved as her cries settled. She looked at Annika's body again. Her mouth was open, and she was struggling to breathe.

"Ricky, whatever you're going to do, do it now!"

There was another burst of thunder that shook the cave as the demon pods turned red. Annika's center pod was still blue, but it was fading.

"They're taking Ally's soul!" Gabby screamed.

"Gabby," Ricky said as he pulled her hand up and waved her dagger in front of her face. "Stay with me. Just don't hesitate."

Ricky rushed at Strand and knocked him over, but Strand was still fast and they struggled. Gabby looked at her blade, snapped, and rushed toward them. She slammed her dagger in and out of Strand's temple, then dropped the weapon, horrified as he fell.

Annika's eyes rolled to the back of her head as her pod's blue glow diminished into a soft light.

"NO!!" Gabby screamed.

Ellie was standing near the pods, defeated. Ghost Girl

was still inside Shadow's pod, embracing his essence and continuing to squeal with glee.

Ricky reached into his pocket and pulled out the amulet necklace that Carlotta had gifted Gabby back in the New Orleans voodoo shop. The amulet she in turn gave Ricky to protect him, trusting him to save Ally if she couldn't.

Ricky placed the amulet around Gabby's neck.

"What are you doing, Ricky?" Gabby asked.

"Returning the favor. Ally needs her mother to raise her."

Ricky picked up Gabby's dagger from the ground and handed it back to her.

"What you just did to Strand. I need you to do the same to me," Ricky said. "Just not in the head, please."

He pointed to his chest.

"What are you talking about? No, Ricky! I can't!"

"Do you want to save your daughter?" Ricky asked, but Gabby was too shocked to move.

"Gabby!" Ricky yelled, grabbing her by the face. "Do you want to save Ally?"

Gabby's lips trembled as she looked at the pod, seeing the last of Ally's soul being drained from Annika's body, gasping for breath.

"Gabby, this is the only way! Who's more important to you? Do it. For Ally! For me!"

Gabby screamed in agony as she thrust the dagger through Ricky's chest. His upper body flinched backward as blood gushed from the wound.

"Ricky, no!!" Ellie yelled.

"Mia!" Ricky screamed. "Don't let my soul escape. Keep me here."

Mia understood. She lifted her arms and at first felt nothing, but as Ricky's face drained of color, she felt it.

There was no darkness surrounding Ricky. It was light. A pure light like Ally's that she sensed inside Annika's body. Ricky's soul was free. She could feel it being pulled into the next world, but she realized what Ricky wanted and grasped it tightly, pulling it back to the cave.

Ricky's essence was now transparent. He turned back to Mia.

"Hit me, Mia."

Mia didn't flinch. She raised her hands and threw everything she had into Ricky's exposed soul, redirecting everything he was directly into the pods. He required no medallion filter. His soul was clean.

Ricky dissipated, and his energy combined with Mia's flew into the pods, followed by a piercing howl of pain.

Ricky was inside the Shadow Demon's pod.

Ricky's soul wrapped around the container, and he took the power he felt, now enhanced with the spell he had swallowed, and threw out all of his energy.

"Now, Gabby!"

Gabby took her beads of darkness and threw them toward the pod. They shattered on impact, and Mia thrust the contents into the pod as Ricky's light pulsated throughout. The Shadow Demon fought back, trying to wrap itself around Ricky's soul.

Ricky didn't fight back.

"Come on, demon! Hit me with everything you've got!"

The Shadow growled and bared its teeth, and Ricky let it bite into his own soul, its energy combining with his.

"Help me, Mia! Use the skull!"

Mia realized what he was doing. She grabbed the sugar skull and placed it on the table, then threw her energy into it. Mia pushed, then she pushed harder. The skull rose and hung in midair, taking the combined energy still pulsating through it from the prayers for the children and Mia's power and creating a bright green stream that hummed as it flowed into the pod.

The glowing pods filled with bursts of lightning, turning multiple colors and finally exploding as the skull shattered into countless pieces.

As the flying shards of the pods and shattered skull cleared, Mia and Gabby looked up.

Ricky's soul stood by the table and the Shadow Demon stood by the stream. The Reflection Demon's face was mirrored in each piece of scattered debris.

Gabby grabbed Annika's body and ran behind the stone table with Mia and Grace. Annika wasn't breathing.

The Shadow Demon inched closer to Ricky. *You. Destroyed everything. Paid with your life. We will eat your soul.*

The shards of reflective debris rose in the air and flew towards Ricky as Ellie stood beside him.

"On a normal day, I would agree with you," Ricky said. "But this is no normal day. When I was alive, you could use my own fear to defeat me. But you no longer have that advantage."

Ricky turned and glanced at Mia.

The fear beads.

She stood and threw the beads toward the Shadow Demon. They cracked open as they hit the rocky ground beneath it.

The Shadow Demon flinched. He looked around, confused. The floating shards of the Reflection Demon spun around Shadow, unsure of what was happening.

"I'm guessing you've never experienced true fear," Ricky said. "How does it feel?"

The reflection shards flew at Ricky and Ellie, and they felt the pain as they landed.

"Mia," Gabby said. "Can you bring those glass pieces back together and remove the reflections?"

Mia stood and concentrated only on the Reflection Demon and its parts. Just as she had taken the pieces of its darkness and formed them into one central mass, she repeated the same with the debris. She brought them into a central blob and coated it with darkness, reducing the reflections to a few exposed pieces.

The containers that Mia had created within each demon glowed. They were partially filled, but she knew it wasn't enough power. Not without the rest of Ally's soul.

Ricky grabbed Ellie's hand. "They still need souls, Ellie. I think we should give it to them."

Ellie understood.

Ricky threw himself into the Shadow Demon's soul container and Ellie did the same with the Reflection Demon.

As Ricky entered, he screamed. "Mia, pull Ally's soul out!"

Mia reversed all she had done. Instead of pushing Ally's soul into the containers, she held on to what was inside the Reflection Demon and pulled. She took the soul energy and sent it through the medallion, filtering out the darkness it had built up in the brief time inside the demon. Then she did the same with Shadow.

Mia combined the energy and threw the rest of Ally's soul back into Annika's body.

Ricky took his remaining power and let it grow. He spread it around himself, clenched his fists, and squeezed. He turned toward Ellie and spread his energy to her as well.

The soul containers within each demon shook and cracked as they expanded. The demons screamed in agony.

"Now you will fear me," Ricky said. "My darkness and my light!"

Ricky combined all his energy with the darkness, while Mia threw all her remaining power toward him. The soul containers within the demons exploded, expelling Ricky and Ellie.

They all stood on the fallen forms of the Shadow and Reflection demons. Ricky reached down and grabbed Shadow by the throat, shoved the demon's face into his open mouth and bit at him, pulling out chunks piece by piece. As each part of the Shadow Demon's darkness touched Ricky's pure soul, it dissipated. After a few more bites, the Shadow Demon was no more. Ricky only had to touch the Reflection Demon for it to break into pieces that broke into ash and floated away.

"You were always weak," Ricky said as the final part of Reflection Demon broke away.

The Demon Brothers' reign of darkness was over.

Annika gasped.

Gabby and Mia looked down at her as her nearly emaciated face filled with color and life. She opened her eyes, revealing a deep green color that glowed with her regained soul.

"Mama…"

Then her eyes drained of color and her face turned black.

"No!" Gabby screamed.

Annika's little hand reached out and flattened against Gabby's cheek.

As her tiny body withered, Gabby's chest felt like it was going to explode. Annika spread her tiny fingers along Gabby's face, and Gabby sucked in a breath as Annika's body turned to dust.

Gabby's vision went dark and when it returned, she

was standing inside her sister Teri's house back in Texas. Teri and her kids surrounded the bed, watching Ally, who was on her back and gasping for breath.

"I think this is it," Teri said as she lifted Ally and held her. She and her children sobbed and none of them noticed Gabby in the room.

Then Ally's head flew back. The color on her face returned like Annika's had only moments before. Her tiny body expanded and her bony little arms and legs filled into chubby rolls.

Teri and the kids gasped. Ally raised her head and looked directly behind her aunt, right into Gabby's eyes.

"Mama!" Ally screamed as she stretched out her arms. "Mama!"

"Ally! My baby! Ally, it's Mama. I'm here!"

Just before Gabby could grab her daughter, her view again faded to black, but she shrieked with joy as her vision returned to Hollow Rock.

She fell to the ground, sobbing, as Mia and Grace held her.

"She's okay!" Gabby said. "I saw her! She's alive! Ally's alive!"

The color in the room went dark, and they looked back to see Ricky and Ellie standing in a white light.

Gabby regained her composure and she and Mia moved toward them.

"Ricky, I don't know what to say," Gabby said. "I just saw Ally. She's fine. My baby's fine."

"I know," Ricky said. "I'm not sure how, but I could sense the moment she regained her soul."

Gabby looked at Ricky and Ellie's transparent forms. "This wasn't supposed to happen like this, Ricky."

"It's okay," Ricky said, smiling. "I found the love of my

life again. We can be together forever now. If that's what she wants."

He looked at Ellie and she smiled, laying her head on his shoulder.

"I've never felt more at peace," Ellie said. "I like the sound of forever, Ricky."

Ricky turned back to his friends. "Thank you, Mia."

"For what? It's my fault you're dead. Why all this happened."

"No, Mia," Ricky said. "Don't you see? Without you, we could have never stopped them. It was supposed to be you. It was supposed to be the three of us. No one else could have done this."

Mia nodded, trying to contain her emotions.

"Do me a favor," Ricky said. "Live your life and go be happy. Don't let anyone take that from you. I floundered for so long and lost what was most important to me, and I know how lucky I am to have her back. I wish you could feel what I feel now."

"I'll try," Mia said.

"Ricky," Gabby said. "I don't know what to say. How to thank you for saving us all. You gave my Ally back to me."

"We all did this. We saved each other."

"You don't have long," Mia said. "Is there anything we can do?"

"There is one thing. Find my sister and mother. Check my backpack. There's something there for Myra. And for Mom. Tell Myra everything. Don't leave out any details. Tell her I did it for her and I hope she'll understand. Tell her I love her and I'm sorry I won't be coming back, but I'll watch over her if I can."

He pointed behind them.

"Can you bring that to me?"

They all turned to see Ricky's first sugar skull on the ground, facing them. Once again, it proved it was indestructible.

Grace picked up the skull and handed it to Mia, who held it up in front of Ricky's face.

Ricky and Ellie raised their hands, and the eyes of the skull emitted a brief blue glow.

"Give her the skull," Ricky said. "Tell her not to be afraid and that I'll always be with her."

The white light around them brightened, and Ricky and Ellie started to fade.

"Ricky…" Gabby said.

"It's okay, Gabby. I'm glad we met and did this together. Now you can be the mother I never had. For Ally. For you."

"Goodbye, Ricky. I'm so sorry."

"Sorry?" Ricky said as he and Ellie faded away. "I get to be happy and feel love for an eternity. Who could ask for anything more?"

Chapter Thirty-Eight

GABBY, Mia, and Grace removed Ricky's body, then set Hollow Rock on fire. As it burned, Mia called the police while Gabby threw in the altar they created. Grace joined them to take down some of the skulls they had placed along the path.

The police bought the story that Strand had murdered Ricky after kidnapping them since they had found video evidence of Grace's kidnapping. Gabby stated she had killed Strand in self-defense.

No charges were brought against them.

Mia and Gabby agreed to fulfill Ricky's wishes together after Gabby got to spend some time with Ally, and Mia took a few days to heal with Aunt Grace and her family.

On the third day, Tino showed up at Aunt Grace's house. Mia didn't let him inside but walked out to the porch to speak with him.

Tino started talking before she could.

"You're not answering my calls, but I heard about what happened. I told you that man was a psycho. But that's not why I'm here. I can't lose you, Mia. You're the best thing that ever happened to me. I'm sorry. I'm so sorry. I know I've been an asshole. I just thought you'd give it up some day. You know how I was raised."

She started to interrupt, but he kept on.

"I get that's not an excuse. I know that. I told my Dad I didn't want to lose you. And you know what he told me?"

Mia held her tongue. She didn't want to say anything because she didn't think she could mention his father without going into another angry tirade.

"He said that you weren't worth it. That no woman who didn't listen to their man was. But I told him that was why my mom left him and why he couldn't ever keep a relationship. I told him I was an idiot, and that I wasn't going to be miserable the rest of my life just because of how he raised me."

Mia tried to disguise her shock as she felt a lump build in her throat.

"I was wrong, Mia. I love you and I don't want this to be the end. I'm going to work as hard as I can to change. I want you to be with me. To have our kids. You're my future. Stay in school. Do whatever you have to do, but let me be there to protect you."

Mia didn't say anything for a long moment as she dug in deep into her emotions and thought about all that had happened to her in the last several weeks.

"No," Mia said, trying to keep her voice from cracking. "I don't need you to protect me. I could have killed you and your father the other day."

"It doesn't matter—"

"It does matter. Things have changed. I may not be able to return to school, but I'll transfer if I have to, even if it means moving."

Tino fell to his knees. "With everything that I am, I promise you I'm not lying. If my choice is to change or to lose you, I'll change. I know it won't be easy, but please, give us another chance. If it means waiting for you to finish school or to do whatever you have to do, I'll wait. I'm yours, Mia. I was so wrong. I know that now."

Mia saw Tino's eyes water. She had only ever seen him cry once when his mom left, and the sight of it almost broke her. This was the man she had hoped and prayed for. The man she'd always wanted. Maybe he really could change.

Mia knelt down to meet his face and kissed him before leaning back.

"Tino, it makes me happy to hear you say what you just said, but the thing is, I've changed. And I can't give this another few years just to find out these were just words you never meant. Words you said to keep me."

Tino's face went pale. "What, what are you saying?"

"I'm saying I deserve better. I've always deserved better. As much as I've wanted to hear this our entire relationship, I just don't believe you. I should have left you a long time ago. I'm not going to put my life on pause and hope you mean it."

"You can't do this."

"I am doing this. If you've truly changed, maybe we'll be able to try again in a few years."

"You expect me to wait for years?"

"I have. What I hope is that you are capable of change, even if that means you make someone else happy in the end."

"You can't do this!" Tino's eyes turned red as his anger rose. A familiar emotion she'd witnessed too many times when he didn't get his way.

Mia raised a finger, and Tino stopped.

She made no effort to harm him or boil his blood. The finger was simply a reminder that she could.

"Maybe someday," Mia said. "But no more. Not until I know what I want. I owe that to myself."

Then Mia stood up, and the sadness left her. She turned and went inside and didn't look back as her eavesdropping aunt and cousin Bianca hugged her, knowing she always deserved better.

And finally, Mia did, too.

Epilogue

MIA FLEW to Texas the following day, meeting Gabby at her sister's house, where she finally met Gabby's family.

The moment Ally saw Mia, she reached for her and squealed in delight, squeezing her little arms around Mia's neck and showering her with kisses. Mia sensed she somehow understood all that had happened.

Mia and Gabby left that same evening, taking Ally with them on a road trip to the west.

Ricky's sister Myra and mother Lori, who was now a few years clean and sober, greeted them the morning they arrived. The family was still under witness protection, so they were the only five people that attended Ricky's funeral that afternoon.

After the services, the group returned to the house and Gabby and Mia sat down and told them every detail, as Ricky requested.

Finally, Gabby showed them Ricky's backpack and pulled out the sugar skull. Myra gasped as she saw it, but Gabby told her Ricky wanted her to have it, and they believed he left a part of himself inside.

Gabby and Mia left the next day, forming a bond with Ricky's family that would last for the rest of their lives.

Later that night, Myra placed the sugar skull on her dresser and thought of her brother as she fell asleep.

At 3 a.m., Myra woke up to a bright light. As her eyes opened, she realized her entire room was lit up.

She thought she heard a voice and turned toward it. The sugar skull was floating a few inches above her dresser with its eye sockets glowing a bright green.

Myra got up and walked to her dresser, then grabbed the skull and lifted it up to her face. She stared into the skull's glowing eyes and smiled.

Myra kissed the top of the skull and placed it back on the dresser.

"I love and miss you, too, Ricky. Please tell Ellie I said hello."

THE END

Acknowledgments

My Reader Team

David Riskind
Michael Sawyer
Mari Molina
Belynda Chapa
Pam "PMoney" Marino
Daisy Ruiz
Thank you for sticking around all these years.
Y'all still rock!

Author's Note

This is my second series finale, and it was so satisfying to bring the characters together for one final confrontation with the Demon Brothers. I also really enjoyed creating their origin story.

After bringing Ricky and Gabby together at the end of The Sweet Skull, I had to decide if there would be another new protagonist for the final book. It wasn't too difficult to decide, since the story pretty much demanded it needed Mia.

Balancing each character's arc and piecing them together was one of the coolest things I've done as a writer. Thank you for going on this Sugar Skull ride, and I hope the payoff was worth it!

Please feel free to contact me for any feedback or just to say hello!

About the Author

Manuel Ruiz is a life-long Texan with a passion for reading, video games, and music. He works in IT, plays in an 80s band, and owns way too many toys. He writes teen and adult fiction, usually with a supernatural twist, and loves to keep his readers on their toes.

Manuel lives in Central Texas with his family where he spends time giving the characters in his head something fun, dark, and interesting to do.

Also By Manuel Ruiz

The Sugar Skull

The Sugar Skull

The Sweet Skull

The Shattered Skull

Printed in the USA
CPSIA information can be obtained
at www.ICGtesting.com
LVHW030337100724
785083LV00013B/789